The Ex-Mrs. Hedgefund

JILL KARGMAN

the
Ex-Mrs. Hedgefund

Dutton

DUTTON
Published by Penguin Group (USA) Inc.
375 Hudson Street, New York, New York 10014, U.S.A.
Penguin Group (Canada), 90 Eglinton Avenue East, Suite 700, Toronto, Ontario M4P
2Y3, Canada (a division of Pearson Penguin Canada Inc.); Penguin Books Ltd, 80 Strand,
London WC2R 0RL, England; Penguin Ireland, 25 St Stephen's Green, Dublin 2, Ireland
(a division of Penguin Books Ltd); Penguin Group (Australia), 250 Camberwell Road,
Camberwell, Victoria 3124, Australia (a division of Pearson Australia Group Pty Ltd); Penguin Books India Pvt Ltd, 11 Community Centre, Panchsheel Park, New Delhi—110 017,
India; Penguin Group (NZ), 67 Apollo Drive, Rosedale, North Shore 0632, New Zealand
(a division of Pearson New Zealand Ltd); Penguin Books (South Africa) (Pty) Ltd, 24
Sturdee Avenue, Rosebank, Johannesburg 2196, South Africa

Penguin Books Ltd, Registered Offices: 80 Strand, London WC2R 0RL, England

Published by Dutton, a member of Penguin Group (USA) Inc.

First printing, April 2009
10 9 8 7 6 5 4 3 2 1

 REGISTERED TRADEMARK—MARCA REGISTRADA

LIBRARY OF CONGRESS CATALOGING-IN-PUBLICATION DATA
Kargman, Jill, 1974–
    The Ex-Mrs. Hedgefund / by Jill Kargman.
        p. cm.
    ISBN 978–0–525–95098–1
    1. Rich people—Fiction.   2. Adultery—Fiction.   3. Divorced women—Fiction.
    4. Dating (Social customs)—Fiction.   5. New York (N.Y.)—Fiction.   I. Title.
    PS3611.A783E93   2009
    813'.6—dc22   2008042999

Printed in the United States of America

PUBLISHER'S NOTE
This book is a work of fiction. Names, characters, places, and incidents either are the product of the author's imagination or are used fictitiously, and any resemblance to actual per-
sons, living or dead, business establishments, events, or locales is entirely coincidental.

Dedicated with xoxos
to
My loving family
and
To the Chères—my Kikis—the best friends in the world.

Acknowledgments

First of all, I want to worship the amazing Trena Keating, who is a brilliant yummy mummy of three–slash–editor in chief—I bow down to you and Lily Kosner for all your incredible insights and wisdom. To the incredible ICM posse: Jennifer Joel and Amanda Urban, plus Josie Freedman and Elliot Webb on the "leff coass." Special thanks to Steven Beer and Mary Miles of Greenberg Traurig. Megakudos to Lee-Sean Huang for help making the graphs, and a special shout-out of major thanks to my anonymous Hedge Fund Deep Throats for the Wall Street crash courses and juicy tidbits, plus amazing supporters like Amelia's mom, Laura Tanny, Jacky Davy, Lisa Jacobs, Aviva Drescher, Tiffany Dubin, Carrie Karasyov, Janisse Tio, Tara Lipton, Alexis and Philip Mintz, the Heinzes, the Bevilacquas, Dan Allen, Jenn Linardos, Michael Kovner and Jean Doyen de Montaillou, Suzanne Cleary, Allison Aston, Beth Klein, and especially Carol Bell and Barbara Martin.

And to my Kikis: All of you inspired me to write this ode not just to finding *amore*, but also to true friendship, and I love you so much: Vanessa Eastman, Jeannie Stern, Dana Jones, Trip Cullman, Lauren Duff, and most of all, Lisa Turvey for all your genius early edits, notes, and advice.

Last but not least, my family: Willie, Mom, Dad, and all the Kopelmans and Kargmans, especially my LC—thank you for being the best, most supportive husband—and to Sadie, Ivy, and Fletch, I love you, my little nuggets.

The Ex-Mrs. Hedgefund

The Mrs. Hedgefund Rolodex
of Favorite Words, A to Z

A is for Armani, Aston Martin, Aman Resort, AmEx (Black)

B is for Bonpoint, Bergdorfs, BOTOX, Bulgari

C is for Cartier, Chauffeur, Chanel, Citibabes, Concierge

D is for Dolce, Driver, Doorman, Dior

E is for Emaciated, Endowment, Envy

F is for Fendi, Frette, Furs, Frédéric Fekkai

G is for Gucci, Golf, Goyard

H is for Housekeeper, Helicopter, Hamptons

I is for iPhone, The Ivy, Italy

J is for Jacadi, Jewelry, Jimmy Choo

K is for Kelly Bag (in every color)

L is for Lanvin, Louboutins, La Perla, Lobel's, Long/Liquid Lunches

M is for Missoni, Mercedes, Manicures

N is for Nina Ricci, NetJets, Nannies

O is for Oscar de la Renta, Opera Tickets

P is for Pilates, Porthault, Paris, Pricey Parties

Q is for Quantity, Quality

R is for Rive Gauche, Rachel Roy

S is for Swifty's, Saks, Season Tickets, Skybox, Second Home

T is for Tiffany, Teterboro, Third Home

U is for Ungaro

V is for Vogue, Valentino, Van Cleef, Vivier, VIP List

W is for Whatever, Whenever, Whomever I Want

X is for Xanax

Y is for Yellow Diamond, YSL, Yacht

Z is for the Zone, Zegna, Zenith

1

New York, 2006

"Have you heard of the new Divorced Barbie? She comes with all of Ken's stuff!"

I t is 1789. An ethereal mist rolls through the gray-smudged streets as coiffed heads are rolling into baskets at the Bastille. The muddied, bedraggled, and oft-diseased onlookers cheer in every Parisian alley. Dawning is the day when preened, brioche-nibbling, wig-powdering royal schmucks no longer shall prance the palace courts in ornamented couture; the chasm between the upper crust and the crumb-eaters is closing with each crisp slice of a once-bejeweled neck, to the thrill of the roaring crowd.

As a raging Broadway geek, I had seen *Les Misérables* probably twenty times, but the music was even sweeter when a limited engagement briefly reopened on Broadway recently. It was packed with tourists and fanatical theater-worshippers like me, and I relished the airtight lyrics and live voices versus my well-worn CD. Seeing it again was like enjoying a short season of a favorite fruit you know you can't savor next month—blood oranges for your ears.

Even in the decade since it last appeared on the Great White Way, a lot has changed in our gritty city. In New York, a glistening new empire was raging, full of the same boundless excesses and sheltered luxuries in which cosseted royals reveled. I thought how lucky I was. Not only because we are now rid of gangrenous wounds, lepers, and inefficient sewer systems, but also because even if there were a class pyramid like the one they had in old Europe, I knew I would be at the triangle's apex, safe from the storm of clamoring mobs raising tattered flags and angry voices. No, I'm not a blue-blooded queen; I'm a normal, down-to-earth, non-over-the-top gal. But I must confess: I am a hedge fund wife.

But wait!

Don't let go of that guillotine rope!

I'm not like the rest of them. I promise. I am not some skeletorious trend-splashed fashion victim or five-foot-eight Xanax tablet with a face. I look my thirty-four years and have not succumbed to the BOTOX needle or boob lift, despite the 9.81-meters-per-second force of gravity taking its toll. Okay, some of my friends are a little OTT, but some are very down-to-earth, and their favorite thing about having money is giving it away. While I must admit, a gal can obviously love the perks of not stressing about dough, there are some drawbacks to the world that I inhabit. Namely the incessant quest for perfection at all costs. In every way—perfect kids, homes, bodies, *lives*. Many of my friends are slaves to their appearance: nips, tucks, $600 creams made of sheep's placenta, trainers, lipo, the works. Anything to be fabulous. But I myself am more drab than fab. More J.Crew than J. Mendel. Sometimes I'll stare at a fashion spread and wish I knew how to work a look like that, but even though I could maybe afford the crazy price tag, I could never in good conscience do it; I'm just not wired that way. I grew up in a well-off but supergrounded, relaxed family in Boston, where people didn't flash cash—my dad is a sweet-natured retired pediatrician and my loving late mother was the epitome of warm elegance rather than opulence, class instead of crass. Sure, a few classmates of mine were megamillionaires (back when that was a big deal), but they made their chauffeurs drop them blocks before school out of an embarrassment of riches. Now in New York I regularly see Rolls-Royces with kiddie car seats glutting the street in front of my son Miles's school. In Boston, the entrepreneurs really created products and didn't show their money around Versailles style. The father of a girl I knew invented the nail clipper; another developed the lawn mower as we know it—patents that still yield serious buckaroos, but none of the families were advertising it. Even though many of my parents' friends had money, there wasn't the flamboyant arrogance I see now.

You see, Manhattan is a different beast. Fortunes are made on people moving around money, not widgets. Very few companies create a palpable product, something you can hold in your hands. It's all about trading, investing, forecasting ups and downs in those markets. Nothing annoys my husband, Tim, more than when he asks what so-and-so does and I blithely respond, "Oh, you know, Wall Street." He tries to calmly explain that there are titans of private equity and mere cold-callers, a spectrum of skill and wealth. But numbers now blur into hieroglyphics for me, despite my A+ in BC Calc in high school. It's as simple as this: I have zero interest.

More than once Tim has given me a mini-crash course—basically verbal Sominex—on the differences between traders who trade stocks versus commodities (like pork bellies and the all-famous Frozen Concentrated Orange Juice in *Trading Places*), versus venture capitalists who invest in small companies with high-growth potential. And then there are the current reigning titans, the kings of ka-ching: the hedgies. What my husband and his brother, Hal, do is all very mysterious and, well, to me, boring. Hedge funds, which are not really regulated, are based on an exorbitant "two and twenty" (or "three and thirty," depending on how well they do) percentage of fees and profits, resulting in lots of boys with lots of cash. All anyone knows is that these guys are minting it, and that the culture, even if clueless about what they actually do, is obsessed.

Fashion designers are telling E! Television that their inspiration is "hedge fund chic." Artists at the Miami ArtBasel Fair rub shoulders not with other artists or their dealers but with their new buttoned-up clientele, who fork out millions for a formaldehyde-suspended pig or a splatter-painted panel. When people ask what Tim does and I respond, "Hedge fund," they say, "Oooooooh," and I cringe, embarrassed; these funds are on people's lips and brains and are synonymous with piles of gold bricks. Not to mention people with no brains: There is even a new book, *Hedge Funds for Dummies*. Like their Gekko-y eighties counterparts, these guys love the money. Greed is good, so it was said, but these days, bragging is better. It seems that every guy my husband works with needs the latest phone, newest car, biggest house, to show off; there's no modesty—it's in-your-face, loud and clear, volume to eleven. And that's how they like it. As do the women who chase them. But while most women would secretly wear Nikes under their Vera Wang bridal dresses so they could sprint faster down the aisle to marry one, take it from me: There are sacrifices.

First of all, the MIA husband syndrome. Tim has to travel all the time, so I'm often solo after Miles's tuck-in with my remote control, learning way too much about Hugh Hefner's three girlfriends on E! or wincing at a taped tummy tuck on the Learning Channel (dashing any desire to have one, despite slight paunch). Then, when Tim is in residence, we have to go to a million "functions." Hedge fund events, charity balls, Tim's co-worker's sister's wedding. The more money you have, the more friends you get, Tim jokes, but he loooves being the life of the party. Me? I'm way more boring. While he likes going out and sampling aged scotch or expensive wine, I prefer . . . Frozen Concentrated Orange Juice.

All of this is a terrific boon for my field of interest: charity work. There is so much money out there, and the dough coupled with the mounting social ambition yields a prime moment for raising money, so I've thrown myself into my volunteer work for the hospital, getting people to come to our benefit and raising tons of funds. In fact, I've raised so many Benjamins that Susan in the development office whispered I was being groomed for the board. But of course, there's a charity version of mutual back-scratching. It means that everyone who donates or buys a ticket to my event then asks me to buy one for their cause as well, resulting in a full calendar of going out.

These events can be fun, sure, but lately the whole black-tie thing has gotten worse, spiraling out of control to the point where we can conceivably be out five nights a week. Sometimes I worry about how easily lying comes to me in terms of wriggling out of attending. It's truly almost like breathing. *Hi, it's Holland. I'm sooo sorry, but Tim and I can't make your Night of Wagner at the Opera because we have friends in town!* Or: *Gosh, I'll have to miss your museum luncheon—I have a doctor's appointment, bummer!* Come to think of it, it's really just minifibs to spare people's feelings, because I generally much prefer small, intimate gatherings to stuffy formal fetes with penguin suits and pearl chokers.

And take luncheons, for example. I have a strict *no-luncheons* policy, which can be tricky in Manhattan, and thus involves at least weekly lies to various hedge fund wives who invite me to their interminable afternoons at La Goulue or Sette Mezzo. Let's face it: The word "luncheon" is "lunch" plus "eon" because it takes eons for the darn thing to end. My last was a Museum of Natural History luncheon that went on so long, it was as if the gigantic T. rex dinosaur jawbones bit a humongous bloody chunk out of my day. Whether I was giving tours at Miles's school, working at the hospital writing fund-raising letters, or simply running the house, my time was in scattered pieces like the fossils. So I feel zero guilt as I rattle off faux excuses to various invitations that would no doubt be the equivalent of social root canal.

But lying to Tim was different.

My husband of seven years knew me so well, I had to avert my eyes when I spewed out some invented plan, tending to a supposedly errant cuticle or lip gloss touch-up rather than look him in the eye. It had come to this since our last major fight a month ago.

"I don't think you quite understand, Holly," he yelled at me, brown eyes ablaze. "You are NEVER to speak to Kiki again. Ever. She is *out* of this family. She left my brother and she's a tacky little bitch. The Talbott family sticks together, and if Hal has booted that slut from his life, we do the same. Delete her from your Outlook. That garbage Kiki Talbott is Out. Of. Our. Lives."

He slammed the door to his bathroom. I heard the shower go on and closed my eyes, knowing that despite his fervent militaristic command, my best friend—my now ex-sister-in-law—was most certainly not going to be dumped in the trash.

We had married two brothers, the scions of Comet Capital, a thriving New York City hedge fund. When I first met Kiki Silverstein, I wasn't quite sure about her—she was kind of a loud-mouth, wearing a leopard-print Dolce&Gabbana coat with big gold buttons, huge Rachel Zoe–esque sunglasses not unlike an insect's compound eyes on top of her head, and five-inch platform tranny-esque black patent leather heels, rattling off a laundry list of orders to her assistant through a headset on her newfangled shiny cell. She ran a manicured hand with dark red nails through her shiny dark-brown shoulder-length hair and had a bit too much eye makeup on her crystal blue eyes. While Posey, Mary, and Trish, my circle of New York mom-friends I'd met through Miles's school, were incredibly refined and traditionally "ladylike," Kiki was brassy and sassy and had edge to spare, with a gutter mouth and a sick bod she flaunted that immediately put all guys' minds in the gutter right beside her language. But little by little, I saw that beneath the windup doll that cracked everyone up with her hilarious zingers and often scathing one-liners was a gentle, nurturing, warm soul who, in the six years of her marriage to Hal, truly grew to be family. In fact, despite how polar opposite we were, she became the sister I never had. And I couldn't excise her from my life just because Hal did.

Kiki had told me that when they first met, the sparks that flew between her and Hal were practically atomic. They shacked up for days, with Chinese food takeout cartons outside her door the only proof that they were not dead. But they had never felt more alive. Madly, passionately in love, they went at it in coatrooms, at other people's parties, even in the handicapped bathroom stall at her tenth high school reunion. When I first met her, I felt removed from the whir and buzz of their shared sexual heat. I was puking my brains out, pregnant with Miles and feeling about as alluring as a cinder block, while Hal kissed and licked her ear and probably pawed her beneath the table. Tim and I were like an old preppy couple, relaxed into three years together and so excited for the stork—definitely in love, but not minks in the sack like old times. Come to think of it, Tim had never pawed me under the table.

But slowly through the years as those electric currents flickered, faded, and then zapped out, Hal began to push Kiki away. He became cold and distant, obsessed with discussing Tiger Woods's latest tournament during dinner rather than lusting after her the way he once had, and Kiki and I found ourselves a couple of golf widows languishing every Saturday and Sunday while our husbands hit the links or flew off to watch the latest PGA tournament.

About two years earlier, on a winter weekend trip to Palm Beach, I clued in to how truly miserable she was, despite the fact that she turned every head by the Breakers pool in her Burberry string bikini.

"I fucking hate it here. This place is all Newlyweds and Nearly Deads," she said, from under her enormous sunglasses. "It's so damn humid in this goddamn state, I get off the plane and I'm in Florida but my hair is in Cuba. I always look like dogshit here; my skin, my hair. The state even looks like a big dick. And the moment I land here, it fucks my whole look."

I pointed to Miles so that she'd halt her incessant cursing.

"Oh, sorry, Milesie. Aunt Kiki said a bad word." She exhaled, looking at her watch as Miles smiled mischievously, then ran off to play on the dunes with his friends. "Ugh, can you fucking believe this shit with Hal and Tim's golf? That sport could not be more torturous. It's watching grass grow. It's men with hideous pants walking," Kiki lamented. "I'd rather gnaw on my own liver than take up that tartan hell. Sorry, I know you hate my cursing."

"I don't mind; it's just when Miles is here, that's all."

"Oh, please. Even when he's not here you say 'sugar' instead of 'shit.' You're such a good girl," she teased, patting my head. "I'm a naughty influence."

"I know, you say that I'm repressed and should lose my edit button. Fine. The golf thing *sucks*. It sucks sugar," I teased. "But they work so hard, and if they can blow off steam . . . ," I offered in Tim's defense.

"Please. Hal can blow *me*. For a change." She looked off at the horizon as Miles played capture the flag with the other kids. "Holly, if I tell you something, do you swear not to tell Tim?"

"Of course," I promised. "Come on, I never tell Tim anything you tell me."

Kiki took off her glasses and looked at me. Her big blue eyes welled with tears. "Hal won't sleep with me. It's been months. I don't know what's going on, but I feel like Marie Antoinette. Minus the rolling head. There's no head in my life. He won't even let me—" Her eyes seemed to glisten with the dew of fought-back cascades.

I felt terrible for her. But more than that, I was shocked. She and Hal had been self-professed "rabbits," and for *them* to have such a sexual dry spell was unimaginable.

"It's just a phase," I said, putting my hand on her shoulder, trying to soothe her as she wiped away one escaped drop from her heavily mascara'd eye. "Tim and I have had that. It's normal."

"I'm not so sure," she said, wiping more tears away from her long, glistening lashes. "He came to my family's seder and was so distant and rude. My parents and brother were appalled; he treated me worse than Pharaoh."

But as time wore on and two more years passed, both Tim and I knew that things between Hal and our sister-in-law had seriously cooled. We had gone out to one of our weekly foursome

11

dinners, and when Kiki put her arm around Hal, he brushed it off—in front of us. Even Tim noticed and commented on how harsh it was, but said that his brother was overworked and stressed out with The Fund, which was almost like a mistress to both of them. Seriously, sometimes I found myself getting so jealous of the darn laptop, I wanted to chuck the goddamn thing out the window. It could be 3:37 a.m. and I'd think Tim was getting up to pee, and then I'd hear him clacking away; the chirpy *shwing!* of an instant message had become like a jackhammer to my eardrum. Or at the airport, minutes before they would close the flight, he simply had to run into the Admirals Club for just a second: more clickety-clacking. BlackBerries in restaurants. Cell phones at dinner parties. You get the picture. And through all of it, Kiki was my sharer in disapproving head shakes, tsk-tsks, and eye rolls from horrified observers, forcing us to whisper embarrassed comments like, "C'mon, sweetie, no texting during the Broadway show."

So it was a surprise, if not a total shock, when she sat me down at Sant Ambroeus on Madison Avenue one warm June day. "I'm filing for divorce from Hal," she said, dramatically clearing her throat and looking me in the eye. "I've fucking had it with being Mrs. Hedgefund."

2

"My ex-wife was a cardiac surgeon. She ripped my heart out."

"Going once . . . going twice? Lot twenty-two: SOLD for seven hundred fifty thousand!" Delicate claps from the chic tuxedo- and gown-wearing crowd echoed the gavel's podium bang.

Was I at an art auction where a Damien Hirst was just hawked? An Etruscan vase? A Schlumberger honeybee ring? No. It was five days before Kiki told me the stunning news of her split from Hal, and the two of us were at the spectacular annual spring charity benefit for the Lancelot Foundation for children's hospitals, at which Comet Capital, along with every other big hedge fund in the city, had taken a table inside the Puck Building in SoHo. For the past four years I'd worked on the committee with Posey and Mary, and we had fun planning it, and the event raised more money for charity than any other evening in New York City. It was very interesting to see the inner workings and politics when the event involved huge egos and huge wallets; for example, Hugo Lovejoy cut an extra check to Lancelot to ensure that this year his table "wasn't in fucking Siberia." By the way, their table previously had hardly been by the kitchen's swinging doors—his wife, Pippa, simply needed to

13

be in the front row this time. Or, as Hugo said it, "So she can see the auctioneer sweat."

Here's the rule for the seating: The bigger the fund, the closer their table to the stage where the action was. There was the auctioneer calling out the astronomic bids, speeches by heavy hitters, and a Rolling Stones performance (lot fifteen, singing "Jumpin' Jack Flash" with Mick, Keith, and the gang, went for $1.2 million). Other lots included Fifteen Minutes with Warren Buffett ($700,000) and A Bowl of Matzoh Ball Soup cooked by Rachael Ray ($675,000). Lunch with Charlize had just garnered three-quarter mill.

Kiki thought it was all terribly "yawnsville," but I found it to be fun, definitely much better than most events. It was exciting, like Wimbledon for the hedgie crew, with heads turning as the auction bids volleyed higher and higher in order to impress colleagues and rivals.

"Lot twenty-three: Vive La France: a private jet to Paris, a stay at the Ritz Hotel, couture show tickets furnished by the houses of Chanel, Valentino, Lacroix, Nina Ricci, Gaultier, and Lanvin."

Paddles went up as nervous wives rubbed their hands together in gleeful fits, envisioning potential Parisian shopping marathons. Beside Mary and Trish, Posey waved at me across the room, beaming as her husband made the opening bid.

"I have one hundred thousand. Do I hear one-fifty?"

New paddles entered the fray.

"One-fifty. Do I hear one seventy-five?"

Kincaid and Peach Saunders plunged into the bidding war; he of Lightning Capital, Kincaid rolled up his sleeves: "Two hundred!"

14

"Please, that woman wouldn't know style if it bit her on her WASPy flat ass," moaned Kiki to me in a whisper. "It's like Chico's exploded on her. What a fucking waste."

"Kiki, shut up!" Hal commanded angrily.

I was holding Tim's hand, which I squeezed when his brother snapped at Kiki, but he just stared straight ahead. Yikes. I looked at Kiki, who sat with her arms crossed, clearly wounded from being reprimanded so publicly.

Then, Mac MacMonigle, from RockyPeaks Capital, raised his paddle as his wife, Jessica (and her new boobs, courtesy of Dr. Hidalgo), beamed proudly. Paddles also flew at tables taken by megafunds like Cerberus, Centaurus, and Firebird.

The honcho of Lava Capital jumped in around three hundred grand, and then Gianni Fasciatelli from WinStar took the bidding up another notch.

One aside: To add to my abbreviated explanation of hedge funds, let me also say that an element of the scene is also the funds' names. Because I'd seen all these paddle-happy people a million times at various industry events such as this one, I knew almost everyone—and their companies' monikers. At the very same event a few years back, Kiki and I plopped at a votive-lit cabaret table during cocktail hour and developed a chart on little napkins of how one could create his own hedge fund name.

It's quite simple: To create an impression of maximum grandeur, one takes a **Lofty Locale**, often celestial or geographic (COLUMN A). Or appropriates an element from **Greek Mythology** (COLUMN B) or the name of an **Elite Town** or **Resort Destination** (COLUMN C). That word can be used alone or combined with a **geological** or **topographical**

HOW TO NAME YOUR HEDGE FUND

A Lofty Locale	B Greek Mythology	C Elite Town or Resort Destination	D Geological or Topographical Element	E Group's Final Name
Star	Apollo	Sankaty (part of Nantucket)	Crest	Management
Galaxy	Pantheon	Cos Cob (part of Greenwich)	Hill	Capital
Wave	Cerberus	Katama (part of Martha's Vineyard)	Point	Partners
Fire	Zeus	Hobe Sound	Mount	Ventures
Moon	Artemis			
Sun	Olympus			

*Note: Optional "POWER WORDS" that conjure greatness can also be utilized, including FIERCE ANIMALS (Eagle, Cougar, Tiger, Jaguar, Panther), MATERIALS OR OBJECTS THAT CONNOTE STRENGTH (Steel, Fortress, Stone, Cannonball) or SWORD-WIELDING BADASSES (Pirate, Guard, Knight).

element (COLUMN D) before adding the group's final name (COLUMN E).

Results: StarPoint Capital or Cos Cob Ventures or Apollo-Crest Management. You get the picture.

Whatever the custom formula, A, B, or C+D+E=ego+**penis extension**. Unless someone just wimps out and uses his last name or initials, this is a surefire way to peg how every fund got its name.

"Lot twenty-four: SOLD for six hundred thousand to the gentleman in front."

Gag. It was Petri McNaughton's snooze of a husband, Roy, from EverestPeak Management. Everyone at their table was patting him on the back like he'd accomplished something. All he did was shell it out—very publicly, I might add—for a frigging trip. Petri beamed. Posey and Trish rolled their eyes. While my friends sometimes had the odd excessive expenditure, they were pretty much down-to-earth by New York standards. Some people we knew socially would occasionally go a tad too over-the-top, but they weren't even in the stratosphere of Dish McNaughton, who, rumor had it, once sent Roy's plane to Maine for live lobsters for her daughter's preschool class. For show-and-tell.

After three more lots (including a victory for Mary, whose hubby bought her a day of shopping with Cate Blanchett and a trip to her facialist), Kiki grabbed my hand and led me off to the bathroom, aching to get a break.

"And can you believe that schmuck who blew a million bucks for yoga with Rebecca fucking Romijn?!" She put on her bright red lipstick and adjusted her tan cleavage. "I guess that's, like, twenty bucks for these guys."

"Please. Tim wants to bid on that week racing McLarens upstate," I complained. "I told him it's one thing to leave us if he has to go away on business, but how do I tell Miles that Daddy's gone again because he has to race cars?"

"Hal wants that, too. I guess they'll go together and you and I will have some fun. Screw them. We can go see all those geeky Broadway shows you wanted to catch up on."

We lingered gossiping in the bathroom until Emilia d'Angelo, the ultimate hedge fund wife, entered. Emilia was the most put-together, perma-blond clotheshorse around, and her son Prescott was in Miles's kindergarten class at St. Sebastian's. Posey, Trish, and Mary were close friends with her, and so, by proxy, I was as well. I was always friendly, but she was a bit high profile in her spending, incessantly flaunting her wealth. Within one breath, she'd "casually" mention the ski house in Gstaad, the Gin Lane Southampton estate, the G5, and *My Honey's Money*, their yacht based in the Caymans. Posey once joked that the d'Angelos' boat made her mere 150-foot vessel look like a dinghy. Posey and I had become fast friends when our sons were in nursery school together at Carnegie, so when she quickly embraced Emilia, I came along. Since their husbands worked together and played golf all the time in Southport, and Emilia, Mary, and Trish's sons knew one another from their nursery school, we all kind of became a clique, reinforced by always seeing one another at events like these. We'd also shared many fun hens' dinners during all the hedge fund conferences when our husbands were away, trunk shows in one another's homes for a friend's new fine jewelry or handbag line or kids' clothes, even the occasional couples' weekend at the Mayflower in Connecticut.

But Kiki never understood my friendships with them and considered them lockjaw preppies. Maybe because she was hipper and a bit younger, but also, I suppose, because she didn't have kids, so she didn't quite grasp how much we had in common, whether it was teachers, school gossip, fund-raisers, or sports games. Plus, Posey and I often snuck off from the mommy posse and went to get a glass of wine; we even had our own secret miniplaygroup, which we called Tots'n'Tonic. During those winter months, when our guys were two and three, with ants in their pants, I thought I'd have to check into Payne Whitney.

"Hi, ladies. Marco just bought me the Hermès Alligator Trench!" Emilia beamed. "It's all handmade from one gator hide! Can you believe it?"

Kiki always said Emilia probably weighed in at 102 pounds and got down to double digits when she took her massive diamond ring off, which was all I could think of as the refracted light off her rock blinded me while she tucked a lock of hair behind her ear.

"Congrats," I said. She always seemed to be going on and on

about all her stuff. Luckily the rest of my friends didn't seem to do that and were a bit more discreet.

"See you tomorrow at school," Emilia replied, smiling, and exited.

"I wish I could throw her in the Everglades and have all those gators chomp her ass," Kiki said, fishing for a cigarette in her clutch.

"They'd still be hungry," I countered as I applied lip gloss.

"Touché." Kiki laughed. "She's no more filling than a fucking cracker. She's like a human Triscuit."

"I feel bad. She's nice, though," I offered, guiltily. "She just, you know, tries too hard to impress."

"Barf. Your whole mommy world is like these clones. They look fifty in their thirties; I mean, what's up with that? The silk scarves, the cashmere cape thingies with the ruffle or fur piping, hellooo, AARP!"

Kiki's hemlines were more like early twenties in my friends' opinions, I'm sure. But while my sister-in-law was the polar opposite of some of my friends, I was somewhere in the middle, seeing both sides of the coin. While I wasn't as edgy as I used to be (not that I was ever as daringly cool or as much of a risky fashionista as Kiki), I still had more pizzazz than most of my circle. Yes, I had long dirty blond hair and the requisite Tory Burch getups, but where the other ladies sometimes veered off in Republican wife territory, I sometimes went back to my semihipper stylings from my magazine days when I'd buy fun cheap dresses from hole-in-the-wall shops or well-worn rock tour T-shirts. But those days were behind me; not that I was a conformist or anything, but I was a mother and definitely had to dress up more often than not given the functions I had to attend by Tim's side. And when I was socially off the hook, I just wanted to be comfortable and not stress about getting decked out, hence my boring uniform of jeans and a blouse, a plain shift dress, or a skirt and cashmere T-shirt. But I must confess, sometimes I missed that feeling of being young and daring. And while I wasn't going to sport Paris Hilton–length minis on one end of the spectrum or my friends' matronly floor-length fur coats on the other, I knew I could be somewhere in the middle of both extremes. Emilia was the type who simply made too much of an effort. Every hair in place, every accessory of the moment, always fancy, fancy, fancy. Even her son was fancy. I swear, I once heard Prescott, as he was being picked up the last day before Christmas vacation, saying, "Mummy, are we taking the Cessna or the G4 to Lyford?" When Emilia replied that, *alas*, it was the Cessna this time as their Gulfstream was in California getting reupholstered in chocolate suede since he had gotten stains from his Milano cookies on the tan couches, he grouchily snapped "Aw, man! *Shucks!*"

But a lot of these women felt that this was the role they were cast to play: preened, polished, perfect—many of them dressing not for their husbands but for one another, glossed and glamorous and without human flaws. Foreheads were tight, thanks to 'TOX from Dr. Pat; asses were cellulite-free, thanks to Dr. Dan. Breasts were perma-pert, legs vein-free and hairless, skin smooth. There were lasers, lipos, and lips plumped, nails polished, feet massaged. Many retained makeup artists for black-tie engagements such as this one. Picture the larger-than-life cheerleading squad who ruled main hall by way of Madison Avenue and Avenue Montaigne.

The bathroom door opened and I could hear the auctioneer's booming voice echo through the marble stalls.

"Lot thirty-three: Get to Play a Dead Body on *Law & Order*. Value: priceless."

A jolt surged through my body. I had previously told Tim I didn't need a thing and not to bid as he'd already given a generous donation. But then I looked at Kiki instantly grinning—bingo, that was my all-time favorite show. Tim knew that during his extensive travels, I often just settled in for the night, hanging in the courtroom with Jack McCoy and the gang. No one—not the dork bloggers, or people with crushes on Chris Noth—*no one*, loved *L&O* more than I. I knew every plot. Memorized so much about the law that actual lawyers thought I was a judge. Was in tears when Jerry Orbach died. I bit my lower lip and smiled at Tim, and he knew immediately that I would love to be that corpse.

We walked back to our table, and there was Tim, paddle raised.

"Fifty thousand! Do I hear fifty-five?"

The bids rocketed skyward, and finally, at one twenty-five, I leaned in. "Tim, honey, it's okay. I don't need it."

"No, I'm getting this, Holly. It's the perfect gift for you, hon!" He raised his paddle. I knew it was for charity and probably tax deductible in some way, but it was all so outrageous.

Milton Summers from MajesticMount, a rival hedge fund to Comet Capital, shot Tim a look and raised his paddle. Sheesh. Now it really was a penis-measuring contest.

"Honey, seriously—I don't even need to be—"

"Holly, hon, quiet," he said, while staring down Milton. I hated it when Tim got competitive. The entire ballroom, in their decked-out luxe lace gowns and custom–Tom Ford penguin suits, were now watching the paddles with anticipation. But I knew, as did everyone, that poor Milton had had a year from hell. Not financially, of course, as his company's continued windfall landed him in the *Times* Business Section almost weekly.

But his wife, Lola, very humiliatingly had left him for the pilot of their private jet. Talk about giving new meaning to the word "cockpit." She was a prominent socialite-about-town who had once been an actress. Some had whispered that "actress" was code for stripper and that they'd met when she was on the pole, but it turned out that was a rumor and she'd just been waitressing in the financial district and had served the right guy his latte. He was smitten instantly. Poor schnook.

"Two hundred and fifty thousand dollars! Do I have two seventy-five?"

The crowd was hushed, with baited breath, and turned their diamond-covered necks back and forth between jumping bids. This was all to show Milton Summers he didn't give a damn about hemorrhaging money.

Finally Milton dropped out. He looked over at me and smiled and shrugged as Tim pumped his fist in victory and high-fived Hal. Nice. My husband's unstoppable paddle-wagging had resulted in his cool parting with half a mill. Tim believed in the Golden Rule. Though that has changed in the last generation or two. When I was growing up, it was that Do Unto Others thing. But now it's shifted a bit. So that it's He Who Has the Most Gold, Rules.

"Timmy, you did not have to do that—" I said, stunned.

"Anything for you, hon," he said, giving me a kiss on the cheek.

It was a very hefty gift to the charity, and I must say, I was secretly ecstatic. Buffett Schmuffet—this was the best lot by far. There I'd be: amidst the staccato, menacing *doink-doink* sound, which I'd read was originally designed to echo a jail cell slamming shut. Camera crews would shut down a city block for the shoot as a makeup person would make me look extra-pallid and cadavery. It would be the coolest cameo ever. But in the midst of my prime-time reverie of trench-coated detectives hovering over me with the flashes of faux–forensic photographers, I had to wonder: Had Tim been generous so that his beloved wife could be a chalk outline on national television, or so he could beat out MajesticMount? Tim loved a lot of things. I knew he loved me. But he also loved being number one.

3

"My husband and I separated for religious reasons. He thought he was God and I didn't."

"What do you mean you *met someone?*" I bellowed, not even a month after our lunch at Sant Ambroeus. I blurted it out so loud in Orsay that I had to re-ask in a low-key murmur, as if taking back my bellowed indignation.

"Shhhh! *Holl*, Jesus! Why don't you broadcast to the whole fucking place? I think those anorexic moms sharing one tea sandwich over there didn't hear you! My God."

"Sorry."

"Listen, you know we had issues for so long now and I was bursting. We met a few months ago. I almost told you at the Lancelot auction last month, but it was too crazy. I had hit my breaking point in a loveless marriage. And now there's no turning back because I knew I wouldn't have the balls to leave Hal unless I left him with my body. I didn't sleep with this guy before I filed the papers, I swear. We just kissed. But I knew that if I betrayed Hal, there would be zero possibility of reconciliation on his end, and I would be free."

"I can't believe this . . . ," I trailed off, staring at the cookie plate but too paralyzed to reach for one.

"Why? I mean, it's not like I'm even in love with Gustave or gonna marry him or anything."

"Gustave?" I asked. "You cheated on Hal with a guy named Gustave? What, is he a poet? Massage therapist? His name might as well be Thor! I can't believe our family is splintering. . . ."

"Hello? *It was just a kiss!* And if I wanted judgments, I'd have laid this on Sherry Von."

She was right. I shouldn't judge her. While they were extremely close brothers, Hal and Tim were not the same person, and I had no idea what Kiki and Hal had gone through behind closed doors.

Sherry was Sherry Von Hapsburg Talbott and we called her Sherry Von because she *always* used her whole name, lest plebians forget she was of aristocratic ilk on the Continent, whence her illustrious crested-blazer ancestry hailed. Even her weekend L.L. Bean bag was monogrammed "S. Von H. T." I mean, everything was Von this, Von that, Von *yawn*. She was a raging ice queen and made family gatherings so unbearable with her snobbish yammering and pronouncements from on high that one begged for an ejector seat, Dr. Evil–style, that would suck her through the Oriental rug into the chasms of darkness. Was I being harsh? No. She really was that bad. Her sons tuned it out, talking business the whole time, while Kiki and I were stuck with her running commentary on everything from "unsightly" Oscar dresses to those "godawful Democrats." Being with her was like having that incessant crawl at the bottom of your TV screen. But in an oversized font. In fluorescent yellow.

It was Kiki who got me through every family dinner we had to endure. Selfishly, my first thought now was how I could possibly handle Sherry Von without Kiki by my side. And while I'd sometimes feel bad for Sherry Von, who was widowed at fifty-three when Tim's dad, Chuck, died in a heliskiing accident, she always managed to take my sympathy and warp it into a complete lack of understanding of how someone could be so cold. Granted, her marriage was not exactly the warm, loving nest my parents had; Tim had always told me his father was this larger-than-life Wall Street legend, world-class athlete, and the consummate charmer, while his reserved wife never doted on him or their children the way my mother always had. Despite all her family wealth, and as the ultimate hedge fund wife, Sherry Von was a fundamentally unhappy soul, a malcontent who never nurtured and probably never was nurtured.

"You just know that bitch is popping Dom corks right now," Kiki said, probably correctly. When Kiki and Hal began their firestorm romance, Sherry vented to Tim and me that Kiki was "not our kind," i.e., Jewy Jewstein from Five Towns in Long Island (or, as Kiki's hilarious and equally colorful dad, a Jacuzzi salesman in Ronkonkoma, would pronounce it, "Lawn Gyland"). In fact, Sherry Von previously had referred to all Jews as "Canadians" when she needed to employ codespeak. And now Kiki had given Sherry just want she wanted: validation.

"I think the second best thing about this is that I don't have to see that evil vitriolic slag anymore." Kiki laughed, sipping her wine. "Though I do feel bad leaving you in that fucking Locust Valley quagmire alone."

I tried to keep up my end of the conversation, but I was reeling with devastation and shock that Kiki was really and truly moving on and there was 0.00 percent chance of a reconciliation. See, being with Kiki was like having a pocket stand-up comedian. Her every observation was geniusly funny, and acutely accurate. My heart suddenly felt like it was ten pounds of lead as she blithely spoke of Gustave and all the sex she had missed for years with frigid Hal but would now be free to have. I simply sat, trembling. I knew the Talbott family was cultlike in its team quality of sticking together and that Kiki would be on the outs and big-time. And because there was no glue of a child to keep her somewhat in our orbit, I was certain that Sherry Von's pronouncement from on high would be that Kiki was dead to us.

4

"FOR SALE: Wedding Dress. Size 6. Worn once by mistake."

The fallout from Kiki's affair was, indeed, nuclear. The first time I saw Sherry Von post-divorce was a few months later at Thanksgiving, in Locust Valley, at Hillendale, the family manor, which was not unlike the Cleary compound in *Wedding Crashers*, though I wish there had been some fun goth brother or drunken grandma to liven stuff up. The only remotely quirky or interesting presence was Hubert, Sherry Von's devoted gay southern assistant–slash–driver–slash–chief of staff. He worshipped the ground she walked on, despite being treated like crap by her, and tended to her every whim, whether shipping her Louboutin heels to have the laces fixed, booking her at-home pedicure (God forbid she be spied with her feet naked IN PUBLIC!), or simply fastening a ruby necklace. Hubert was immaculate: French cuffs; a quiet, soothing aura; and only kind things to say. Every other word out of his mouth was "divine," and I loved him. My crappy Banana Republic dress? "Divine." Miles's vocabulary? Divine. I wondered how on earth he put up with Sherry Von's moods and barked orders.

Hubert had overseen the dining room's divine décor for the evening: Over pumpkin pie served by Sherry Von's staff (who wore full antiquated outfits with the frilly white aprons and caps like the ones you get in a prepackaged "French Maid" Halloween costume), sterling Puiforcat utensils clinked against fine Baccarat china, and fine wine was quietly sipped from Yeoward crystal. The table was immaculate. The food: impeccable. The flowers: richly arranged in subtle hues, their fragrance filling the air. The vibe: filled with the bitter flavor of rage. As soon as Miles went into the den to watch *The Wizard of Oz* on TV, Sherry Von unleashed her own flying monkeys of wrath. Finally, after a dramatic drawn-out silence, Sherry Von spoke.

"I always knew she was garbage," she pronounced.

I felt my stomach drop.

"Mother, please, let's just enjoy dessert," Tim interrupted.

"NO. I won't be quiet for Holland's sake."

I always hated when the spotlight was on me. I got instantly toasty on the back on my neck, cringing from her gaze. And Sherry Von always called me Holland, my real given name, which was my mom, Lillian Holland's, maiden name. I could tell that for Sherry Von, the more sedate "Holland," versus the staccato "Kiki," seemed less playful and more fancypants. Even after years together, with everyone on planet Earth calling me Holly, I was only Holland to Sherry Von. Which would be fine since I loved my name, but I just knew her shady motivation for clinging to it was reinforcement that I came from what she considered to be an *acceptable* family versus Kiki's. The Silversteins, meanwhile, were a fun, spirited, hilarious crew. Kiki and her two brothers would never call their mom "Mother" the way Tim and Hal did. Which was another reason I felt a kinship with her from the start: I knew she hailed from a more affectionate, caring family, like mine, despite Sherry Von's nose in the air about her clan's stature or lack therof.

"You were thick as thieves, you two," Sherry Von said, pointing a skinny, bejeweled finger at me across the grand table as Hubert quietly refilled her wineglass. "You fought for her acceptance, and now look! DISGRACE! She *cheated* on our Hal. She brought filth into their bed."

I looked at my lap, shuddering. "There was no 'bed.' They just kissed," I began in her defense.

"Cheating," pronounced Sherry, "cheating is a MORTAL SIN, in my book, Holland. After all those vows that courtesan pledged at that tacky wedding with that horrible chair dance, after all those oaths before our friends, she HUMILIATES us. And she has the GALL to challenge the prenup!"

Said prenup was signed by both my ex-sister-in-law as well as yours truly. It was a Stone Age–style offering of a million dollars, with more depending on years spent together and number of children. Since Kiki's number of offspring was zero, she was to take the mil and walk. Kiki didn't want to milk Hal, but she wanted to buy an apartment and move on, so she challenged for a little more. Most women go for half the fortune (which was probably around $100 million), but Kiki just wanted the whole thing done with pronto.

"It's not all black-and-white," I feebly ventured. "Sometimes things don't work, and there are always two sides—"

The fiercest hurricanes could not temper Sherry Von's meteorological reaction.

"NOT. IN. THIS. FAMILY. HOLLAND. TALBOTT!" She always spoke with full stops between words, for effect, not unlike an earsplitting trumpet blaring short bursts; I had actually noticed Tim grifting off this pattern of speech of late as well, and I did not enjoy any like-mother-like-son parallels. It was Sherry

Von's trademark punctuation vehicle in which to fully deliver her accentuated fits of ire. Her frail framed quivered and boiled with fury as she cleared her throat and narrowed her eyes, glaring at me as if I were committing high treason.

"We. Stick. To. Gether!" (table pounded on "gether") she continued. "And if some disgusting earthworm of a whore crawls into our homes and deceives us, we turn our backs on that worm FOR. GOOD. She is FINISHED in this town, finished! No clubs, no boards, nothing. You BETTER not allege that there are 'sides' here! There is ONE side! The. Family's." And with that, she threw her hand-stitched monogrammed linen napkin on the table and stormed off.

Sheesh. The way she spoke it was as if we were the Corleones.

"Holy shit, Holly, why don't you just FedEx my mother to the cardiologist," Tim said as he bent to finish his pie.

"Sweetie, I'm sorry, but she's insane. That whole 'mortal sin' crap. It's not so cut-and-dried—"

"Yes, it is." Tim took his arm off my chair. "I know you guys were close, but she cheated. That's the point of no return. My mom's right, Holl; there aren't 'two sides' to *every* story. No matter what Hal did, she shouldn't have crossed that line. I hope you think about that if she tries to reach out to you."

Little did my unsuspecting husband know, I'd been talking to her almost every day. In the wake of press coverage swarming buzzard-like over the gutted antelope of their marriage, Kiki needed to vent about what the gossips were writing. As the family is high profile—Sherry Von sits on almost every major board in the city: MoMA, Metropolitan Opera, New York City Ballet, New York Hospital (which had changed its name so many times, it currently had, like, seven words on its letterhead)—Page Six of the *Post* had picked the scoop right up, complete with the bold headline **SPLITSVILLE FOR HEDGE FUND PRINCE**. Kiki, who had been kind of a high-profile party girl herself pre-Hal, was still working as a publicist, having started her own firm in her mid-twenties pre-marriage, and was now doing better than ever, so her being photographed by Patrick McMullan out and about made the family even more pissed than before. See, publicist is not an acceptable hedge fund wife job. Example profession charticle:

HEDGE FUND WIVES' CAREERS

COLUMN A (acceptable)*	COLUMN B (unacceptable)
Stay-at-home mom with 24/7 help	Publicist
Docent at the Met	Fashionista
Jewelry designer	Nightlife impresario
Handbag designer	Actress**
Editor at glossy monthly	Editor at weekly tabloid

*Note: even column A careers cannot be *too* successful lest they threaten the husband and the ability to be present as arm candy at countless hedgie events.
** Unless she's won a major award (Oscar, Emmy) and stopped working, i.e., Grace Kelly saying her best role was that of a mother caring for her children.

Publicists court press and attention, which WASPy matriarchs, like Sherry Von, avoid. Kiki and Hal's wedding had gotten a ton of press, much to Sherry Von's chagrin, as she pronounced sending wedding photos to magazines uncouth. She believed your announcement should *only* be in the *Times*, and then you should never appear in the papers again until it's your obituary.

There was some leeway for the occasional cameo on Bill Cunningham's charity party page in the Sunday Styles section, but that was it. Before I got married, I worked at two monthly women's magazines covering music and writing features on musicians. It was far more acceptable than Kiki's party-and-flashbulb-centric milieu, but hardly Sherry Von's world, either, and the second I got pregnant, I was encouraged to quit. It's not like I was obsessed with my daily grind, so I happily threw myself into motherhood and never looked back. Okay: Sometimes I've looked back. For one, I always used to see bands. I knew every new act, hot track, and trend. Now I was out of touch; when I tune in to the MTV Video Music Awards I don't recognize half the names, whereas I used to know everyone who cleared their throats by a microphone. I have a very eclectic musical spectrum, loving hard rock and Broadway show tunes and a little in between. Tim loves classic rock, which I abhor; he favors the Eagles most of all, and their music is like a cheese grater to my ear. Plus, aside from seeing new hot bands, I also missed interviewing illustrious people—I'd written about indie rock bands and British invasion groups, and had done cover stories on everyone from Gwen Stefani to countless bubblegum teen pop idols. I always secretly dreamed of one of them asking me to write their biography. I found profiling people fascinating, and sometimes wished I had kept a toe in the work pool rather than cut bait altogether; sometimes deep down when I was with all the other moms or volunteering or doing tours at Miles's school I was dying to scream, *But I'm not just a mom, I'm cool! I used to see bands three nights a week! I don't play "Baby Beluga" for my kid, I play vintage R.E.M.!* But I had no regrets.

Kiki, on the other hand, loved her work and could never quit. And she was very successful, with all kinds of high-profile accounts from fashion houses to car companies, each one trying to penetrate the young, cool scene in New York. Even before she married Hal, Kiki was a name around town, known for her lavish parties, for being a muse to Zac Posen, even for a fling with Christian Slater in the nineties. A high-profile marriage only added to her omnipresence in the party picture pages. So now in the foaming wake of the divorce, the press was lapping up every detail about lawyers, possible prenups, and the epic battle that would ensue. One reporter had even called me at home, but per Tim's instructions, I simply answered, "No comment," then apologized (not in Tim's instructions) before hanging up.

It wasn't until I met Kiki for one of our secret lunches that I realized how dark and dirty Tim's family would play it. Kiki had a college friend from her U. Penn sorority who was in New York for a day of meetings. As she ran around town, the friend started noticing the same guy in a brown suit cropping up at various points throughout the day. Paranoid, she took the train to SoHo, always looking in store windows' reflections to see if he was still there. He was. Finally, in the middle of West Broadway and scores of people, she spun around and came face-to-face with the man, demanding to know why he was following her. Surprisingly, he admitted he was a private investigator and said he was sorry but was just doing his job, tracking Kiki and trailing her pal for added due diligence.

Upon hearing this, back at her apartment, Kiki paused and had a Keyser Söze–style flashback of various people watching her around her neighborhood. There was a guy buying fruit next to her at Gourmet Garage who showed up at Barneys, which was odd since it was by the Goyard corner, where men didn't often lurk, and then he was even walking by the Lexington Avenue window of Simadi, the hair salon where she got weekly blow-outs. The pieces fell into place, and she realized the Talbotts had hired a sleuth to dig up dirt on her.

"So I've put the brakes on with Gustave and any other guys, for now," she told me just before Christmas at La Goulue, looking both ways at the preened yummy mummies slurping their liquid lunches. "I could give a shit what the papers say, but it's this freaky investigator shit that wigs me out. I feel like Sherry Von has called in the CIA."

"Listen, there's nothing they can say. You haven't done anything wrong; you're separated and you've filed for divorce."

"But it's such a double standard. I have to be very discreet. I finally got out of a frigid marriage and I still can't see anybody or they'll label me a whore. But I'm no gold-digging slut. I work, and I just so happen to be kicking ass. I just hired Ellen Barkin's attorney. Two can play hardball."

And hardball she played. She landed a fair settlement, won the acrid, unhinged, fiery fury of Sherry Von Hapsburg Talbott, and got herself a fresh new start.

5

"An ex-spouse is like an inflamed appendix. It causes a lot of pain and suffering, and when it's removed, you realize you didn't need it, anyway."

In January, just after Kiki and Hal's divorce was finalized, I exhaustedly trekked home after a particularly chilly day in the park (though I am one of those people who is always cold, as in sweatshirt-on-the-beach cold) watching Miles in his Super Soccer Stars class. We ordered in a pizza, as I was too lazy to cook (read: heat up Citarella takeout). One of the good things about marrying the son of Sherry Von is that he never expected me to whip up some insane dinner in full apron mode, 1950s style—the only thing in her life his mother ever made for dinner was reservations.

Tim was away yet again, this time in Oregon at some giant convention center–slash–hotel, so I was in a pattern of tucking Miles into bed and then facing the question of what to do with myself from 8:00 until midnight, when I fell asleep. I had already booked our sitter just in case I wanted to escape and have one of those luxurious dinners alone at Etats-Unis wine bar, something I occasionally treated myself to when Tim was out of town. So when Posey called me and asked me to join the other hedge fund conference widows for dinner at Sette Mezzo, I was game.

When I got to the restaurant, our normal window table was full with Trish, with her trademark bright red shoulder-length hair and strand of pearls; Emilia, dressed to the nines; raven-haired Mary; and smiling Posey, who waved through the window as I approached. Once we all kissed hello and ordered, the sport of choice commenced: killer people-watching. It was like golf for women.

After a few minutes, in walked a nervous Millie Lange. After a quick smile and greeting by our table, she walked with an older woman—who I guessed was her mom or aunt—to the back of the restaurant. All the women swooped like hungry vultures on the bloody carcass of poor Millie, a mom whose sons were in the second and fourth grades in our school, who had just gotten divorced due to her husband's excessive cocaine use, which even stints at Promises, Paradise, Passages, and Cirque Lodge couldn't remedy.

"Poor thing. Ugh, I mean, who's gonna go for her now?" scoffed Emilia, hand through her coiffed mane. "She has her sons, thank goodness, but what guy would want that baggage?"

"Well, maybe she could get some older guy," offered Mary, with a look of concern across her freckled, black-Irish complexion. "You know, some rich gray-hair type in his fifties or sixties, and then thirty-seven will seem young to him!" I knew that Mary, like Posey and me, hoped Millie would land on her feet. But New York is a tricky town for women *d'un certain âge*, as Sherry Von likes to say.

Posey had testified that Millie Lange came from a very powerful old–New York family and that luckily she would have plenty of money and enough influence to maintain her social standing.

"Her father was a huge ad guy. Like CEO of one of the big agencies. He invented the Energizer Bunny."

"Come on," I said, snorting up my Sprite.

"Seriously," said Trish. "And it's still going and going and going, that rodent."

"It's so funny," I mused. "Who would have thought a rabbit with Corey Hart sunglasses banging a big drum would become an icon?"

"There's no accounting for random successes," said Posey. "Just look at Teenage Mutant Ninja Turtles. I mean, how bizarre is that? *Billions*."

"Oh, check it out, Cassidy Freedkin is sitting in the corner." Emilia subtly gestured, sipping her Chianti.

"I heard she's chairing the NACHO benefit at the Waldorf this year," said Trish. "She just hired two publicists to get herself more 'out there,' she told me."

"It's so weird," whispered Mary. "I assumed that since she's so obsessed with New Yorkers Against Childhood Obesity, her daughter would be, like, rolling into the room à la Violet Beauregard! But she's the skinniest one at Ballet Academy East! Her mom won't let her NEAR that vending machine. Instead she buys her ten-packs of shiny stickers to distract her from the Nutter Butters."

"I know, I mean I could rake the leaves at my farm with her kid!" Trish laughed.

"Meanwhile, Cassidy looks great," remarked Posey.

"Yeah," agreed Emilia, looking disappointed. "What's she doing, South Beach? Atkins? Macrobiotic?"

"I heard she's big on the Two Finger Diet," whispered Mary.

There were a few more sightings: Kincaid and Peach Saunders loudly ordering risotto with "a double helping of white truffles" for everyone at their table of eight; Chip Berlin and his wife,

Patty, sitting mute, not speaking for their entire dinner; and Mac McMonigle and Kent Quick and their decked-out wives going through four bottles of wine and laughing way too loudly.

"So sad," said Emilia, leaning in. "I hear Chip Berlin has a standing high-priced hooker at the Ritz-Carlton every Thursday afternoon!"

"I heard that, too!" exclaimed Mary, flushed with gossip high.

"How does she not know?" asked Trish, eyes aflame.

"Ostrich syndrome, just denial," said Posey. "Or maybe she does know and doesn't care. She gets her lifestyle. . . ."

"Yeah, I mean, where's she gonna go?" said Emilia.

"You always know everything," I told Mary, who beamed.

"Well, I'll admit I am privy to a ton of scoop. But let me tell you girls this: For all the stuff that's going down in this town, we don't have a thing on the Greenwich hedge fund scene. That place appears perfect, with the lawns and the four blond kids and the golden retrievers, but we were out there this weekend and let me tell you, some of these gals were doing lines in the changing room at Round Hill!"

"No!" gasped Posey, hand over mouth.

"Yes," continued Mary, leaning in. "And in the bathroom at Polpo, too. The DEA could do a full-on raid, I swear! You know that guy Burke Lockhart from Triton Partners?"

"Wait, the guy who has five daughters and won't let his wife stop until he gets a boy?" asked Trish.

"Yes. And while he's making her into a baby factory, he's in his Ferrari getting BJs from the wife of Kent Colgate from SaturnRings Capital!"

"You lie," I said, stunned.

"I'm telling you, we city rats are tame next to those preppy country mice."

"Here's to staying in the city!" said Posey, raising her glass. We all clinked glasses and cheered our sometimes odd but definitely fun urban existence.

"Oh, and speaking of BJs, get this," said, Mary, eyes ablaze. "Corbett walked in yesterday after school and said, 'Mom, Richie Frank told me where babies come from.' So I asked him where Richie said babies come from, and he said, 'The daddy sticks his penis in the mommy's mouth.' I said, no, darling, that's where *jewelry* comes from!"

We were all howling. All in all, it was a great (if a bit raunchy) night.

I got home and flipped on the television. My other husband was David Letterman, but he wouldn't be on air in forever. And the barrage of depressing reality TV was too much to bear. I hit the guide button and scrolled down to find—YES!—*Sixteen Candles.* Jackpot. It was amazing to me that I was now more than double these kids' age and yet in my head they were still the same age as, or even older than, me, as if frozen in time from when I first saw them in fifth grade. And, oooh, Jake Ryan. Someone spatula me off the carpet now. That last scene, with the cars scooting away in every direction leaving only his red chariot, chills. So many teen movies nowadays have just fast-paced zingers, insta-comebacks, and Teflon-skinned bad-asses who never let anything get to them.

What I loved about the John Hughes movies was the characters' vulnerability, that *everything* got to them. Like real teenagers. The beauty was in them not knowing what to say—they didn't even dream of zapping out the pithy one-liner. It was the biting of the lower lip, the anxiety of wrong-side-of-the-tracks-ness, and the palpable insecurity that was so real to me. Not because zitty teenagehood was finally a distant memory, but because in some ways it never goes away.

Basically . . . I married a John Hughes hottie.

But instead of the kiss over flickering candles, frozen in a snapshot of happily ever after, I still sometimes felt like an outsider in Tim's world. When I was single I was hardly a party girl, but I loved being at music venues, seeing rock bands, and just feeling part of this huge giant city I'd moved to. Tim's world was way more rarefied, sort of a homogenous, preppy, athletic petri dish within this bubbling cauldron of diversity. In a way it's kind of amazing we even intersected at all, seeing as how I was writing about music and more drawn to nerdy musicians and writers and he was in what I considered to be the more robotic world of finance. But that's the magic of New York: You can go through any revolving door and you never know who you'll bump into on the other side.

This is how we met: a Wall Street party in the financial district.

When I first saw Tim, I was living with my roommate, my best college friend, Jeannie, who has since moved home to Boston. Even though we were smart and educated, we talked about boys all the time and primped together for Saturday odysseys around town. We were always up for anything. If we weren't going out to see a band, we'd all hit the phones and call around to see what was going on, and one particular night we ended up at a random party in what's now called SoChiTo (South of Chinatown, not to be confused with WeWa, West of Wall). New York had so many newly gentrified ghetto-to-gold neighborhoods, I couldn't keep track. But I remember having to look the address up on my map, as it was the first time I'd ever been there and the rental building was the first of its kind in that then-creepsville area. The space was big and boxy, the music was good (some trendy DJ "spinnin' it"), and the skyscraping view was twinkly and mesmerizing. But it was one of those parties where all the good ingredients still made up a crappy stew. Plus, I didn't feel well at all—my chunder was mid-esophagus and rising. Unlike the anonymity of, say, a bar or a music venue, parties were often bizarre two-degrees-of-Kevin-Bacon social Venn diagrams where you bumped into random people you knew tangentially and you couldn't just be free to listen to songs or dance; there was too much small talk, too much "how do you know so-and-so?"

Did I have some kind of social anxiety disorder like the people on that drug commercial with all the warped, stretched-out faces? Why did I occasionally get nervous at parties? Sometimes I could have a blast, of course, but the newness—that feeling of starting over—always haunted me until I grew at ease with my surroundings. The elevator door opened and there were two signs, for apartments A to H and J to P, but we heard the din of music, voices, a breaking glass, and a collage of muffled whooping, "heys," and "what-ups" before we could remember which letter we were looking for. Back then, there was always this excitement turning the corner into a party; even with the best of friends at your side, there was a nervousness of anticipation. And the anticipation turned to sheer dread when I beheld the scene: I detested this kind of crowd. It was mostly carbon-copied Wall Street dudes chugging beers in their fleece'n'khakis and girls named Muffy and Steph with blond bobs, black velvet headbands, and tragic Lilly Pulitzer–meets–Ann Taylor concoctions, slumming it on their first night downtown in eons. There were cashmere Ralph Lauren sweaters spanning the spectrum of punch to celadon. There was so much cable knit in the room, they could have started a branch of Time Warner.

R.E.M. blared, and there was a keg and towers of those red

and blue plastic cups with the white insides. I never could stomach a beer—the taste conjured cow pee, not that I've tried bovine urine, but one can imagine. So I always opted for wine, no matter how cheap. So there I was as usual, all dressed up, sipping Gallo, looking around an all-white cookie-cutter apartment punched in the face by Pier 1, on husband safari. Jeannie and I might as well have had binoculars to scope the prey—we weren't that subtle. My laser beams were honed to cut through the masses of fleece-covered former frat boys burning off steam from their Wall Street analyst jobs and in search of a non-wasted one who seemed more mysterious Jake Ryan than rowdy jock.

Then in walked Mark Webb, the quintessential rowdy-jock-cum-date-rapist type, whom I had once met through a friend who'd gone to UVA with him. Mark was an analyst at Goldman Sachs who had a lust for money that rivaled his carnivorous sexual proclivities. How can I describe Mark Webb? Here's a try:

MARK MATH

(James Spader as Bad Guy)
× red Porsche
× π
÷ calling San Francisco "Frisco"
= the blond Cobra Kai dude in *Karate Kid*

But alongside Mark was Tim. Gulp. He was . . . everything. I bit my lower lip and ran a hand through my blond hair, which was slightly too long at the time. He was gorgeous, with a bright smile that necessitated shades to behold. Not that he had huge Nancy Kerrigan Chiclet choppers, just superwhite teeth. And this was pre-Rembrandt, people. He screamed movie star. After circling each other throughout the night, we ended up meeting, and it was one of those conversations where an hour speeds by and soon enough your friends are standing behind him winking at you as your blush grows hotter.

TIM MATH

π (J.Crew Catalog)
$\div$ lacrosse stick
$\times \Sigma$ (Michael Schoeffling in *Sixteen Candles*)
$-$ vest

We hooked up that night (tonsil hockey only, no advanced bases), and the next day, with a spring in my step, I regaled the roomies with my re-lived lightning bolt of crushdom, delighting in every detail of his hand on the small of my back to putting me in a cab to the last kiss through the taxi window. I was twenty-four and he was twenty-nine—almost thirty!—a man.

And now it was ten years later. Sam and Jake (Molly Ringwald and Michael Schoeffling) conveniently disappeared for the most part, so that we don't have to know them all grown up; they are frozen in that idealized time of lower-lip biting and candlelit smooches. No diapers, work crunches, and business trips hovered in their romantic midst. Tim would be forty in two months, hotter than ever, but me? My forehead looked like Freddy Krueger had dragged his razor-edged claw across it—there were four deep grooves that I was strongly considering Restylane to remedy. Above my nose there were those creases they call the "elevens," two vertical lines so deep, you could row a canoe down them. Why did guys get sexier when weathered?

Most hedge fund wives were early adopters of line fillers, microderm, and photo-facials, and by thirty they were all going under for the little snips of saggage here and there. I, on the other hand, was way too freaked out by needles and photos of Jocelyn Wildenstein to even go that distance. And why should I care so much about staying young? I'd already socially kind of put myself out to pasture. It was funny: Tim was the total life of the party, greeted by hugs and high fives all around when he entered a room, just like Kiki. Hal was a bit more reserved, like me. I guess opposites attract. Sadly, the glue binding Kiki and Hal had dried up and worn off, and I wondered what the future held for Kiki. Poor thing. To be "out there" again, ugh: my *nightmare*. I hoped she didn't have some rude awakening that all the guys our age now wanted twentysomethings; Kiki seemed so confident and excited about being free, but I couldn't imagine anything worse. I loved being married. The only thing Tim and I ever fought about (aside from radio stations and my clandestine relationship with Kiki) was my desire for one more kid; he liked our small nest as is and I would have loved another nugget, but I felt blessed to have Miles and Tim—our little family cocoon was so safe. I couldn't even fathom being back in the bar scene or at some Grolsch-stinking incubus of a party. I rarely, if ever, got nostalgic about those years. Maybe because I know I never missed any opportunities, and my life was pretty much right where I'd hoped it would be at thirty-four candles.

6

"*Women might be able to fake orgasms, but men can fake whole relationships.*"

—Sharon Stone

A few weeks later, in February, Tim and I were going on our weekly date night. Well, it had been weekly originally, but in the last year it had devolved into monthly, since Tim was traveling so much for work. I got my hair done and went to meet him for a drink first at the Knickerbocker Club.

But when I got there, I found him seated in a club chair by the fire with none other than Mark Webb, his UVA buddy from St. Anthony, their quasi frat. Mark was now the ultimate hedge fund guy, and when I walked in, he was showing Tim his new watch. Everything about Mark, from his tie to his custom shoes, was, in a word, slickster. He was unbelievably attractive, but in that exaggerated way that was too manly man, too chiseled, like Gaston in *Beauty and the Beast*. He had the cocksure swagger of some kind of superhero (*Hey, darlin': Snow Queen Vodka, rocks, no fruit*), but he was just, quite simply, rich. Filthy rich. Thirty-nine, he had never married, but bragged incessantly of his conquests and sexploits. Stewardesses on private jets, his trainer at E2 (the ten-grand-a-year fitness club), and countless slashies—models–slash–actresses. Slash–waitresses.

"So the new 650 series is what you have to get—" pronounced Mark.

"Are we looking for a new car, honey?" I probed.

"Not this second, no, but Mark always knows the latest on it all."

He sure did. Here's the thing about the hedgie guys—there's always the newest, greatest, must-have new thing. Down to cuff links.

HEDGE FUNDER TRAPPINGS

CAR HE DRIVES AROUND BMW	**CAR HE GETS DRIVEN AROUND IN** Mercedes S550

CAR HE USES AS A TOY ON WEEKENDS
Aston Martin DB Series

WATCH (black tie) Franck Muller	**WATCH (day-to-day)** Rolex	**TIE** Charvet or Hermès

SPORT Squash and Golf	**SPORT ON VACATION** Heliskiing in the Canadian Bugaboos

CAFETERIA Lever House	**SUMMER HOUSE** Hamptons	**WINTER HOUSE** Aspen

CATCHPHRASE "Wheels up"	**WINE** Petrus	**DRINK** Snow Queen Vodka	**SHOES** John Lobb

MILESTONE BIRTHDAY BUDGET
Half Mill to Infinity

For Mark's thirty-fifth birthday, he had rented out the Puck Building and had an over-the-top black-tie meltdown. Caviar and champagne were everywhere, exotic dancers with feathered headdresses that rivaled Vegas, the DJ from Studio 54, Tiffany party favors, and cringe-inducing lap dances from the New York Knicks cheerleaders.

As a married woman, I sometimes found it vaguely threatening how much he spoke to Tim about his colorful sex life. It went beyond the obnoxious observations everywhere we went ("Holy shit, look at the cleave on that chick, that's a fucking cup-holder between those babies! I could stash my Corona in there! Or somethin' else, heh-heh."). It was a general toxic pull away from the domestic tranquility of marriage. Even when it wasn't about T 'n' A (which was rare), it was always something about jetting off to JazzFest in New Orleans, or Vegas for the weekend, or his wild adventures, such as bungee jumping off cliffs in rural Peru—escapades that I knew Tim missed since we'd had Miles.

"So, Holly," Mark said, leaning in conspiratorially. "You got any hot friends for me?"

"Well, my friends are all married now—"

"Oh, come on, none? What about that chick Frances? She was smoking."

"She's engaged."

"Bummer, man! Hey—guess who I just saw on the street coming over here?" asked Mark with a glint in his eye. "Heidi Klum. Man, what a fucking fox."

"Yeah, she's gorgeous," I added in agreement. "She's had three kids and she looks amazing!"

"THREE kids?" said Mark, with a horrified grimace. "Oh, well, fuck that, she's ruined, man. Doing her would be like throwing a hot dog down a hallway."

I was ill.

Tim laughed at the visual, but I was insulted and disgusted. No doubt I was clearly a "hallway," too.

"It . . . isn't really like that," I countered defensively.

"Whatever. That poor, scarred dude. Seal. Three kids through there? No matter how well he's hung, that's like putting a Tic Tac in a whale."

This would have been a moment, on behalf of not only the stunning Heidi Klum but all "ruined" mothers everywhere, when I would have very much liked to take the sterling tray of snacks and bash his cheekboney face to a bloody pulp.

Next, he started dumping on their "friend" Sly Fisher's plane.

"It's so lame, we went to Lester Hamm's private island—got some serious poontang down there, holy smokes—but the jet is so old now, maybe his returns aren't what he says."

He went on and on about this and that model of private jet, essentially counting everyone's money, which my mother always said was something one should never do. By the time he finished his incessant spiel, I could pretty much figure out the hierarchy of flying in his elitist eyes:

"WHEELS UP" HIERARCHY, ACCORDING TO MARK

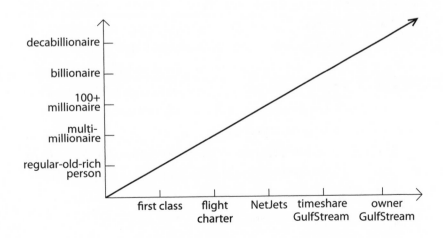

49

My only way out was to pull the ejector seat.

"Oh, sweetie, look at the time! Our reservation at Nello is in five minutes, so we should probably go."

Tim looked down at his, yes, Rolex. "Oh, yeah, Mark, care to join?"

Huh?

"Nah, I'm hooking up with some guys from ThunderPoint Capital downtown at this new restaurant, Midas." Phew.

"Next time, man—"

I was furious with Tim for even offering to include Mark in our date-night dinner, so we walked around the corner to Madison in silence as I thought about how much I actively loathed Mark Webb. He was everything I detested: devoid of values, voraciously materialistic, and loathsome to all thinking women. He was a huge partyer, a male slut type. But not all hedge fund guys were like that. I'd studied the scene up close, and Kiki and I had decided that there was a link between the style of the guy and the type of hedge fund he worked in.

For example, at quantitative-style funds, where mathematical formulas and computer software helped determine investments, at the helm was a nice, power-nerd type, who loved his wife and kids and didn't care about "the scene." Contrastingly, both the "global macro" type firms (who put their wedding rings in their pockets on Boondoggles) and the equity hedge funds (preppy white-shoe types, including scattered "Tiger cubs" from the once all-powerful Tiger Management) were way more life-in-the-fast-lane: jets, cars, wine, women, and song—the works.

Mark was the worst. And he was one of Tim's best friends on earth. Granted, their relationship wasn't close to what I had with Kiki: It was more about bonding through partying. Many of Tim's friendships were just about having fun or showing off and spending money on boy toys and adventures.

The excesses of the cultural moment made everything seem ripe for the picking; the money made everyone around me feel like they had a complete carte blanche of moral elasticity, and like their AmEx Black cards, the sky was the limit as to what they could pull off. Or should I say the lowest rung of Hell's circles was the limit—there was no sin they couldn't get away with. New York was a bacchanal of the rich and obnoxious, a Falstaffian brew of hedonism and material excess: no boundaries, no breaks—just high octane, high speed, all the time. I knew the economic law of gravity held that what goes up would inevitably come down—for every boom there would be bust—that's why it's called a business cycle. But on the horizon, despite forecasted downturns that we were headed for Bearland from Bull, there was no sign of humility or fear or slowing down for these hedgie boys. I only hoped that the world in which Tim rolled, especially given his friendship with assholic Mark, wouldn't be a bad influence.

7

"My husband and I were happy for twenty-five years . . . then we met."

A few weeks later, a production assistant from *Law & Order* finally called regarding my small-screen debut, but my excitement would have to be on hold, as they wouldn't shoot my glamorous rigor mortis self for almost a year. As winter's chill started to thaw, Miles and I took a fun trip to Disney World over April break while Tim was at a management directors conference in Duluth. It was something I'd sworn I'd never do, but it was actually fun. I'd never felt so thin. Everywhere I looked people were eating fried cotton candy. Like regular ol' cotton candy was too healthy. They would dunk the pink plumes into vats of boiling oil, then dredge it out with tongs: hot fried sugar. Only in America. You could almost hear the people getting fatter.

When we came home from our vacation, Miles started extended sports after school—two hours longer than the former school day. I had such a lump in my throat watching him board the bus at 7:55 a.m., knowing that I wouldn't see him again until 5:00 p.m., and I needed wild horses to not be a loser mom who runs to the window and puts my hand on his tiny paw through the glass. I was going to be on my own now more than ever. It would be a season of working out, eating right, and feeling good. It was going to be a spring of Me Time.

I blithely lied to Tim about my whereabouts whenever I wanted to see Kiki, which was every week. It was actually getting easier and easier to lie to him because he was traveling so much. When he'd check in on the phone, we'd talk mostly about Miles's cute comments about school or how Tim's meetings went, or which errands I'd run. So when he was in Chicago for two days, it was perfect timing for me to help Kiki move in to her brand-new loft in TriBeCa and get settled.

She'd decided to swap her temporary uptown digs for a hipper new space, the physical move echoing her mental turning of a corner, the crisp white paint like a big, open, three-thousand-square-foot clean slate. It was younger, fresher, and far away from what she called "the reversible name, roman numeral set" uptown.

"Those fucking gray flannel drones on the Upper East Side, I won't miss those," she said, raising her glass at Bubby's after we'd unpacked the last of her gazillion boxes. "Stiff everywhere except their cocks."

I almost spat out my cheese grits (a last-hurrah pre-diet) but contained myself, looking both ways for eavesdroppers to her comments. "It's like Kim Cattrall said on *Sex and the City*," she continued. "'The higher the roman numeral after their name, the worse they are in bed.'"

"Nice, Keeks," I said, semihorrified by a potential septuagenarian listener nearby. Kiki seemed to have a microphone implanted in her larynx. And while I loved her brashness, quiet lunches were kind of impossible.

"Hey, what time does Miles come home today? Why don't you come with me to Williamsburg? I'm looking at this Tauba Auerbach drawing for the living room at Pierogi Gallery. Will you come with? Pleeeease?" She begged like a seven-year-old wanting ice cream, her blue eyes yearning and her beautiful face tilted to the side. I could often see why men fell at her feet when she switched on the charm and went from vixen PR viper to innocent pouty pretty girl; they were snowed by her confidence and power but then loved that she played the vulnerable beauty card for them.

I looked at my watch. I had three hours. "I can come, but . . . how will I get home?" I wondered aloud.

"Holly, news flash: It's Brooklyn, not Mars. You said you used to go there and see bands all the time! What happened? Now it's like you and Tim fucking think you'll burst into flames if you cross a bridge! Trust me, they have oxygen over there, you'll be fine."

I know, I was lame. But when you don't normally make the trek, even if it's geographically close, it feels like oceans away. I didn't want to disappoint her, though. "Okay, okay, I'll come," I conceded. "I always loved Williamsburg."

"Me, too. The guys are so damn hot," she purred. "Last week, I screwed this guy I met at Lux, and when I woke up I was so disoriented, I needed a fucking compass. I went to go to the bathroom and saw the Manhattan skyline out the window and almost fainted. But I started walking and got my bearings and, I'm telling you: the restaurants, the galleries, the clothing boutiques—all amazing. I'm obsessed."

"So why didn't you move there instead of TriBeCa?" I asked, semireeling over her roll in the hay with some random dude.

"I'm not that obsessed," she said. "I like somewhat gentrified. Not edgy-now, nice-in-ten-years. I'm thirty-two; it's too late for that grunge shit."

An easy fifteen-minute ride on the train later, we hopped out onto Bedford Avenue. And Kiki was right. The energy was palpable. The people all seemed a decade younger. Even those in their thirties looked like kids, thanks to hip outfits, various facial piercings, and tattoos aplenty. I suddenly felt like one of those uptown crones Kiki spoke of, but I was excited by the whole new world. I watched a bunch of guys carrying their guitars up some stairs to a practice space, and a crew of miniskirt-wearing girls with funky-colored hair and bloodred lips popping in and out of stores. I remembered having the same feeling when I went to Kings Road in London in 1983. It felt cool and raw, and even though I was a tourist passing through, I got excited that there were people doing something punky and different. This time, though, instead of looking up at them as older, cooler people portending my adulthood, it was more of a bittersweet looking back. I was the older one, and they held all the promise of becoming artists and musicians or prostitutes, who knows. But they sure did look amazing.

"It's up here," Kiki said, gesturing as we walked around the corner toward the gallery. "I think it's like two blocks down on the left—" She froze. Halted in her Manolo Blahnik'd tracks.

Uh-oh, great. I couldn't entirely keep the whine out of my voice. "Please tell me we're not lost, Kiki. Because I have to be home to get Miles in a couple—"

She silenced me by calmly putting her hand on my arm and squeezing firmly.

"Ow!" Her grasp clenched my wrist. "Holy sugar! That hurts!"

"Shhh," she commanded in a mute daze, grabbing me even harder.

I was about to complain again when I noticed her huge, widened eyes staring in a forty-five-degree angle across the street. What? Was there a mugging in progress? Slowly I turned my head to follow her fixed gaze as she pulled me back into the shadow of a parked van. My eyes landed on what she had beheld, the sight that had made Kiki, the most talkative person on planet Earth, silent, the vision that had caused the most nonstop, kinetic, ants-in-her-pants live wire stop cold, turned her normally warm hand to ice on my wrist: It was my husband making out with another woman.

8

"When I meet a guy, I think, Is this the man I want my children to spend their weekends with?"

—Rita Rudner

Fog. I have heard people say they've been trapped in one, mired in a cloudy, gray state of catatonic mumbling and grief. It's usually people who have just buried a parent or gone through some horribly traumatic phase. They look back and can barely decipher what they experienced: It was all a tumultuous, blurred frenzy of tear-splattered cheeks and zombie-esque marching through life, detached from the humdrum of the world around them.

I had experienced that thick, enveloping fog when my mother died eight years earlier. And here it beckoned again, enveloping me in its chilly, bleak clutch. I shook as Kiki propped me up. I was spinning in a vertiginous emotional free fall. I remembered the jolt of first meeting Tim and falling love with him—my head was spinning then, too, but with the elated, dizzied Tilt-A-Whirl fueled by the heart, infusing a buzzed high to my every breath. Now it was in reverse: The little tweety birds were flying around my head counterclockwise. Or better yet, kamikaze-style, into the ground. And that bouncy heart of mine? Pounding blood through me as if each vein carried the Orient Express. Was I dying? It felt like it.

The hours that followed were a pastiche of taxi, hyperventilation, bridge toll, Kiki's hand rubbing my back, and the muffled sounds of her cursing. It was as if I were frantically drowning underwater, hearing her voice and muted honking horns through a thicket of waves. I don't think I was even crying. Yet. Just glazed over. Like some of the pill-popping moms I'd seen on Park Avenue en route to Pilates.

My little dreamy family cocoon had cracked. And it wasn't a beautiful, vibrant-hued butterfly that flew out. It was a sickly, wan, gray, fraying moth. Too bad my effing husband couldn't keep his very hungry caterpillar in his pants. I shuddered with rage.

Kiki wanted me to lose my edit button? It was history now.

"I can't believe he did this to me. That fucking asshole," I squeaked as Kiki and I staggered into my apartment. She walked me down the hallway and positioned me in Tim's office while she proceeded to ransack the contents of his desk as I quaked on the tufted leather cognac couch.

"What are you doing?" I asked, watching her rip through every drawer like the Tazmanian Devil.

"Tim told you he'd be in Chicago till tomorrow, right?"

"Uh-huh." I slumped back into the couch, staring at framed pictures of Tim, Miles, and me in Italy a few years ago: in Venice on a gondola; in Pisa, pretending to hold up the Leaning Tower; by a monastery in Padua.

"Good. That means we have twenty-four hours to gather as much information as we can. He probably already has his money hidden, fucking bastard."

"Wait, wait, Kiki—slow down. Maybe it was . . . a fling. Or—"

"Come on, Holly. I know this is so heinously painful, but you have to act now to self-protect. If he was banging Russian whores like Barbara Ceville's husband, he wouldn't concoct fake trips. You get action at lunchtime. This isn't some courtesan doling out nooner blow jobs in the W Hotel. This is a mistress."

A *girlfriend*? Like . . . a whole other relationship? No, no, no, no. He loved us!

"I'm giving you the List. Meg McSorley gave it to me—she was my friend's friend who ended up being my divorce adviser. The woman who got me through. You have to call the twenty top lawyers in town—today—and make appointments. That way, he can't hire them. It would be a conflict of interest if you're already in their books as a potential client—"

"Hold on—Kiki, slow down. I'm really out if it right now, I . . . don't know about d-d-d—" I couldn't even say it. I could barely process what I'd just witnessed, let alone entertain the concept of divorce. My parents had been married for thirty years until my mom died of heart disease at age fifty-five. My dad lived in Florida and had wealthy widows throwing themselves at him, but he never bit; he loved the memory of my doting mom more than life itself. So how could I, coming from a perfect family, be headed for splitsville? It was too crazy! This was not my life. Maybe I'd confront him and he would freak and beg for me to stay. I had to at least see what this was all about before calling lawyers. The crazy part is that Tim was the person I'd call whenever something bad happened—I almost wanted to call him to cry about what I was going through. My body felt both heated, charged with boiling rage, and chilled with an icy grip of devastated sadness. I watched Kiki, who was cracking file cabinets and opening stacked boxes in a frenzied hunt for God knows what. My eyes focused behind her, on an eight-by-ten wedding photo, grainy and black-and-white, our faces smeared by the kinetic twirl on the dance floor, my veil wrapped around us in a gauzy ethereal sheath, binding us together. We were partially obscured by the white tissuey wave, but you could see our faces beaming through the delicate tulle. As I looked at the picture, which so captured the beauty and joy of that moment, my eyes gushed for the first time, recollecting the paralyzing vision on Wythe Avenue in Brooklyn. He was kissing that girl and holding her as he once had held me. Clearly what bound us together was not a wedding vow stronger than oak: Our bond now seemed as wispy as my veil, as fragile and transparent as its lace border.

9

Lady Astor: Sir, if you were my husband, I would poison your drink.

Winston Churchill: Madam, if you were my wife, I would drink it.

"Uh-oh . . . Bingo."

Kiki looked up at me, gripping a nondescript manila envelope.

"This is exactly what I was looking for." She held it up, looking almost dismayed by her eureka moment, a discovery she had wanted to make but was then unhappy to unearth, like someone whose job it is to deep-sea dive for dead bodies. You're successful when you locate one, but the find is extremely unpleasant.

I got up and staggered across the room to see what she was holding. Nothing special. The return address was GTP Mortgage, LLP, on Oakdale Avenue, Suite 4300, in MacLean, Virginia. So what? I stared at her blankly.

"See this? Looks boring and tedious, right? Some dumb financial packet you put aside for Tim?"

"Yeah. . . ." We got tons of stuff like that. I never cracked them. I never dealt with the finances. When tax return time came, I just signed on the dotted line where the yellow stickers with red arrows told me to.

"This is how Hal did it, look—" She opened the envelope to reveal a packet with two CDs. The discs appeared to be normal, unmarked in their jewel cases.

Huh?

"See, this is how they mail them. Top secret, in an unmarked envelope. Like Ticketmaster, since they don't want people to swipe concert tickets. You know, they send them from some P.O. box in Iowa or something?"

I nodded, vaguely recalling how in college I had chucked some Smashing Pumpkins tickets by accident, thinking the envelope was some junk-mail solicitation for a magazine subscription or political campaign.

"These hedge fund guys, they order these kits. It's how to plot your exit. They cost like a thousand dollars and this guy instructs you how to start laying the groundwork."

I still had no idea what she was talking about. Kiki walked over to Tim's Bose CD player by his desk and popped one in.

"Hello," a man's voice spoke crisply. "This is Lachlan McDonald. And with these divorce secrets for high-net-worth men, you'll be ahead of the game. These guidelines will instruct you how, over a one- to two-year period, you can be armed with information on arranging finances and understanding the reality of the divorce process. Back in the day, a caveman would simply kick his wife out of the cave. Now, the woman gets half the cave. . . ."

Mr. Lachlan McDonald droned on as I started panting. Harder and harder. I meandered back to the couch, where I melted down completely. So it wasn't some trashy whore; it was phase one of Operation Leave Holly. My hands shook. Kiki came over and hugged me as I wept in silence, a silent hysterical cry like toddlers in the moment before the air comes back out of their tiny lungs accompanied by an unbridled piercing wail. All we could hear over my retinal faucet were McDonald's introductory tips:

DIVORCE RULES

1. All's fair in Divorce. It is a War.
2. NEVER forget that the root of the word "uterus" is the Greek root *uster*, which means "hysterical." Women, fueled by their uncontrollable emotions, will want revenge when you leave them, so you must be prepared.
3. You must start by selling major assets like your home; rent something smaller so that her lifestyle is diminished.
4. Dissipate proceeds from asset sales and borrow money to create marital debt, which will also be her obligation to repay.

Blah blah blah. On and on and on it went, a tricky litany of fox-like ways to hide money, a dizzying verbal collage of words like "offshore" and "deferred compensation."

"You see," Kiki said soberly, putting her hand on my knee. "These bastards planned it. Yes, I kissed that guy, I filed the papers, but I found Hal's computer cache with Web sites like mensdivorcesecrets.com and divorceprep.com—he was already thinking about bailing, so I bolted before he could take the year or two this asshole tells them to plan."

Could that possibly be true? I staggered toward Tim's desk, which I previously couldn't bear to look at. I looked at the closed drawers, potential keepers of more secrets, a dormant volcano that could spew the lava of hot lies were I to explore them. And yet with Kiki beside me, I exhaled and got on the floor and opened them.

At first, it was the usual boring taxes, investment research information, and other yawn-inducing legal and financial documents. As I sifted through the files, I started to think maybe this was a fluke, a whim on Tim's part. Once we talked about this, I'd discover it was some onetime thing. Maybe she was a high-class hooker? He loved our family! Maybe he was just getting his rocks off. . . .

But then I saw a brochure for a Relais & Chateau spa in Oregon. Huh?

"What's that?" Kiki said, as my brow furrowed.

"Tim was just in Oregon. But he said he was at some huge convention hotel. This looks awfully romantic and luxurious for a business meeting."

Kiki grabbed it and perused the high-gloss photos of body wraps, massages, mahogany four-poster beds, and couples dining by candlelight.

"This was *not* business. It was *bidniss*," she scoffed, clearly nauseated. "Monkey business."

I sifted through folders, envelopes, Pendaflex files—each containing mystery receipts—La Petite Coquette, a lingerie store on University Place. One If by Land, Two If by Sea, a romantic restaurant where one would never do business, on a MasterCard I'd never seen before. My head spun, my tongue dried, my gag reflex triggered.

"I-I don't know what to say," I sputtered, zoned in my pile of piecemeal clues that the man with whom I'd shared a bed literally was leading a double life.

"Say you'll call the lawyers. Two can play at this game, Holl."

I wanted to die. I obviously wasn't truly suicidal and could never leave Miles mommyless, but I got it into my head that if Tim came home and found my dead body, he'd be sorry and would weep to the gods for atonement. There were more than a few Upper East Side suicides that were legendary, and often were caused by husbands upgrading to trophy wives or losses of fortune.

I gathered what strength I had to pick up Miles. Seeing him almost made me dissolve again into tears, but I summoned every last ounce of energy I had to hold it together and take him to Dylan's Candy Bar on Third Avenue. I had heard kids of divorce are more spoiled; I guess this was part one of indulgent sugarfests to come. He beamed as he got his crystal Baggie and started scooping pieces from the various bins with the tiny shovels. Kids with backpacks from all the different schools crammed the aisle, eyes ablaze, mouths watering, as mommies and nannies reined in the small-handed grabbers and gobblers. The Wonka-esque megastore was a candied kaleidoscope of lollipops, chocolates, every jelly bean shade in the color spectrum. And yet through my new eyes, it was all slates, grays, and blacks and whites.

10

"Bigamy is having one wife too many. Monogamy is the same."

—Oscar Wilde

"Mommy, thanks for the PEZ. I love you!"

"I love you, too, sweetness. But Milesie, you should love me even if I don't buy you the PEZ. We have to love each other no matter what."

"I know. Can we read *Frog and Toad*?"

"Sure, lovely." We curled in his bed with a pile of books as I choked back tears. The innocent words of friendship and simple values buoyed me as I got through the final pages, kissed his forehead, turned on his dinosaur night-light, and closed the door. His little noggin would soon be matted with the sweat of sleep, peaceful and restorative. I wondered if I'd ever slumber that like again in my life.

Kiki had offered to come over and be with me, but I was so wrecked I just wanted to crawl into bed. As I lay there, not even twelve hours after my life-altering revelation, I started going back. I thought of each and every business trip. It was then that I first had a Keyser Söze flashback of my own: recollections of his "day trip" to Cincinnati, or that supposed conference in Utah. Was there even a board meeting in Wichita, Kansas? Or that boat ride with no cell reception with a client in Nassau? It was all lies. Like Chazz Palminteri, I mentally dropped that teacup—my heart, my happiness, my history—and it shattered to the floor in scattered pieces I couldn't even begin to sift through.

Just then, the phone rang. I sprang into action, pouncing like a puma to the caller ID screen. Tim. No way was I going to pick it up. I let it go to voice mail, which I furiously dialed a minute later. The computer voice alerted me to my One. New. Message.

"Hey, Holly, it's Tim. I miss you guys. Chicago's busy and really warm. Looking out my window now at the Sears Tower. I'll be back tomorrow night, can't wait. Love you guys. Call me if you're up, but I'm pretty pooped from these meetings all day and might crash. Love you."

Fucking liar. In all my years, I was never a curse-word kind of gal. But this whole debacle morphed my tongue into Kiki times ten. That fucking assholic, deviant *serpent* had packed countless lies into probably every voice mail he'd ever left me. In St. Louis: "I'll say hi to the Arch for you." In San Francisco: "I'm looking at the sun setting over the Golden Gate Bridge." The Eiffel Tower. Big Ben. That was his stupid modus operandi: drop details of his surroundings. He probably even checked the paper and saw it was unseasonably warm in the so-called Windy City. I bet he was lying naked with that slutbag and winking at her while he uttered those patent falsehoods into the receiver. "I'm pretty pooped from meetings." Yeah, how about pooped from porking your skank? I oscillated from frothing vitriol to self-pitying grief and back again every second. What would I do? How could I cope? For years I had looked at my few single friends through a lens of pity and relief that it wasn't me. And now it was.

I thought of my childhood friend Natasha in Boston who had gone through this, but she had no kids. I had baggage. Not just baggage, Vuitton trunks of baggage: what will probably be a messy divorce, a kid, and the clichéd anger of a woman scorned. I opened my e-mail account and looked back to find Natasha's e-mail detailing her meltdown. A choice excerpt:

"It's like they say, Holly: Infidelity isn't the cause of a split, it's a symptom something is wrong."

Of course all I could think of was *When Harry Met Sally* and Billy Crystal's response to the same line: "Yeah, well, that symptom is fucking my wife." I had no idea what was wrong with our marriage. We had occasional sexual dry spells compared to how we used to be, sure, but nothing was "wrong." I read on.

"I guess subconsciously I knew divorce was coming. . . . I could smell it in the marriage. Cliff started plotting and planning, I could just sense it. And you're living and sleeping with your enemy. It is like a bad movie-of-the-week on Lifetime. You check his wallet for receipts belonging to a secret credit card. You watch his fingers as he checks his cell voice mail to figure out his password. . . . You check his voice mail with the password and hear girls calling. . . . I wanted to catch him cheating, so I had a girlfriend of mine call him and ask him out. Cassie called him and pretended she was a one-night hookup who was calling for more action. He bit. I flipped."

But the strange thing was, I never felt like I was sleeping with the enemy. I had confessed a few months back to my father that I sometimes felt a growing void between Tim and me, but it had since passed.

"You and Mom had good moments and bad moments, right?"

"I'm not going to lie to you," my dad had said. "Not really. It was always wonderful. The whole marriage. That's not to say there weren't times we were tired or maybe had disagreements here and there, sure. But it was never work with Mom. I hear people say marriage is work, but Mom never made it feel that way."

I heard his voice drift off. Even though it had been seven years since she'd passed away, I knew his voice could crack at any moment. My father was such a sensitive, kind, and gentle man that I knew when he lost her that in some ways, he'd never recover. I know people can deify those they've buried and that my dad was still and always would be in love with her, but after thirty years, I had assumed that, like all marriages, theirs had had peaks and valleys.

And while I knew some of our valleys were definitely deeper within the last year as what I thought was Tim's work had intensified, I never, ever clued in about the plotting—the CDs, the affairs, the fake phone calls, bogus business trips, and lame alibis. I was the dumbest, most clueless woman on the planet, or Tim deserved an Academy effing Award. Either way, I had been duped. As someone who always thought she was so damn smart, that realization made me cry the most that night.

11

"I think men who have a pierced ear are better prepared for marriage. They've experienced pain and bought jewelry."

—Rita Rudner

The next day, I awoke dreading the confrontation. In anticipation of Tim's arrival home, I got my hair done and looked like a million bucks. Okay, maybe a thousand. Pesos. But in my fractured and weary state, it was the best I could do, and I needed to feel put together to face off with the man who I thought was my partner but was in fact a complete and total stranger.

I had been distracted all day, running errands in zoned-out autopilot mode, grocery shopping and making dinner with Miles, and after tuck-in and bedtime, I waited. He was probably jamming in one more shag pre–return home. Via the Brooklyn Bridge, not LaGuardia. As I sat there, flipping through the daily pile of catalogs, I felt newly distant from the shiny smiling families who wore matching pajamas, each page marked at the bottom with a 1-800 number you could call to order up their synchronized sleepwear and a slice of their familial bliss. For some reason, even if the stuff was not my taste, or was even outwardly hideous, I loved getting in bed at the end of the day with catalogs.

Once in a while I'd order something, but usually it was the bed-time equivalent of the morning's snooze button—a way to wind down slowly and zone out in front of monogrammed towels or key fobs or knapsacks, toted by perfect all-American children and their carpooling parents. I wondered if as a single mom I'd find the same brainless bliss in those colorful pages, or if I'd chuck the catalog into the trash. I turned the page and found a picture with the dad kissing the mom's head while she cuddled with the two kids, all four swathed in matchy-matchy huggable fleece.

Tim hadn't cuddled me like that in a while, I supposed, but when did that stop? Here you are, a team, and then you just have completely separate lives? I know fatigue and travel and busy schedules all accelerate the slow drifting apart, but when I looked back it seemed like a blink-of-an-eye mutation. This is the man who fathered my child, kissed my belly as it grew swollen with a flesh union of our marriage, and watched our son come out of my vagina. I know it sounds gross and graphic, but that's what marriage is: the real deal. Unedited. The stuff after the sunset: the screaming baby at 3:00 a.m. It's bonding through not just the rush of cheek-flushing romance but the viscerally human times, the ugly, the sick—the things beyond the white wedding—the stuff that starts Monday morning. The sharp betrayal gutted me so thoroughly that I threw up a little in my mouth when I heard the jingle of Tim's keys outside the front door.

He walked in, complete with rolling T. Anthony suitcase, and found me on the couch.

"Hiiiii, honey!"

Normally, I would have leaped up and hugged him, his cute floppy hair a welcome sight after a few lonely nights. I always marveled over how gorgeous he was, especially when he returned home from a trip and I had missed him.

A meek "hi" was all I could muster, shakily.

He unzipped his bag and pulled out a teddy bear wearing a Chicago Cubs jersey for Miles. *Such genius planning*, I thought. He always came back with various city-emblazoned souvenirs.

"Milesie asleep?" he asked.

"Mm-hmm," I answered.

"What's wrong?"

Where to begin? I couldn't look at Tim, so I looked at the huge brown eyes of the teddy bear.

"So, what, do you have your assistant order the local teddy bear online and ship it so that you have a gift to bring home?"

"Holly, what are you talking about?"

"Come on, Tim. That's what all the culprits on *Murder She Wrote* and *Law & Order* say when they are first confronted. Don't say, '*What are you talking about?*' Don't insult me. I may have been an idiot for however long, but I've caught on now."

His faux-incredulous smile suddenly flattened. Aha! He knew I knew. And now he'd beg for mercy. He'd think of not coming home to Miles and a real home with food in the fridge and hand towels in the powder room and catalogs!

"Listen, Holly . . . we have to talk." Nota bene: any sentence that begins with "listen" or "look" equals chiming death knell for your relationship.

"About how you're cheating on me?" My heart rate spiked, waiting for him to greet my accusation with a laugh, proclaiming its falsity. *It was all my imagination! Or It meant nothing! Or It was the first and only time and it was a huge mistake and I totally regret it!*

I was met not with these protestations but rather a long exhale. Another bad sign.

"How did you know?" was all he could ask, soberly.

So there it was. No denials, no sweeping it under the rug. That weirdly pissed me off even more.

"How did I know? I FUCKING SAW YOU, that's how! You

72

were making out! On the STREET, no less! With that trashy whore, after EVERYTHING I have done for you, given you! How the hell could you betray me like this?" I screamed. I stood up and looked at him, channeling my rage into a laser beam shined into his eyes as I squinted my own. "You HUMILIATED ME with that tart. I am THE MOTHER OF YOUR CHILD! How could you do this?" I stunned even myself that there were no tears accompanying my diatribe; the only moisture was anger-infused perspiration and possible burst blood vessels in my face.

Tim was breathing heavier but maintained control.

"Holly. Calm down."

"DON'T TELL ME TO CALM DOWN! You faked a business trip? How many times did you do that? There are twenty major league baseball bears in Miles's room. Is each one a different slut you nailed?"

"AVERY IS NOT A SLUT!" he yelled back, forcefully.

Wow.

Avery?

Somehow, even though Kiki had guessed Tim had a mistress, I still felt like anyone outside the marriage was some disposable pair of legs. But she wasn't. She was Avery.

"Oh, gee, I'm so sorry to insult your HOME-WRECKING WHORE!"

"Holly, stop it."

"You come in here and DEFEND that SLUT YOU PERSONALLY GAVE A STREP THROAT CULTURE TO ON THE STREET?!"

"I know you can't understand, Holly, but I'm sorry," he said, shaking his head. "I love her."

Hiroshima.

I never. Ever. Expected to hear those words.

At that point, quite simply, I crumbled. Burning, lava-like

thick tears cascaded out, flooding my face as I wailed like a child. Tim tried to comfort me, but I slapped his arm away "GET OUT!" I screamed, shaking.

Tim looked at me sadly. Part of me did want him out that nanosecond, but the other half wanted him to run to me on bended knee and beg forgiveness. To sob and fight for his family. But his mouth simply turned down into an apologetic frown.

"Sorry, Holl," he said simply, and obeyed my instructions to turn and leave.

I cried myself to sleep that night. And many, many, many nights afterward.

12

Woman #1: My husband's an angel!
Woman #2: You're lucky. Mine's still alive.

The following weeks were a Kleenex marathon of hermit dwelling. I met with Kiki's divorce lawyer and filed the paperwork, if a *Night of the Living Dead* drone can fill out forms. I made the painful phone calls, which were gasp-inducing to all, who proclaimed "NO! You guys?" and "Everything seemed so perfect," and of course, "WHY?" I wanted to be a lady about the whole thing and not sling the mud of Tim's indiscretions, but from my wounded tone, people gleaned the dirty details and accurately sniffed the scent of another woman.

After dropping the bomb on my cute Dad, who was quiet, clearly dismayed, but supportive, it was the call to my maid of honor, Jeannie, that was the hardest. She had been there the fateful night we met, winking at me behind Tim's back, holding her white wine and smiling; she knew we would get married.

And now she was as in shock as I had been; when I told her, she promptly burst into tears.

"I don't believe this! Oh, Holl . . . I'm so upset. That asshole!" I heard her sniffle and pull tissues from a box. "I would have expected that from his loser friend Mark Webb, but never Tim!" Jeannie had had the pleasure of getting hit on by a shit-faced (or as Sherry Von would say, "overserved") Mark at our wedding. He was, along with all six of Tim's Wall Street groomsmen, so trashed that he was doing the Tom-Cruise-in-*Risky-Business* run-and-slide-on-knees move across the dance floor at our wedding reception—albeit in tux in lieu of boxers. Clearly, as it is always all about him, our wedding reception may as well have been his living room, the way he was carrying on, front and center. When his fifth slide actually knocked down Lauren, one of my other bridesmaids, Tim told him it might be time to head home.

"You know," I told Jeannie as I twisted the curly phone wire around my finger, which still bore my wedding ring, "I secretly thought that after Mark's behavior at our wedding, he and Tim would grow apart. That through the years we'd pull the feeding tube on that friendship. But they're still best friends, and I can't help but blame Mark a bit—he's such a louse, such a bad influence."

"Honey," Jeannie said soberly. "You can lead a horse to water, but you can't make him hump it."

"True enough." I laughed, eyes welling anew with fresh hot tears.

"But still, that whole world Tim rolls with, it's this Boys Club in finance. They're all the same. Dirty jokes, booze, and obviously women on the side. It's the hedge fund culture. The I-can-get-away-with-anything money. I thought I got a good one, but they're all the same."

"I'm so sad, sweetie." I heard Jeannie's voice break. I was touched she was so traumatized on my behalf, but it killed me to hear her cry for me. "I'm just so appalled. I mean, even if he begs you to take him back, you won't, will you?"

Obviously the fantasy was comforting. He'd wake up, wonder what the hell he was smoking, and bolt back, hysterically
imploring me to forgive and forget.

"We have Miles. I don't know."

"Hey, I have three kids. And after that whole Governor
Spitzer debacle, I told William in no uncertain terms that if he
ever pulled that shit, I'd be out the door."

"You don't know till you live it, I guess," I replied, zoning
into space. My skin was tight and itchy from the streams of tears,
and while both Jeannie and Kiki were indignant, thrusting the
girl-power mantras in my direction, I felt only weak and scared
and alone. The only way I could even get myself to breathe was
to have a melodramatic emotional seal-off à la Princess Butter-
cup: *I shall never love again.*

The night before Tim and I were to preliminarily sit down with
our lawyers, I got a shocking buzz from the lobby doorman—
"Mrs. Sherry Von Hapsburg Talbott is here to see you."

My heart skipped a beat. Well, unlike Kiki, I supposed I
wasn't to be frozen out, if she was paying me a house call. I knew
from her reaction to Kiki that she abhorred cheating, so she must
have been mortified by Tim's behavior.

I opened the door to find her immaculately dressed, even in
the heat of early May, in an Oscar de la Renta cream sheath, alligator Kelly bag, and Tom Ford sunglasses atop her highlighted
head.

"Hello, Holland." She said my name as if it were Newman
saying "Jerry" on *Seinfeld*. Why the acid?

"Come in, Sherry. Please, sit down. Can I get you anything
to dr—"

"I have one thing to say and I won't waste your time with

small talk or niceties," she said, chin skyward as she brushed a blond lock from her suspiciously wrinkle-free forehead. "Holland. You are making a huge mistake."

I was stunned. "I beg your pardon?" I had never uttered that phrase in my life (it seemed so old-school), but I was indignant that she had walked into my house and pronounced these words.

"You have a child. A family. Talbotts are all about The Family."

I was aghast.

"Well, I *thought* we had a great family," I responded, trying to hold it together. "But unfortunately your son betrayed us."

"I have some news for you, Holland Talbott," she said, every syllable infused with ice, wagging a crooked ring-covered finger in my face as if instructing me on a life lesson. "Boys. Will. Be. Boys. You didn't have to go and call him out on it. How positively juvenile. Women have been looking the other way for millennia. You do what you have to do to keep the family together."

At this point I did something I never thought I would ever do; it was actually more of a Kiki move: I laughed in her face.

Her face morphed with rage. "Do you think this is FUNNY?" she stammered.

"Sherry, are you joking? This is not 1953. I'm not going to just take it and live a total lie! He took her to the hotel where we honeymooned, for God's sake!"

"Oh, please. Grow up!" she commanded. "You think you're the first one to have a husband with something on the side? Men have needs. This is life. Marriage. Family. You have a son. My grandson. And you will alter the course of his life if you proceed with this NONSENSE!"

"It was your son who proceeded with 'nonsense' when he broke our marriage vows! The ones you so ruthlessly indicted

Kiki for breaking, remember? What happened to the whole cheating-is-evil diatribe when Kiki strayed, huh?"

"That was different. She was the wife. And furthermore, she never had children. You have a responsibility—"

"To Miles or to you? To not have the world know both your sons failed at marriage?" I started to exit my lobotomized-with-grief state and become simply livid. "You can't show up here and tell me to stay with Tim when he's 'in love' with someone else—not even sleeping with random women but, in fact, enamored of one! How dare you lecture me on family?"

"For hundreds of years there was no divorce in the Von Haps-burg or Talbott families, and now you and that trash Kiki come in and leave our traditions of strong families in shards!"

"*Strong*, really? Living a lie for the sake of keeping up appearances? That's weak! You may have chosen a life that is all about image and what people think, but I wasn't raised by a mom like you. My late mother was the epitome of strength and would have never endured humiliation or betrayal like this. Please. Leave. Now."

"You will be sorry," she said calmly, turning to exit. Before the door closed, she placed a polished manicured hand on the gold knob, forcing it ajar. "Just so you know, Holland, you cross this family, and you're finished in this town."

"It's not a *town*. It's New York City. There are millions of people, so I doubt you can get all of them to freeze me out."

"Correct, millions. *Millions* of young women: It's a jungle out there for someone your age. Good luck trying to get someone to love you again. You should have just looked the other way like everyone else instead of making this big mess for yourself, for all of us. You'll never get anyone as good as Tim to marry the likes of you." She looked down at her diamond-encrusted Cartier watch. "Well, Hubert awaits me downstairs. Good day, Holland." With that, she closed the door

I hated her. I wanted her to meet Hannibal Lecter in a dark alley. I wanted barracudas to gut her alive, crocodiles in the Everglades to chomp her to shards, Batrachotoxinous dart-poison frogs to pounce. She was dead to me. But unlike in breakups where there were no kids involved, both she and Tim would be bound to me forever. With no-kid splits, the spouse and in-laws can exit your life completely, eventually drifting out of vision like Wilson, Tom Hanks's volleyball companion in *Cast Away*. But through Miles, we were tethered forever.

Sherry Von, I could happily bid adieu to, but Tim, for some crazy reason, I still mourned. Maybe it was because it was the nail in the coffin on my youth and that innocent love. . . . Was I pathetic that I still loved him as much as I detested him? I couldn't just switch off that current. That night was the first of many that I went back to the beginning of our relationship in my head. I couldn't reconcile what he'd just done with the guy I first fell in love with. I pictured him that first year we were dating, his fluffy hair coming out from his baseball hat like wings. He was such a nugget. A nugget, by the way, is not a fried piece of chicken eyelids for sauce dunkage; it's a huggable, heart-fluttery, sweet, yummy thing. Generally, it's a baby ("look at that cute nugget stuffed into the little snowsuit"), but sometimes a really nice, affectionate, huggable guy can be a nugget. Tim Talbott was the crown prince of Nuggetdom. He was cuddly, caring, teddy bearish, and loving, and, until now, he made me feel taken care of. Except . . . when he talked about business with a rabid competitiveness, which he did more and more through our decade together. As his success increased, so did his bravado. Talks about Miles or movies were eclipsed by how killer a trade was for the company. As he became giddy about his accolades in the press (a *New York Times* profile on top hedge funds cemented his ascent), I sensed him getting in-toxicated by power. I missed the cute nuggety parts of Tim, the parts that were loving and protective, the parts that were fun, the parts that once made me think I'd be happy with Tim on a desert island forever.

But life is not a desert island. Life has cad clients who cajoled out the worst. It has mothers-in-law and mergers and acquisi-tions and sports bars. And Avery. And now, what was left of our little oasis was gone.

The next day, I showed up at the hospital to meet with the devel-opment office about the next year's benefit; under my leadership cochairing, we'd raised $3 million for our event at the Waldorf and I'd even launched a sold-out Young Patrons after-party for the under-forty set.

Susan, the department head, who worked full-time pro bono (her husband was a Wall Streeter, so she waived the nominal sal-ary), sat down with me in her office.

"Holly," she said, taking my hand nervously. "I'm afraid I have some upsetting news."

"What?" I wondered, terrified—maybe she had been diag-nosed with something?

"I got a very upsetting call this morning. I feel awful. . . ."

"What happened?"

"Mortimer DuPont phoned. I guess . . . unfortunately . . . I, um, understand that Mrs. Von Hapsburg Talbott phoned him, and they . . . said they are going to pass on having you join the board."

You could have knocked me over with a benefit RSVP card.

"*What?*"

"Holly, I am so sorry. I told him that you have done more

81

than any of these women, that you've raised the most, have been here till all hours writing personal notes and stuffing envelopes, but he simply said that we can't cross Mrs. Talbott. And he just wants to start fresh with the benefit next year."

"Wait—start fresh? So you're saying not only am I not getting on the board even though I've done the most work, but I am also booted from the event I helped create and launch?"

"Holly, trust me, I am sick about this. It is so unfair. But my hands are tied; I mean, Mr. DuPont is head of the board and built the whole new wing. This whole thing is so disturbing."

"So I am barred from even doing volunteer work! This is crazy. I raised tons of money!"

I knew the board was a serious honor that would involve the New York slogan of "Give, Get, or Go"—give tons of money, get it by raising it from your friends, or hit the road, Jack.

"I guess he said that so many donors do business with the Talbotts and might not want to take sides if you call upon them or something."

"I'm sorry—take *sides*? Giving to the hospital because I ask them is not taking sides!" I was so enraged, I thought I would pop a blood vessel.

"Listen, you are preaching to the choir," Susan said, taking my other hand as I began to cry. "This is all politics. I guess they're worried that so many people you would be soliciting are linked to Tim through investments or whatever. It's so unfair and ridiculous, but please know that once the dust settles, I'm hoping you can still work with us in some capacity—"

Great. Morty and Sally DuPont, rumor had it, possessed not one, not two, but three private jets through his company, Solar Partners. He gave sky rides to the Bushes and other pals up to Maine or down to Hobe Sound, and there was even Fifth Avenue lore that Sally had once sent Rubies, her beloved infirmed purebred Pomeranian, *alone* in the leather-appointed 757, to a canine diabetes specialist in Chicago. And now, these titans of not only industry but also, apparently, charity were booting me from my own volunteer work. I rose from the table, offered a weak hug good-bye, and wandered home in a trance.

As I entered my apartment, my breath became dotted with whimpers as I staggered in a Frankenstein-like walk to the phone.

Heart pounding, I called Kiki to report Sherry Von's pop-by and subsequent sting operation.

"That fucking Mayflower BITCH!" exclaimed Kiki, in even more of a rage than I was. "What does she get out of blackballing you? What the fuck does she want from you?"

"I told you. She wants me to play nice, look the other way, and stick together."

"So, what, she just thinks Tim can have his cake and fuck it, too?"

I was cripplingly weary with the turn my life had taken. It was truly as if it were someone else's plummet, all in bold font, tabloidy and rank. Was Sherry right? Was I being too rash in confronting him? Should I have waited it out and seen if the affair would fizzle, and keep our family together instead of shining a floodlight on his indiscretions? But there was no room for second chances when Tim wasn't even begging—or asking—for one. There was no remorse, no dramatic throwing of his blubbering, weepy carcass at my feet in penitence. There wasn't even a meek apology. Tim left me no choice. And Miles . . . my eyes welled with tears thinking of Sherry Von's poisoned words, her suggestion that I somehow am a shitty mom by clipping our family apart with the long, sharp scissors of divorce. I collapsed on the couch and cried to Kiki, weeping in a way I hadn't since my mom died. I took deep breaths and exhaled staccato air through my lungs, my body shaking.

"It's okay, honey. You are strong. Like your mom, you are a rock, and you one hundred percent are going to get through this," Kiki said in such a confident but calming way that I was sad she wasn't a mother—she would have been a natural.

Thank goodness it was summer vacation and I could just hole up while everyone else swung golf clubs or skied far away. Then I could roast with the rats in the city that summer while they all hit the Hamptons or the Vineyard or Newport and not face the masses until the fall; hopefully by then I'd be somewhat cobbled together to deal with the public scrutiny of being La Divorcée.

"There will be no public scrutiny," Kiki said.

"There won't?" I asked meekly. "I just know all those perfect moms are going to have a pity party for poor dumped Holly," I lamented, imagining their condescending pats on the back as they gripped their husbands even harder.

"No. Because I am going to help you," pronounced Kiki. "You are going to be my project," she promised.

"What do you mean?"

"You are the best mother to Miles. You organize his life: his playdates, his Super Soccer Stars, his TechoTots computer lessons, his Petite Picassos art class—and I am going to do that for you."

"How?" I wiped the tears that had spilled and settled on my cheeks, rendering my skin tight and hard.

"I'm going to help you press the restart button of your life. Makeover, new hair, new clothes, new confidence, the works. We are going to show that bitch Sherry Von that she was wrong—*plenty* of guys would kill to be with you. I will be your social quarterback. And while our loser ex-husbands are watching the NFL, we will be making our own plays."

"Kiki, I really appreciate that, but I'm such a mess right now, I don't even know where to begin."

"I do," she said. "Repeat after me, one hundred times: Nina Ricci short yellow dress. Nina Ricci short yellow dress. Nina Ricci short yellow dress . . ."

I knew she was referencing Reese Witherspoon's post-divorce Golden Globes dress, which she rocked on the red carpet, proving philandering Mr. Philippe a total raging idiot. That frock was a symbol to all divorcées that they could take an emotional beating and still land on their five-inch Roger Viviers.

"She did it. We can do it. I don't have a kid, so I can be in the driver's seat. You just work on pampering yourself, building yourself back up. I will take care of everything."

"Kiki, I love you. What would I do without you?"

"Listen, it fucking sucks. You're basically in hell right now, express train, zero stops. There's gonna be crying and more crying until your tear ducts look like the Sahara. But you have to wake up and breathe in and out and get through those heinous days. It will obviously take a while until you feel whole enough to even function let alone date. And then even when you're ready, every bad date, you'll be sitting in the back of that taxi crying. But every good one—whether it works out or not—will give you a glimmer of what your life could be like. Romantic and exciting. I know I made the right choice leaving Hal. You have more to work through because you didn't have a slow deterioration like we did. But trust me, you will triumph over this noxious toxic sludge of a moment. You will push through it and fucking shine on the other side. It's like that river of shit the guy crawls through in *The Shawshank Redemption*. You'll cry and barf and get through this horrible tunnel and then you will be free of all this pain. I swear to you."

I just prayed she was right. Because at that moment it felt like a thousand football fields of misery ahead of me.

———

The next few months brought ten chopped-down trees' worth of tissues, long talks on the phone with my only other divorced friend, Natasha, incessant meetings with lawyers, a battery of Tim's assistants packing up his things for the Carlton House on Madison Avenue (where Wall Street titans shack up post-divorce), and a planned date to sign final marriage-dissolution documents. My heartbroken father flew into town to console me and help me through navigating my prenup and guide me to take the high road and ask for what was only fair. While the Empire State was "no fault," Tim's whore-bangage couldn't help me at all; in fact, it was the same legal consequences as if I had been banging my trainer at David Barton. My dad stayed up with me into the night, wiping my tears. "Honey," he said, "let's think this through. I know you're hurt, I know you're angry, and while part of you might want to make him pay, you don't want to make Miles pay emotionally. Your mom and I never had any of this kind of life-style, and we were fine."

And my dad was always right. Like my mom, he was a calmer, nobler soul than I, who wanted to gut Tim for all he was worth . . . but it wasn't worth it. Not for karma, or even Miles, but for the fact that I was too tired for the fight. I didn't feel like rolling up my sleeves to duke it out. Even though I was blood drunk for some kind of revenge, I didn't want to punish Miles by suing for custody, so I let him share fifty-fifty with weekends and Wednes-day evenings. Financially, because of our ironclad prenup, I was hardly entitled to what I ended up scoring: our beloved apart-ment.

Tim, out of guilt, gave me the whole thing and agreed to pay the maintenance, but because it was well beyond the money stipulated by our contract, that was all I'd get. Child support for Miles, sure, but good-bye Bergdorf's charge card; adios clubs, even David Barton gym membership. My lawyer said I could have probably fought for some of these, but I just wanted the whole thing done. I didn't want to give Sherry Von any more ammo—I was sure she was steaming I got the apartment, since she'd been the one who'd found it for us; it had once belonged to a prominent socialite she knew from Locust Valley. And I loved it. I had decorated it myself, and it was a constant in Miles's changing life. And since Tim was always away so much, anyway, we were both used to it being spacious for the two of us, but always cozy, with the third bedroom functioning as a TV and toy pit with Miles's art station and an easel. Home was everything to me, especially because I had grown more into a nester than ever, and I wanted one touchstone that would remain sacred. Luckily Tim didn't fight me on it.

But as for all those other perks of being a hedgie wife, I never really was so obsessed with all that excess. Did I really need to call one of Tim's assistants to get theater tickets or make that reservation? I'd call myself, so what. I was almost relieved to eliminate the middleman. And, sure, on a rainy day it was great to have a driver, but sometimes it was fun to get soaked. I loved my walks. Walking in New York is one of my greatest pastimes, and so many wealthy wives miss out on that pleasure. He could keep it all. I had my pride and wasn't going to beg for more, even if it was my due.

When Tim and I finally entered the offices, each flanked by our lawyers, we briefly locked eyes. I looked down quickly to try not to cry. I soberly stared at the dotted line, and as the ball rolled through the ink and onto the paper, I realized the shock had subsided and clarity was taking its place through closure.

After he signed, my lawyer simply said, "Okay, then."

That was it. A decade together and a Tiffany fountain pen pierced our matrimony like a silver scythe.

"Holl—"

I looked at him, his lips folded together in a stern grimace. "Sorry."

Saying nothing, I blinked back tears as I opened the door and left.

My dad came back to visit for a couple days and we stayed up through the night as we both cried, me for my marriage, he for my mom, for the past, for easier times. I told him how even when I was fighting to swim back to the shore of stability, after ten strokes I'd realize the forceful current of grief had dragged me twenty strokes farther out to sea. I was weary and thought I'd drown.

"Honey, remember the utter despair you felt after Mom died?" he asked.

"Yes."

"You thought you could never function again in the world without her. And it was hard, terribly hard, for all of us, but we soldiered on. You can do it, you will do it. Not just for Miles, but also yourself. You're young, you have your whole life ahead of you, and you need to be strong."

Leave it to dads to hand out the tough love. He was right; I could wallow in self-pitying misery till the Crypt Keeper giggled in my face with his sharpened sickle or I could buck up and jump back into life. I only wished my mom was there to help me through this second dark chapter.

But as time passed, when I breathed in and out, it took less effort. It used to be that when my alarm went off, I'd immediately feel a two-ton weight upon my chest. But then, little by little, it was one ton. And then half. And less. Until slowly I became more anesthetized to the gut-churning pain. Sheer agony became blunt pain became discomfort. And soon enough discomfort morphed into tolerance for my situation. And once I started to get used to everything, I started, step by tiny step, day by day, to feel that if I squinted hard enough, I might be able to make out an infinitesimal ray of light in the distance. When I looked back on how far I'd come from not wanting to get out of bed, to pulling myself together and dealing with it for my son, I knew the future could only get less and less gray.

Kiki had been right: I would get through this. As Miles and I lay in bed one night, I read his stories until my own eyelids grew heavy like his and I ended up passing out next to him. And in the reverie of watercolor illustrations that danced in my dazed head, the color that emerged in the distant swirl was yellow. Sunny, Nina Ricci yellow.

13

"She's been married so many times, she has rice marks on her face."

—Henny Youngman

If my life were a movie, this is when you'd cue the *Rocky* or *Star Wars* music. Something majestic. Something grandiose forecasting my rise from the emotional ashes of my scorched home! Okay, so maybe the long days were peppered with a few random crying fits in Starbucks. I also tended to weep and get full-body shivers when I found one of my neighborhood accounts closed; I didn't think Tim would stoop to literally shutting down house charges for banal things like toothpaste and combs, but he did. "Sorry, Mrs. Talbott," the old guy at Zitomer's replied. "I'm afraid it's been shut down." Ditto at Clyde's Chemists, Citarella, the hardware store, even amazon.com rejected my one-click all of a sudden. The spigot was turned off completely. Horrifyingly, when I went to buy Miles's favorite steaks from Lobel's, I bumped into Emilia d'Angelo—with her chef—selecting filets mignons for a dinner party. We chitchatted and then the sweet man I'd been buying meat from for a decade looked at me sadly and said my house account had been shuttered. I saw Emilia pretend to play with her Bulgari necklace and carefully study the sirloin, but I knew she had overheard. I would now certainly be the talk of the next Sette Mezzo gathering. I guess it was like Sherry Von said: You're either part of The Family, *Godfather* style, or not. I was now clearly Fredo floating face-down in Lake Tahoe.

Soon after my denied beef, the news hit the press. Not to the extent of Kiki's split, since she was more glam and high profile than I was, but we were included in a column on megadivorces in both *W* and the local society mag *Quest*, both with photos of Tim and me at various charity benefits chaired by Sherry Von.

I looked at my smiling younger face in those photos; I wished I could have warned that girl what was coming down the painful pike.

But for every downer moment I had—wondering what to do with my wedding album, my ring, our family photos—I had a pep talk from Kiki. It was she who told me how to sit Miles down and tell him that I loved him more than anything on planet Earth and that Tim and I both adored him as much as ever. It was she who gave me my new gym card with a bow on it, and a new colorist, Juan, who insisted, with her by my side, that I needed to get blonder again, and lose the mousy mommy shade I'd sported for eons. Thanks to Kiki's coaching, the past months had been a montage of fitness, pampering, and Holly-centric laser-beam focus. It was a jumble of psycho long walks with Kiki, running the soccer ball in the fields in July with Miles, endless museum trips with him on too-hot days, and pounding the Poland Spring instead of my usual Sprite, which had become my water to the point where a horrified Kiki told me my diet resembled Britney Spears's. It's not that my fingers were oranged with Cheeto dust or anything; I just had . . . rather unsophisticated taste buds for the circle I previously ran in—that of pure protein or liquid lunches and frisée-with-balsamic dinners.

Next we hit Frédéric Fekkai in SoHo and I bit my lip as my long locks were cropped to a sleek bob; then the colorist amped my dishwater blond into a high-octane summery hue of childhood as Kiki stood by instructing him and cheering at the results, which I must confess were amazing and shaved five years off my looks. In two short hours I'd gone from Debbie Downer to Debbie Harry.

Tim requested that post-camp Miles spend a week with him in London, where he would be spending more and more time due to the burgeoning U.K. office. I wanted to fight him and say hell no, as the thought of his skank near my child made me ill to the point of hurling bile. But Tim had been traveling nonstop for close to a month and I couldn't forcibly keep my son away from his dad, especially since he was an only child and had no sibling comrades in the divorce trenches.

So when Kiki invited me to her friend's house in the Hamptons, I decided that rather than roast on the gray asphalt frying pan that was Manhattan, I should go. Kiki had sworn up and down that we could avoid the hedge fund scene out there—that of the $500,000 summer rentals, helicopter landing pads, and polo we had been forced to endure in previous years. The four-inch-stiletto, sunglasses-on-head, tanorexic party set would be over the hedge, so to speak, as we'd hole up alone, especially since I knew the diseased cat was more than out of the bag vis-à-vis our divorce. Even though I was now not loaded, tongues wagged more about the rich than anyone else. I could just see people trying to figure out what I got, who Tim was banging. The rich are more scandal prone, with salacious affairs ranking as the big kahuna of gossip. And a hedge fund divorce seemed to have everyone talking.

One August day by the pool, Kiki and I reminisced about our early days as sisters-in-law.

"I almost fainted when Hal told me about the Black Falcon Club," Kiki said, and laughed, sipping a fresh-mint-infused mojito. "That shit was so fucking brutal. I faked being into it for Hal's sake, but he clearly caught on that crawling through a tunnel lined with bats wasn't my thing."

I had to laugh at the recollection. The Black Falcon Club was a U.K.-based semisecret society whose members were almost entirely hedgies from New York and London, plus a few quirky characters like that old dude in *Contact* who went to outer space with the Russians and funded Jodie Foster's alien quest. Eccentrics, if you will (read: freaks with way too much money). Not unlike Michael Douglas's movie *The Game*, members booked time and paid upward of $100,000 per trip, which began when you were "kidnapped" by the club staffers in a travel adventure that took you to the literal ends of the earth. Tim and I, pre-Miles of course, went to places I hadn't even seen on the Discovery Channel. We hiked on an uncharted island with scorpions as big as my face. We played elephant polo in rural India. Watched the wildebeest migration in Masai Mara. Anaconda hunting. Surfed volcanoes. All places were either way too hot (watching Saiga antelopes cross the Gobi Desert) or way too cold (camping in an icehouse in Greenland), and all made me long for my bed at home.

Not one to challenge Tim's passion for these Black Falcon trips, I shut my mouth and even sometimes, despite the discomfort, got into it. But boy was I elated that I didn't have to do that anymore.

"Fucking Kalahari Desert!" said Kiki, mid-chug. "I think Tim and Hal were so jaded from their childhood at the Ritz and all that cosseted bullshit with Sherry Von that by the time they got to us, they needed to sweat and bleed to feel alive on vacation!"

I smiled, remembering Tim's acute (and accurate) sense that Kiki was unhappy on our many Black Falcon trips together, remarking, "Roughing it for Kiki is when the Four Seasons is booked."

"Well, you know . . . ," I started, somehow feeling oddly guilty at my forthcoming betrayal, as I was sworn to secrecy about all things related to Comet Capital. "Tim and Hal bought the Black Falcon."

"WHAT?!" Kiki was aghast.

"Fifty percent of it. A few months ago. I guess they've been raking it in and Tim thinks they can expand it and go global and stuff. Who knows."

"Gross. That company is so weird and creepy."

"They also invested in O.F.R.I.—remember that lab we visited?"

"No way!"

"Way."

O.F.R.I. stood for Ocean Floor Research Institute and was started by these two guys who were the top underwater explorers looking for sunken treasure. They had made headlines six years before in their find of a 1623 Spanish ship filled with $300 million of doubloons. Now they supposedly had found a ship carrying a treasure from four hundred years ago that was meant as a war bribe to lure an archduke to switch loyalties, but got lost at sea, crashing to the watery depths below with an estimated booty of $5 billion. Tim was all hush-hush about the deal, as he had been competing with rival fund MajesticMount, but he and Hal managed to turn on their Talbott charms and seal the deal, with Comet now owning roughly 30 percent of O.F.R.I.

"You know, I'm not greedy," Kiki said, shrugging. "But what we got is a pittance compared to what they have squirreled away somewhere. Forget their trusts—I'm talking that bullshit 'carry' with Comet. It's so unfair. They're shit husbands and yet we get flushed down the toilet financially."

"Well, we did sign the prenups," I lamented, thinking of how Tim sprang it on me three weeks before the wedding. I was semihorrified, as its existence had implications that weren't exactly till-death-do-us-part, but Tim said Sherry Von made him do it. Her speech went something like this: No signatures, no inheritance. Either way, after all those years of exhausting Black Falcon travel and scuba dives down to quasi-frozen underwater wrecks, it was interesting to realize that if Comet Capital's ship came in (so to speak), neither Kiki nor I would see one doubloon. But in the hot pink sunset of that August sky, clinking glasses filled with minty green refreshing concoctions, neither of us cared at all.

We had never been the gold-digging types, and so we weren't bitter—we had each other. We had met through the two brothers, who were now fading away into the past chapters of our lives, but we remained side by side, closer than ever. I just hoped that after our warm summer sanctuary, I could get through the chilling ice-water plunge of September's reentry.

14

"Marriage is a three-ring circus: engagement ring, wedding ring, and suffering."

The first day of school, heart pounding, I walked beside a skipping Miles, eager to see his friends, as I cringed, wishing I had a Harry Potter–style invisibility cloak. But I couldn't hide; I had to face up to everyone and diffuse any gossip with my big smile and confident composure. In other words, give Meryl Streep a run for her Oscars.

"Hi, Holly," said the perfectly bobbed Mary Grassweather, looking me over. "You look . . . great. How was your summer?"

A loaded silence hung in the air as four nearby moms turned to hear my response. Miles had scampered off to gab with his friends, and I looked at them with a small shrug.

"Well, you know, Tim and I split up, so it was kind of crazy, but I'm hanging in there."

"We heard," said Emilia d'Angelo, with a faux-sadness in her eyes like that kitty-cat poster they sell in Hallmark. "I'm so sorry to hear it. But these things are usually for the best!" Mary, Emilia, and Posey all looked down briefly at their different candy-hued Tory Burch Reva flats in a nanosecond of silence as an imaginary death knell rang over the grave of my marriage.

I had a scarlet "D" on my forehead and could tell I somehow felt different to them now; maybe because I represented the fact that if it could happen to us, it could happen to anyone. There were reactions of shock at the demise of my marriage, patronizing looks of pity on the school steps, and whispers from perfect mommies who saw me as I approached. Women whom I myself had resembled only a year ago when kindergarten had started. I was the first divorcée of the first grade. Well, second, but Kathy Gilles had split from her husband when their son was only two. I, however, was the first singleton of the couples who had arrived intact. Posey was my only organic pal, and in my low pony and occasional sweats I always felt like an outcast from the other women who were so groomed and glittering. And the Cadillac Escalades and GMC Denalis at drop-off always reminded me of this.

Whenever Miles had a playdate and they rode home with his pal's chef-baked chocolate chip cookies and movies for the fifteen-minute trip, he always lamented that we didn't have the same amenities. But I didn't want some dude in my kitchen on call, and not to be cheesy but I liked the idea of Miles daydreaming out the car window, watching the world go by instead of Spider-Man's webbing. I remembered one time, Hubert, Sherry Von's sweet and loyal butler, came to scoop us up. Kiki accompanied Miles and me to Locust Valley in Sherry Von's car, which was equipped with countless DVDs for Miles, all of which were age-inappropriate, skewing too young. But Miles was a captive audience and even though he was six, he preferred Dora the Explorer to green highway signage any day, so he zoned out to the quest to get the little ducky back to his momma, whose nest was perched at the top of a volcano. After the Map sang his round of "I'm the Map! I'm the Map! I'm the Map! I'm the Map! I'm the Map! I'm the Map! I'm the Map! I'm the Map!"

Kiki blurted out, "OKAY, YOU'RE THE FUCKING MAP!" She asked how I could ever put up with that cacophony, and from that moment I knew we would not succumb to the in-car entertainment system that the hordes at drop-off and pickup were screening. Even Hubert, who never complained (and had been through way worse with Sherry Von's poison tongue lashing him when the coffee was too hot or not hot enough), exhaled in relief when I turned off the relentless chirp of our *amiga cantante.*

But because Miles's friends would always run in elite circles and possibly infect him with their yearning for stuff, I knew I had to ground him as best I could and keep his values centered, like the school's teachings did. I adored Miles's school and the unmatchable education it offered my son. But while I loved the soul of the place, I was loath to see all the moms whose husbands somehow worked with Tim—half the class was hedge fund wives. There were other professions, sure, but many—most— were hedgie molls. As I surveyed the school's steps from a distance, I saw everyone preened to perfection, blond locks glinting off the sun from a summer of beachside rays—and amped up shades at Fekkai.

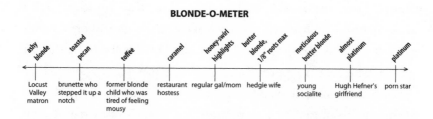

BLONDE-O-METER

But as I saw the blond heads whispering and casting not-so-subtle glances in my direction, I knew that not just good news, but also bad, travels fast: Within yards of the front door where the boys lined up outside school, I knew damn well that word had broken on Tim's extracurriculars to every last mom on those crowded steps, not just the Hamptons crew among whom gossip is texted at the Mercedes wheel between Hay Ground camp and town. My bomb's fallout had even reached those summering on their private islands off the coast of Maine and Canada. But while such salacious revelations would have spurred me to reach out to the poor humiliated wife, I weirdly had the sense that I was somehow diseased when two of the moms looked me over. I tried to change the subject.

"Wow, Emilia, that's a cool camera," I observed, noticing a very sleek futuristic digicam with MoMA on it.

"Thanks!" She beamed. "For a five-million-dollar donation, you too can have one!" she said, in all seriousness. She then looked down, probably realizing (correctly) that post-divorce I was in no position to be a high-roller philanthropist any longer.

"Oh, they're letting us into school," she was happy to notice, puncturing the pregnant pause. "Let's go, Prescott!"

And with that, they ran off to get in line with their sons. Emilia had looked away almost immediately and swept the whole thing under the proverbial rug, as if she needed to change subjects. Were all these perfect women somehow threatened by my split?

It got worse a week later when I heard Trish say to Mary, "Is there anything I can bring tomorrow night? We're so looking forward to dinner, we had such a nice time last year. . . ." Ah, yes. It was Trip and Mary Grassweather's black-tie dinner party in honor of the seasonal equinox on the twenty-first at their penthouse on Fifth. These hedge fund people will find any excuse for a party. Tim and I had met them a few times at birthday parties during the nursery school years, and when a mutual friend told us our kids would be in the same school for kindergarten, they invited us to a beautiful evening at their home at this time last year. I guess I was off the list now. I guess I'd be off every party list now. . . . I was the pariah of St. Sebastian's.

15

"Marriage is the triumph of imagination over intelligence."

Kiki and I were standing in my walk-in closet. Miles was leaving for a sleepover birthday party at Corbett Grassweather's house, and I would be . . . alone. Free to go out on the town with Kiki. Sort of. I gripped my cell phone in case Miles needed me and wanted to be airlifted from the slumber party, which I was weirdly secretly hoping he would.

Corbett's party wasn't just a Spider-Man theme. No, no, no, no—that would be too easy! Too pedestrian! You see, Mary and her husband called the owner of Marvel and arranged for Stan Lee himself to come and do drawings for the boys! And: You guessed it, Tobey Maguire would be "stopping by" for the cake, since now many hedge funds were investing in movies and the Grassweathers had befriended the webbed one by funding a pet project of his. Nice. Here, without exaggeration, are party themes of some hedgie children Tim's friends had thrown for their beloved offspring:

It sounds like I'm exaggerating, but I'm not. I wanted to shield him from the excess as much as I could, but I wasn't going to have him be the only one to miss the parties. All I could do was try and stay grounded in our new family of two. Keep him

HEDGE FUND KIDS' BIRTHDAY PARTIES

ROCK ON WITH RILEY!	Backstage at Gwen Stefani concert	**Party favor:** complete music catalog and autographed t-shirt
HOOPS WITH HAMILTON!	Free throws with the New York Knicks	**Party favor:** basketball signed by full team
LILA: EQUESTRIAN CHIC!	One pony and pony handler per child	**Party favor:** leather monogrammed saddle
STEFANIE'S SPA!	Mani-pedis or massages for the children	**Party favor:** cosmetics case with three tiers full of lotions and potions with custom Stefanie's Spa labels
FRANCESCA'S FASHIONISTA PARTY!	Donna Karan stages a fashion show with the kids as models, hair and makeup done	**Party favor:** cashmere twin set with child's name embroidered
PIERRE'S POWER RANGERS!	Actual Power Rangers from the movie stage a scene in which the kids get filmed acting out battles	**Party favor:** DVD of each child's scene complete with Chyron credits starring your child
LIFE IS A HIGHWAY!	Car-themed party with kids driving mini Ferraris from FAO Schwarz	**Party favor:** remote-controlled electric car with custom airbrush of child's name

centered, read to him about other places outside this bubble. So far, so good: He was a truly loving, good kid with a huge heart and strong values. But as he kissed me at the Grassweathers' and skipped off with his Spider-Man sleeping bag and navy duffel, it occurred to me that he couldn't wait to have me bail. So there I was. Walking home alone to face getting ready to go out like the old times.

I stood staring at my closet wondering what to put on to face the world as a singleton again. I gulped wearily at the prospect of gussying up, until Kiki burst into my apartment, fiercely dressed in a chocolate brown leather mini, a chic cowl-neck sweater, high boots, and bloodred nails.

"Okay! Let's get this party started! We need wine and music."

It had been so long since I'd done this: the revving up pre–night out. Choice after fashion choice that Kiki handed me was about as over the top as a spa day for six-year-olds.

"Keeks. I'm in my mid-thirties. This is too wild," I protested as she handed me a red satin D&G clinger she'd brought. "You don't wear this hem length at my age."

"Bullshit. All those *Sex and the City* girls were older than you and they wore Hermès scarves on their boobs, for Christ's sake!"

"That was a show. And I ain't Sarah Jessica."

We blared songs from my newly downloaded file on iTunes, which Kiki had introduced me to, blowing the cobwebs off my stereo and buying bands I'd never heard of but liked. I'd never felt so old: The rockers who crooned the tunes we shimmied to were a decade younger. And would probably laugh if they saw this mommy ramping up for a Saturday night.

I was oscillating from fear to excitement to cold strength. I knew it was "character building" to be dumped—I never had been ditched before—and I strangely almost found solace in the fact that this was a rite of passage for me; suddenly I was in on the Top 40 chart lyrics about heartbreak. Now I knew what all those dumb happy people didn't—there's a whole subworld of the miserable out there. And guess what? It's so much hipper! Kiki blared the Smiths as I brooded in front of the mirror applying eye shadow. The darkness was making me grow, and hey, everyone probably has one big earth-shattering heartbreak, right? Now mine's out of the way.

And now, along with my thinner frame (the Grief Diet is so amazing), I had something I hadn't had during the sad times in my marriage: hope. Loneliness when there's a human next to you is way worse than alone-loneliness for some reason. When you're single, there's always the accompanying reverie that you'll find Him, that special Dream Guy who will be forever your companion, laugh factory, lover, and, most of all, friend. But Tim and I hadn't even been close friends for a while. Before we had met, I used to see married couples and truly felt like they were little skipping in slo-mo through green pastures holding hands, like they had crossed over into happy-land and knew something all of us single ignoram uses didn't. But years into marriage, I realized that there is no gold-laced border into the land of rainbows and hazy sunsets. It was . . . the same. Or maybe worse. Because then the dream of finding that perfect love was over. And here I was on the outside again, back across that border in the realm of the unattached, where anything was possible. It was terrifying but electrifying.

To get to the way West Village, Kiki and I piled into a taxi, which stank so horrendously that you could toss your tacos. I was praying for the little yellow oxygen masks to spring out of an overhead compartment, but instead I just zoned out on the descending numbered street signs.

When we got to the party in one of the Raymond Meier buildings where one of the Olsen twins formerly resided, there was that crush of bodies that instantly transported me back in time. It wasn't that Tim and I hadn't been to parties; we just went to sedate, catered affairs with mostly married people. Or married people's hanger-on single friends who wanted to be married. This was not that at all; it was a full-on raucous rager, music blaring, lights low, hot-blooded hook-ups hours away. But it wasn't the fleece-and-headbands preppy twenties set, either; it was entirely new to me. There were some younger people, but there were plenty of thirtysomethings as well, just not older drones like uptown. These were edgier, cooler-seeming people who didn't seem to give a shit about aging. In fact, they dressed so young, they seemed younger, whereas the women at Miles's school may have been the same age but instead of vintage band T-shirts and fishnets and mod minidresses, they wore pleated kilts and cashmere twins sets and (gasp!) capes and looked way, way older than their years. I always had been somewhere in the middle—never matronly, but not edgy, either. But seeing people look so cool and stylish inspired me to take more risks and take clothing dares the way I did in college when Jeannie and I would flaunt our assets more than I had as a Mrs.

There was an energy bounding through the loft that I couldn't relate to, but wanted to. Reading my nervousness, Kiki squeezed my hand. She spied her friend Eliza across the crowded space and waved, dragging me behind her through the mass of dancing bodies.

There was a round of introductions yelled over remixes of Nine Inch Nails, and of the faces who mouthed their names over the din, one guy did catch my eye. He said his name was Matt Sevin, which seemed to ring a bell. Lucky seven: I liked the sound of it. There seemed to be a cool twinkle to him. We all sat near each other and tried to chat, but the music was so loud that it was a strain to gab freely. I gleaned he was a music journalist for *Spin* (hot!) and that he lived in DUMBO in Brooklyn, but not much else. I chatted with a few people plopped nearby, but I kept making eye contact with Matt. Finally, when everyone was heading out to some late-night party across town, my mommy clock kicked in, even though Miles hadn't called my cell. I wasn't exactly used to the words "after-party" and slowly felt myself turning into a pumpkin. My eyelids got heavy, and I even let a yawn escape as partygoers piled into the industrial elevator. As everyone hopped into cabs, I could sense Matt staying near our smaller posse, but what was the point of sticking around when I didn't have the energy to turn on the charm? I decided to bid everyone adieu and bolt. As it turned out, my non-strategy proved a good strategy.

"It was fun shouting over the music with you," said Matt flirtatiously.

"Yeah, you, too. Very worth the laryngitis I'll have tomorrow," I said, and smiled.

"Holly, do you want to grab dinner sometime?"

"Sure, I'd love that."

"Somewhere quiet, I promise."

And with that, I had set up my first post-divorce date.

16

Q. What food causes the most suffering?
A. Wedding cake.

Kiki had informed me that while the words "late night" weren't in my vocabulary (unless they involved Conan O'Brien), they were certainly in hers. Having never been woken by the sound of a newborn's lungy cry, she was used to partying hard and had, in fact, gone home with the bartender from the loft party.

"Kiki, how do you do it?" I asked over lunch a week later at Sarabeth's. "Don't you feel creepy about slithering in and out of some random guy's bed?"

"Guys don't. Why should I?" she said, sipping her club soda with a shrug.

"I need time alone. To rebuild," I thought aloud. "And even when I am ready, it's not like I'm going to meet someone serious in some party like that."

"Who said anything about serious?" Kiki mocked. "That is the last thing we need."

"Speak for yourself."

"Okay, I need. I am so not ever remarrying. Ever."

"What?" I asked with surprise. "You don't want to get married again?"

"No. I want to be free. I want to be like a guy. Why the fuck shouldn't I be? Because Doris Days like Sherry Von think we should be there with oven mitts and plastered smiles? I am so not being someone's Mrs. again."

Suddenly I saw Emilia d'Angelo getting up from her booth in the back, followed by Posey, Trish, and Mary Grassweather.

"I just hit an age where I said to myself, I'm just not doing my own hair anymore! Who has the time?" bellowed Emilia, retrieving her sable from the maitre d'.

"That's like me with sweaters," said Mary. "I just got to this point where it's, like, if it's not cashmere, it's not going on my body. You know, life's short, why itch?"

They turned and saw us and immediately started whispering before approaching.

"Hi, Holly," Posey said, coming over to kiss me hello. Trish and Mary did the same.

"Hi, Holly," said Emilia, faux-pity infusing her voice. "How are you doing? You poor thing . . . I've been thinking of you during what must be an extremely difficult and unbearable time," she said, making a sad face like one a child would draw, with an exaggerated downward arch of the mouth, as Mary and Posey looked on.

"She's fine, actually," Kiki said. I was kind of embarrassed because it was obvious from her tone that she wanted to send the gang packing.

"How are you guys? I feel like I haven't even seen you guys in forever." Translation: They had stopped inviting me everywhere. Not that I cared. But Posey's distance seemed to get under my skin a bit more than the other twos'. "How was your summer?" I asked with a smile.

"Uh-oh," chimed in Posey. "Don't get her started on her rental."

"It was the pits," said Emilia. "We get out there, after signing the contract—half a mil for three months in Montauk—unpack the four kids with all their stuff, all the staff, only to discover the central air is kaput. Broke. Unfixable." She threw her hands up, shaking her head at the horror.

"Can you imagine?" added Mary, hand to throat, with an intonation that put the catastrophe on par with the Hindenburg.

"So we just left," said Emilia. "Started at square one. In June. It was awful. Marco took the seaplane out, and we scrambled to find a suitable alternative but naturally all the best properties are taken by then and it'll be two years before our Gin Lane house is ready—it's a total gut job. I'm talking Baghdad. Marco and I are poring over these blueprints every night, it's SUCH hard work. *Plus*, to add insult to injury, we had construction on the apartment here, and there are summer work rules, so we have two crews working day and night, around the clock, don't get me started. You have no idea how incredibly exhausting it is to be presiding over not one but *two* construction sites simultaneously!"

To say that our world was sheltered would be the understatement of the century. But now I saw it more than ever. Here I was, in the throes of a hellish year, and these so-called society mavens have the gall to complain about lives people would kill for. All perspective was clearly out the penthouse window.

As my frenemies Mary and Emilia went to put on their jackets, I said to Trish and Posey that I'd love to catch up and maybe grab a glass of wine sometime.

"Uh, sure, yeah . . . um, things are so crazed right now with Noelle's kindergarten applications, but yeah, let's definitely try—" Trish stammered.

I felt the sting of Trish's semidismissal of my offer. You can't bullshit a bullshitter, and I was the queen of wriggling out of invitations. Looked like I was being dethroned.

"Okay, whatever works down the road when things are less chaotic," I said, letting her off the hook.

She bit her lip and gave that apologetic look for her crazy schedule (but hey, it's New York, we're all busy) and I just wondered if she thought the Divorce Disease was contagious.

Meanwhile, I could tell Posey felt a bit guilty. "Oh, Holl—save the date the thirteenth next month—it's the Winter Wonderland Ball; it's going to be great this year," she offered. Meanwhile, I knew that benefit cost $10,000 a ticket, obviously something I could never afford, not that I wanted to go, anyway. I made some comment about checking the calendar, though we both knew inviting someone to purchase a ticket to a benefit was hardly a gesture of reaching out.

Posey waved good-bye with a sweet smile as she headed for the door, and after the trio departed for St. Sebastian's dismissal, it took all of seven seconds for Kiki to unleash.

"How happy are you to not be around those nasty bitches anymore? Tim had you seeing that crew, what, twice a week?"

"Sometimes more."

At pickup, Miles skipped into my arms and I saw Emilia, Mary, Trish, and Posey all glancing toward me with that look of compassion mixed with fear. There I was, kissing my son hello and handing him some pretzels. That's what my life was to them, a salty twist. And like the carbo-loaded snacks Miles and I munched together, I was their darkest fears embodied.

17

"If variety is the spice of life, then marriage is a big can of leftover Spam."

—*Johnny Carson*

The next week, on the night that Tim took Miles, I got ready for my little experiment: a date, post-apocalypse. I walked into the bar of Peasant, a warm little joint on Elizabeth and Spring streets, and scanned the joint for Matt. Then I heard, above the mild hum of the bar crowd, "See, I think 'Dusting the Stars' was a seminal song that cut through the pop confections and offered them legitimacy, not to mention street cred."

Music journalism lingo 101: "street cred" and "seminal."

The speaker of these words was Mr. Sevin, a tall, lanky, hot guy with painter's pants and a vintage T-shirt. Even cuter than I recalled from the week before.

MATT MATH
(beat-up messenger bag $+$ Andy Samburg haircut $\times$ Elvis Costello glasses $+\sum$ (the Strokes $-$ trust fund) $+$ vintage band tee) $\div$ 3% body fat

"Hi, Matt!"

"Holly, great to see you. And hear you, this time." He smiled and introduced me to his pal, who was called Slam or something weird, I can't now recall, but it was a word and a verb. As we small-talked about the "killer" paninis, the wheels were turning in my head. If only the Carnegie Hill gang could see me now, with a cute Brooklyn boy with vintage Adidas sneaks who looked like the fourth Beastie Boy! He was the opposite of hedge fund land. Thank God.

We ate some of the best pizza I'd ever had, and I felt young again. But every so often reality would set in and I'd feel like some kind of fraud, a play actress. In my mind, the restaurant was a stage and we were acting out the roles of single daters in downtown New York, when in fact I was a weary divorcée. I appeared happy and unattached to the stylish diners in adjacent booths, but I was laden with the burden of bitterness and heartbreak; I worried that if the lights went up on the dimmer, one could see the invisible Scotch tape and staples holding me together like one of Miles's collages. I wanted to seize the day! Drink life to the lees! So I surprised myself by saying yes when he asked me to accompany him to a midnight sneaker auction. Yes. That's right. A midnight auction where they sell highly collectible running shoes. Think Sotheby's for Beastie Boys.

We walked out and I followed him like a sheep down to the subway, where we boarded a train line I never knew existed, arriving twenty-five minutes later in a random neighborhood of Brooklyn I had never explored in my excursions to see bands at various Williamsburg clubs years earlier as part of my magazine job. On the ride, he spoke a mile a minute about his obsession with collectible sneakers and how, like the upside-down airplane stamp worth millions, there were accidental New Balances, Nikes, Reeboks—factory-second samples or limited editions that were never manufactured into lines. He was very anxious to acquire the final lot, a pair of never-seen Pumas that had some kind of metallic stripe. This was so not my life. And I liked that.

I must admit, I was kind of hypnotized by his cool factor, and for the first time in my life I felt like I had to keep up with all the music minutiae he threw my way. I was so used to being the one into music—at least among my set—and this dude was making me feel like an uptight out-of-pop-culture moron. He knew every rapper's exact ghetto and tenement of origin ("it's all about what's coming out of Coney Island right now") and every little rock band's musical recipe ("they're part Blur with a dash of Pogues meets Machines of Loving Grace by way of Morrissey"). The word "seminal" was used eleven times. And I felt, for some reason, this desperate need to please him, like I was auditioning and had to be the coolest, funniest, most ON I'd ever been.

We got off at the Montrose stop and ventured around the corner to a seemingly abandoned office building with looming loft-like spaces that dwarfed my church's cathedral ceilings. Hordes of young-looking people with those black thick-framed glasses (that tend to signify either film student or serial killer) paraded in. There were mostly guys, but the girls there were 'rexi-thin chicks with tank tops over nips, no bra necessary. Their amber henna'd hair was held in place by haphazardly placed little clips, and they had asymmetrical-on-purpose hemlines and blue nail polish—you know the scene I'm painting here. A spiky-haired platinum-bleached DJ in a ringer tee "spun it" in a booth with four turntables as the organizers pushed the Lucite boxed lots onto a makeshift stage. On the dudes: on-purpose mullets, faux-hawks, and guyliner abounded.

I felt like I was on the set of a music video. Fishnets everywhere. Urban Outfitters had thrown up on the whole room.

And I loved it. I was the cut-and-pasted "one of these things is not like the other" person set against a collage of high cheekbones, punk rocker hair, tattoos, motorcycle jackets, and vintage concert tour shirts. Blue light streaked the massive room as people excitedly flipped through the zine-like "catalog" of the sneaker lots, with drawings and cartoon blurbs in cool mini-handwriting about each stellar pair. Surreal but intriguing; people watching extraordinaire. Everyone seemed way younger than I was. This was a center of hot-blooded energy coursing with a youthful buzz of artists and funky stylish gamines. And not a penny of health insurance in the whole warehouse population.

It all seemed very badass until I saw a girl definitely high on something. Even though I'm always clueless about people being high, as it often takes one to know one, I suddenly realized I was among tripping sneaker bidders, and the whole energy changed in my mind, making it all far less interesting.

Fortunately, Matt seemed to be high only on life, and we talked about bands we liked (some overlap) and writers we admired (no overlap). He read only zines and thought *Rolling Stone* was "the devil." While I preferred novels, he strictly read biographies, preferably autobiographies by rock icons or people "who were there" ("Legs McNeil's book is my bible"). His almost-too-tight T-shirt revealed my favorite kind of bod: overbred and underfed, except there was an air of being unselfconsciously self-conscious, decidedly undecided. In other words: messy on purpose.

The auctioneer began the proceedings, with bidders using Reynolds-wrap foil disks with numbers on them as paddles. The price of one pair of Nikes skyrocketed up to $700! A "dealer" bought them.

"Whoa, seven hundred clams for sneaks," I marveled. "Those make Christian Louboutins look cheap!"

"Oh, that's nothing!" scoffed Matt, now sitting very close to me. "They sometimes go for, like, three grand."

Finally Matt's lot came up and he even let me wave the tinfoil paddle.

"Twelve hundred, do I hear thirteen?" asked the auctioneer, who was wearing a headset and vintage-looking Lacoste zipper jacket.

"Thirteen," said a blond-dreadlocked person waving his paddle across the floor.

"Fourteen!" yelled Matt.

"Fifteen," countered Bob Marley meets bleach.

"Do I hear sixteen hundred?" asked the auctioneer.

"Sixteen," said Matt for the final bid, which was unchallenged.

"SOLD!"

"Yay!" I yelped as the auctioneer's fist-as-hammer went down for our victory. We hugged for a second and then walked behind this *Wizard of Oz*-like curtain where boxes of sneakers were piled up. We collected his loot and walked outside.

The streets were empty except for some action outside a bodega down the block.

"They love me there," Matt said, gesturing to the market. "I'm the only customer who doesn't use food stamps." I smiled and said I should get going. I was starting to worry about not getting home; I felt so far away and was getting suburbia panic.

"Cool, I'll walk you to the car service."

"Oh, are there no cabs?"

"Nah, but Rico'll get you a ride. They're fine, don't worry."

We walked down a tree-lined street and turned into a garage where a few men sat around a small table playing cards. They greeted Matt, who asked for a car for me. The dispatcher yelled in Spanish and I heard a reply of *"dos minutos"* on the scratchy CB.

"So when can we hang again?" he asked flirtatiously. "Do you want to go out Monday?"

Shit. "Oh, you know, actually, my fiend Kiki and I are going to the Elton John and Billy Joel concert."

Silence.

Then laughter.

"Oh! You're kidding! HA! That is so funny."

"Uh . . . no," I ventured, "We're going. I usually listen to really hard rock, but as a kid my family always listened to either Broadway show tunes or Paul Simon, Elton John, or Billy Joel in the car."

"You're serious." Poker face on Beastie Boy.

It was as if he thought I was a Martian. Make that a Martian on crack. So I sang out *"Caaaan you feel the love tonight?"* in the middle of the street. Nothing. "I don't know, I love that stuff. I've seen *The Lion King* three times! I'm really into Broadway."

He looked crushed. His eyes darted away from mine and he looked at his watch. Naturally some retro Casio, no doubt a difficult-to-come-by rare score. "Where is your car? I kind of have a headache and I have an interview with The Hives tomorrow, so . . ."

Was he going to leave me there? We stood for a minute in total silence as the fall breeze blew a paper bag across my feet.

Thank God my car pulled up, a burgundy rickety-ass beat-up Dodge with multiple dyed rabbits' feet dangling from the rearview and a gold-toothed driver who looked not unlike a pimp.

"Here's your chariot," he said.

"Well, maybe another night?" I countered.

"Yeah, um, well, things are really really crazy with work stuff so, yeah. I'll just . . . get back to you . . . at some point when I can come up for air or whatnot."

"Oh, okay, well—" I stammered.

He slammed the car door and walked off. I turned around and saw him shake his head through the back windshield. In the mirror the gold-toothed driver barked, "Where to?" and I told him my distant-seeming address.

As we bounced over potholes down the foreign streets, I got a sinking feeling of rejection. Great, I blew it. He frigging dumped me because I like Elton John. I don't believe this. I wasn't cool enough because I was a Billy Joel fan? So sue me! That's not edgy enough? I felt my throat close up a little and I started to cry. Argh.

Shockingly the tough-ass driver noticed. "Aw, sweetheart, why are you crying? Did he do somethin' bad to you?"

"No." I sniffed, wiping a tear. "It was just my first date back after my divorce and I realize I made a huge mistake. I'm not ready. I don't know if I ever will be." I started to convulse with sobs as we crossed the Brooklyn Bridge, just as I did on my return after discovering Tim on whore patrol.

"Naw, it's just rough the first time, you know?"

"I guess, I just . . . think I maybe I'm not cut out for this."

"Aw, you're cute though; you'll be fine."

"Thanks" was all I could muster.

"You want to know a secret, though?" he asked with a wink in the rearview mirror. Wisdom comes from strange places, and after my bad date I was desperate for some insight.

"Okay . . ."

"So maybe not tonight, but sometime, you're going to find a guy you like, but you don't tell him right away you like him, you see, you gotta—"

"But that's a game. I hate games."

"No, no, no, no, no! It's openness and honesty. But here's the key: Always keep ten percent for yourself."

"Okay . . . what does that mean?"

"It means that you always take a little piece, ten percent, that is yours that you don't give. So you, you know, keep your ground. Keep part for you."

Interesting. We pulled off the bridge, and the lights of countless office buildings gleamed against the night. I thought of all the New York men who were working their asses off in some office. One of them could be great for me, if he ever exited his fluorescent-lit gerbil wheel of work before midnight so I could meet him. But I wasn't going to date anyone in finance again. I'd maxed out on stock talk. And the whole competitive fast lane of that old-fashioned boys club world. I needed something radically different and new, someone who did something that actually interested me. Yes, my date had turned out frightfully wrong, but at least I got to escape my pod and see a new mini-universe that is right here in my city.

I got home, thanked the gold-toothed driver-slash-shrink for everything, and bounded upstairs. As I exhaled and climbed into the king-size bed, I couldn't help but feel the muted pain of missing Tim. In bed we always slept like the roman numeral XI, him splayed out in an X and me the line down the side. He was such a bed hog, but even now with all that space, and crisp, empty sheets, I was still a piece of spaghetti down the right side. When I thought about how he used to be there with me, I got an abdominal cramp like I had just run a mile and put my hand on my side, rubbing as if to make it stop. Maybe rabbit's foot guy was right: I had to be my own protector, giving but always keeping some for me as a defense mechanism. I didn't have to try as hard as I did, sitting up straight and laughing at Matt's every wisecrack. This was not a tap-dancing audition, and I had to try not to pour myself, 100 percent of myself, onto the floor at some guy's feet.

In mental playback, I realized I did everything I could the whole night to make Matt like me. And he still didn't. And while that originally sent me into an embarrassed shame spiral, the thought suddenly sparked that I didn't even like *him*. If, at age thirty-three, he was spending hundreds on the lost pair of Holy Grail–caliber Pumas, why was I so into pleasing him? I knew the answer was that in my post-Tim desperation I just wanted *someone*. Anyone. And preferably someone very different from Tim. But Matt wasn't even that great, and I had got sucked into the fear that if I could not even get him to like me, then I really could never get an amazing guy. This, of course, is the dating myth of Dumped by a Dork.

The D by D phenomenon is when you go out with someone and feel like you are doing them a favor and you're psyched because, hey, you're a catch and cuter than they are, so they are grateful—they worship you, try harder in bed; you are their world. Then, just when you've given them confidence, they dump you. You thought they were lucky to have you, but then they unload you. So you wig. Because if you can't please a guy you don't even want, how can you charm a guy you adore?

I guess the answer is, you charm the one that's right for you. Because after trying on all these people for size, you find one that fits. You don't have to tap dance to please them. But still I knew inside that every date would be accompanied by the hope that it would spark into something—and so there would always be the auditioning feeling of having to perform and please.

I remembered my mother's advice to me when I'd been depressed about a guy I liked in high school: "Go for the guys that like you," she said. "No assholes or bad boys. Just know they have to want you and court you. There's one egg for ninety-two million sperm and we have to echo our biology and be choosey! The egg is a microcosm of us; we have to let guys fight for us like in the olden days."

I took a deep breath, burrowed into my pillow, and resolved to try again when the moment arose. But next time I'd be more cautious: no blow-drying my hair, fretting over outfits, and try-ing so desperately to impress. I'd just make like the cliché and "be myself" . . . but always keep 10 percent.

18

"When a woman steals your husband, there's no better revenge than to let her keep him."

I took Miles for some gelato at Sant Ambroeus after school and we walked through the October leaves down Fifth Avenue toward the park. He wanted to run around before he started his homework (yes, *homework*—in first grade), so we went into the park. I watched him climb up the Alice in Wonderland statue on Seventy-sixth Street, and as he sat in big bronze Alice's lap and waved to me, I felt such love for him that I knew I would be okay. Even if I never met the perfect guy, I was raising the perfect guy, and I loved him more than anything.

My cell phone rang, and I looked away from my precious son to fish out my phone and found Kiki on the line.

"Hey where are you guys? I just stopped by your building—"

"Hi, we're in the park by Alice in Wonderland, come by!"

In five minutes Kiki was there, huge sunglasses, spike heels, fur coat, and cigarette, which I made her extinguish. She was larger than life, my friend.

"So. I have another guy for you—"

"We'll see. I'm not so sure I'm ready."

121

"Fine. I have another thought, then. When Tim takes Miles to London for Columbus Day weekend, why don't you come with me to Vegas?"

"Vegas? Are you crazy? No!"

"Why? You're just gonna sit here alone and mope? I think you need to break the rut and get away. I mean *really* away."

I noticed a gorgeous guy with a camera taking pictures of the fiery changing leaves. He then snapped the statue with Miles on it. My kid would end up in some tourist's memory book of New York.

"Isn't this statue great?" asked Kiki, flirtily, to the man, who was next to us.

"Yes, I love this," he said in an American accent. We were both surprised, as he had an aura that was too cool to be local.

"I'm Kiki and this is my friend Holland," she said in a Madonna-style quasi-Brit accent trying to make me sound more exotic than my low ponytail and unglam flats would project, pushing me forward. So embarrassing.

"I'm Elliot," he replied, shaking our hands.

Suddenly his cell phone rang.

"Excuse me, I've been waiting for this call—" He walked to a nearby bench and sat down.

"No worries," said Kiki as he turned to take it. Then she leaned in to me. "Gorgeous, right? Go for that!"

"Please. I don't pick people up in Central Park. Least of all weird tourists."

"Maybe he's not a tourist. He sounds normal."

I stared at her blankly to let her know she was being insane.

"Fine, okay, so, anyway, this guy I met for you," continued Kiki. "It's a friend of a friend. Investment banker. I know, I know—"

"Kiki. What did I say? NO WALL STREET. No hedge

122

funds, no brokers, no one who even glances at the *Wall Street Journal*! Got it?"

"Understood. Back to square one."

I always hated the sound of that phrase. It was like getting that one dreaded wild card in Candyland or Chutes and Ladders and going all the way back down the path to the beginning.

Kiki took Miles's hand.

"I'll race you, Aunt Kiki!" he challenged.

"I'll beat you in my high heels, you little critter!" she taunted. "On your mark. Get set. GO!" The two sprinted up the hill that led to the Fifth Avenue exit as I slowly meandered up. As I rounded the bend in the park path, I saw Elliot, still on the bench on the phone, looking up at me. He waved good-bye, as did I.

That night Miles and I made dinner in the kitchen, chopping veggies for a frittata. I remembered once seeing a T-shirt that read "Real Men Don't Eat Quiche," but I knew my son was more of a man with his big heart and unedited love than most schmucks out there. As we ate our concoction he started telling me about his studies in school. They were doing geography continent by continent and now they were on Africa.

"Mommy, did you know that in some cultures you get married and you don't even know the person? You marry a stranger!"

"Yes, I did know that. Crazy, huh." Little did he know it was the same thing here in the free world. Tim had turned out to be stranger. But he had given me my kid. And I couldn't dream of any child more delicious.

I read him some stories and tucked him into bed, wiping the matted hair from his face after he fell asleep. The thought of him on a plane without me always gave me a coronary, but I'd have to get used to it. As I walked into my bedroom, I started thinking

about what Kiki said: getting away. At home I'd probably just
worry about Miles incessantly and brew and stew about Tim and
whom they were with. Maybe a trip would be nice. But Vegas?
No. I didn't want the pressure to party and have a good time. I
wasn't in a festive mood. But the idea of travel had piqued my
interest; it was a weird time of year, so maybe I could get a bar-
gain. Because I wanted the apartment over any cash settlement,
and I had no new income, I couldn't exactly jet off to some ritzy
destination the way we used to. But maybe a trip would be just
the psychological break I needed. Maybe . . . I could get gelato
from the source. Within minutes I was clicking away online, and
within an hour I was the proud owner of a cheap ticket on Ali-
talia. Two nights in Florence, two nights in Venice. I had gone
with Tim during our first year of marriage, and this would be a
way of starting over: repaving those storied streets with new
memories. That would be more strengthening than partying
loneliness away in Vegas. I would embrace the loneliness instead.
It would be a quick trip, but one that was right for me—instead
of casino lights there would be lanterns; instead of desert, water.
And instead of throngs of slot-pulling, sweat-suited loafers walking on loud carpets, there would be the quiet pitter-patter of my
feet in quiet, twisting, cobblestoned alleys.

19

"The first decade of marriage, you watch TV after sex. The second decade, you watch TV during, and the third decade, you watch TV instead."

As the plane started to descend on the Old World, I was glued to the window, drinking in the different topography and totally new visual flavor. Sometimes, to get out of a rut, you have to fly out, via 777. It was like my passport stamp was a defibrillator jolting me awake after a haze of zombie-like existence as opposed to living. The little rooftops were centuries older than anything at home, and suddenly the U.S. felt like strip mall central next to the rustic charms of Italy. You could highlight and drag one seminice building from Europe and paste it into New York and it would be an insta-landmark. But we had our own brand of magic buildings at home, and while I was thrilled to be abroad, part of me missed the glimmering Gotham skyline already.

I got from the airport to my little hotel, which used to be one family's mansion and was pretty gorgeous considering it cost only a hundred and fifty euros. In the U.S. you couldn't get a twin bed in a crack flophouse for that! Then I saw my room.

To say that it made a monk's quarters look like a baronial spread would not be an exaggeration. So much for the appealing virtual tour online. The room must've been like eight by nine feet, with a tiny doll's bed in the corner, a small drawer set, and a bathroom where the showerhead is above the toilet so you can pee and condition your hair at the same time. There was a tiny *Shawshank Redemption*–style window about the size of a Scrabble board and a framed map of the *città*. Okay, I thought, the plan is not to spend much time in the hotel, anyway.

So I meandered out to achieve my first order of business: gelato. I glanced in the glass-covered bins of two places before I knew I'd struck gold; the coffee gelato in the third joint was so dark, it looked like espresso. Never had I tasted anything so orgasmic. The flavor on my dime-sized spoon could kick the ass of a pint of any coffee in the States. Bliss.

With my dish in hand and bag slung over my back, I trolled the little winding streets, marveled at every church I stepped into, and crossed the Ponte Vecchio to scope out the view of the river. The freezing wind was blowing through my hair and I leaned over the wall to look at the other side of the city and felt so proud of myself that I had come here alone. After years of Black Falcon Club trips with Tim, this felt way more adventurous. I had a small fear that I could be abducted and no one would ever know or remember seeing me, but for some reason I felt braver than I did at home, and my ignorance of bad neighborhoods in Florence sent me exploring for hours in every dark corner. I'd never dawdle aimlessly in twisting gray streets at home, but I was so curious about the random fountain at the end of a stone path, or the hidden palatial town house or a tucked-away mosaic. The sky fell to electric blue, then darker purple, and the stones beneath my feet looked almost shellacked black, like perfect skipping stones but big. An old woman out of central casting was attending to her window box and I decided to walk back through the dim-lit streets, and change before taking myself out to dinner.

I was lured off the non-tourist-trodden path toward a small cove aglow with the orangey flicker of a fun little hole-in-the-wall café. The place must have had a total of thirteen tables, and there was loud music, big plates of food, and happy, *dolce far niente*, life-loving eaters. The one drawback was the gust of smoke, but hey, I was in Italia, so I smiled at the guy who seemed to be in charge. He came over and I did the universal sign for *I am a loser and need a table just for me 'cause I am totally alone in the world* (the index finger up as if to say *one, please*). I got a look of pity and even saw him exchange glances with one of his *amici*, but he sat me in a very cute minitable in the corner.

Two hours later, there were seven people smashed around me. It began ten minutes after I sat down, with two *uomini* nearby who started speaking to me in broken English.

"Why you are alone, signorina?" When I replied in broken Italian, they were very impressed. How did this lonely American *ragazza* know Italiano?

"*Studiava all'università.*" First they angled their chairs toward me, then a cute couple walked in and knew them, so they introduced us. The woman had vibrant blue eyes and jet-black hair and the kind of weathered gorgeosity and extreme facial architecture that women find beautiful; guys don't always agree. We all hung out and they told me places to go, and even gave me their mobile phone numbers. I loved disposable friends. They were like my new best buds, kissing me good night and offering rooms in their homes, and I could be an effing serial killer. Fascinating. In New York, people would probably just whisper and feel sorry for me, and in Italy, they pull up chairs.

The next day I wandered to the Uffizi and waited in an

endless line to get to Botticelli's *Primavera*, which was sadly behind some bulletproof glass, which I found odd–slash–annoying. Some maniac had attempted to slash it. Who are these people? I camped in front and just zoned out staring at the fabrics of the maidens' dancing gowns, hypnotized by the ethereal gauzy haze. The women looked so serene, lost in a milky swell of lightness. And soon I felt as light as spring as well, renewed and fresh.

Seeing the painting, more because it was famous and reproduced everywhere than because I loved it, was like seeing an old friend. Way beyond a familiar face, the works in the galleries were like lost close childhood pals rediscovered on foreign soil. And because I was a lone American woman, these were connections not only to home but also to my past.

I passed an Assumption into Heaven, in which a weightless Christ with luminous skin was making his way to the sky. I saw Titians with blue so saturated and choked with color that it was as if the artist had ground up stones and spread liquid lapis on the panel. Staring at these masterpieces, in *delizioso* Italia, I felt poetic, romantic, with the excited chills that I normally reserved for a movie's final sunset-dappled kiss.

The next day I went to see the giant statue of David, and in the massive hall, there were a hundred *studenti* hanging out. It was funny to see a European cultural icon being treated as some ho-hum regular backdrop, but Miles and his friends often played in the Temple of Dendur at the Met in the winter, throwing pennies, laughing as if they were on a jungle gym, oblivious to the treasures perched among their sneakered feet. If you live with it every day, it may lose its luster. Still, I always loved walking in that looming glass room whose stark interior bled into Central Park's resplendent trees, and I never took it for granted.

I sat on the floor like some of the other visitors, and a guy next to me with a giant sketch pad was drawing a perfect rendition of the statue from our profile angle. It was quite impressive.

"*Molto buono,*" I offered, in pathetic Italian.

"Thanks," he said, smiling. He knew I was hopeless and spared me the humiliation of fumbling.

His name was Marcello and he was a former art student, now a lawyer, who had grown up in Bologna and moved to Florence a few years before with his firm. I marveled at the other great drawings on the layered pages of his pad, and he asked if I wanted to have lunch. He was handsome in a really foreign, dark way, and we talked about America and art and my trip and ultimately, why I was taking it.

"Ah . . . starting over?" he asked in perfect English. "Italy is the best place to do that."

On my date with Matt I hadn't mentioned Miles. Kiki had said I should wait till date number two to drop the mom-bomb. "No need to scare him too fast," she had said. "Rope him in a bit, and then let him know, once he's invested."

We never got to that point, obviously, but walking with Marcello I felt unedited and I talked forever about Miles, and then Tim, popping the cork on my emotional Prosecco. We walked through the little streets and watched the sky fall dark, and he asked if I wanted to come over.

In retrospect, I realize I must've been on crack to just follow him up the three flights, but for some reason it felt like a good idea. The alternative was being alone again, and I was suddenly not into that. We entered his apartment, which I thought for some reason would be a cyclone-hit mess, but it was surprisingly cute and clean, with huge arched windows overlooking a square and a little painter's corner with pots of brushes and an easel. After he closed the door I got that weird rush of being in a total stranger's abode. What was I thinking? He could be Gioffreddo Dahmer! Maybe he'd hack me up and make paint out of my blood and guts, *Red Violin*–style, and brush me onto a canvas.

He brought me some bubbly water, smiled, and plopped down on the couch. What if it was drugged or rufy spiked? It's poison! It was from a glass bottle, Holly. Okay, okay, he's fine. Not Teodoro Bundy. I was being paranoid, I realized, and calmed down a bit. But I apparently still was a little on edge, thinking of people saying, as I would, *"She went up there to his place? Then she's an idiot and it's partly her fault she got raped and hacked to bits!"*

My imagination is a burden sometimes.

Marcello, as it turned out, was not a razor-wielding rapist-murderer. Not Carlo Manson. He was a sweet, honest man who had just broken up with a girlfriend, and we ended up talking about life and relationships for a few hours. I tried to extract little pieces of wisdom from him, but it all mirrored what I already knew, just in slightly different words.

"You trusted yourself to go," he said. "You knew you could not stay and look the other way. As scary as it is to leave the marriage, it would have been worse still to stay and pretend you were happy."

Sì.

"You got it. *E vero,*" I said.

There was absolutely zero sexual tension. We shared only a mutual smile where we both knew we could have had a little *bacio*, but what was the point? It would just be a Band-Aid for two recovering lovelorn souls who were feeling a little small. How fitting that we had met next to a giant David, the underdog who later pulled through. Maybe we would, too . . . but not together.

"Good night, Holly. It was nice spending the day with you."

"Likewise."

I hugged him good-bye and left to go back to my room for my last night before Venezia.

When I arrived in enchanted Venice, it transcended my gargantuan memories. How many things are actually better than you imagined? I've heard people say it was smelly, that there are omnipresent rats, that it was a massive sewer. They all were wrong (then again, I was there in crisp October, not stinky July). Plus, I never saw one rat. Okay, I saw *one*, but it was swimming in the canal and my water taxi driver said, "Don'ta worry, they do notta eat the *turisti*."

I got to my little hotel and immediately called Miles to tell him I missed and loved him. And while I could hear Avery's voice in the background, which made me puke-ready, I took comfort in the fact that my son sounded happy. After we hung up, I unpacked and settled into my room, which was way better than the nun's quarters in Florence—this time it was *bellissima* and my queen-size bed was actually long enough so that my cobblestone-weary feet didn't hang off the end. The large single-pane window was crisply Windexed and much bigger, so the muted splish-splash of the narrow waterway outside could be heard all night, lulling me to sleep like I was in a giant womb. I walked everywhere in Venice, through the charcoal alleyways lined with creepy mask stores. Carnivale must be a really big deal there to sustain so many of them. As a rabid coulrophobe (victim of a paralyzingly traumatic fear of mimes, clowns, and worst of all, ventriloquist dummies), I had goose-bump-laced, violent reactions to the white, spooky, I-am-a-murderer visages.

The next day I walked to San Marco Square and bristled with

a bad case of the skeeves when I saw the hordes of pigeons (i.e., rats with wings). But then I remembered a photo of my mother standing in the very same spot at age eighteen, smiling by the domed wonder of the basilica in front of me. I got a tear in my eye when I thought of her, and how the pain of missing her would never subside. I wished she were there to coach me through this year. But I would summon her strength, as I knew she would have wanted me to.

My final day pre-departure was spent on a gondola. I scanned the striped-shirted men and when a cute old guy smiled at me and called me *bella,* it was game over. I hopped in and was amazed at how he expertly maneuvered me through the tiny canals as if we were a duck. I leaned back in the love seat clearly meant for two and drank in the rooftops and filled clotheslines. Considering that this city in its aqua maze had always occupied such a hallowed place in my imagination, it felt like a miracle to absorb the reality of that moment. This soaring above my own dream gave me something I never expected: the realization that I was not jaded. Things would be fine. Because I was not wounded and scarred enough to be closed off to the details, the visual balms, that make everything feel healed inside. It was as if this trip had peeled off a few pieces of that emotional Scotch tape, and plucked out one or two staples holding my heart to-gether. And as Mario burst into "O Sole Mio" when we crossed under a bridge, I got the rush of knowing my hope was restored. Of knowing some things are better than we dreamed when we book a spontaneous ticket online, and that the lapping water at the shiny boat's side was a symbol that taking a risk can be this refreshing.

20

"I'm a big opponent of divorce. Why leave the nut you know for one you don't?"

—*Loretta Lynn*

The trip was just what the doctor ordered, spiritual Prozac. Even though I was back in the saddle at home, doing volunteer work for Miles's school, I felt like I'd turned a corner. I was happily leading new prospective parents through tours of the hundred-fifty-year-old institution, which was not unlike Hogwarts, but sans capes and wands. It was a highly traditional, extremely rigorous course of study, complete with long white beards, plays by Ionesco, an organic chef in the dining room, and tweed aplenty. The school received a thousand applications for sixty spots. Two days a week I led wide-eyed couples through the mahogany-paneled halls, gesturing Vanna White style at the plaques that bore the names of two U.S. presidents, several accomplished writers, doctors, and an Academy Award winner. The couples all strolled hand in hand, probably thinking how lucky I was to be already "in," when in fact these women would die if they knew how thoroughly un-perfect my life was.

I loved peering into Miles's classrooms throughout the day, like a Where's Waldo–style treasure hunt, from the science lab (in his white coat and safety glasses) to the gym, to social studies, where they were studying South America. After school we walked to the park for his soccer, and as I stood chilly on the sidelines, I got a call from Tim's friend, Lars Hartstreich, from EdgeCreek Capital.

"Holly, I'm so sorry about the news of you and Tim—" He sounded sincerely upset.

"Yeah, well . . . yeah. What're you gonna do? I never thought this would be me, but hey, if you want to make God laugh, tell him your plans, right?"

"Well, Emma and I are thinking of you, and if there's anything we can do, please let us know."

"Thanks. . . ." I paused, signaling that it was okay to cut to the chase; he was clearly calling for something. Lars was a great guy whom I had always liked. But my defenses were still up from the breakup and I still felt antisocial vis-à-vis the hedge fund world, which was weirdly small.

"So I'm calling because I know you said you'd be willing to be a vice chair for the Bankers for Babies gala, and I wanted to confirm you're still on board—"

I drew breath to respond with a lame wriggling out of my commitment, but before I could speak, he continued.

"Holly, I know you've been through a lot, but you always bring so much to these events and we really hope we can count on you. We sent out the invitations a few weeks ago and didn't hear from you, but Emma and I would love to have you as our guest. Please join us. . . ."

"Um, okay," I mustered, before I could think clearly. Shoot, what did I go and say yes for? I didn't want to go! It was all hedgie bores and their quasi-lobotomized wives. I had endured it every year, even serving on the gala committee for the last three, and wanted to shut the gilded door on that whole world. But they had been my friends for years, and I guess it was a knee-jerk reaction to still being included when I had been feeling so out to sea socially.

"Terrific. We'll send the car for you next Thursday evening, then."

"Okay, thanks, Lars. Bye—"

Though I was dreading the evening, I was touched that Lars and Emma would still want me on board despite the fact that I was the jilted ex. I wasn't just a "plus one" arm-candy addition to Tim.

That night Miles and I worked on his diorama of all the planets in the galaxy. As the supposedly nontoxic model paints stank up our den, Miles broke my heart wide open. Talk about the Big Bang.

"Mommy, I know you and Daddy say you will not get back together. But are we still a family? Even with two houses?"

Spear through aorta.

I blinked back tears as the lump in my throat grew into invisible hands that strangled me, rendering me unable to breathe. I gathered myself enough to slowly answer.

"Sweetness, your daddy and I still love you as much as we ever have, and just because you see us separately doesn't mean you don't have a family that loves you. More than anything. You are my whole world. My galaxy . . ." I kissed his forehead and hugged him before he could see my eyes watering.

21

"It's not who you know that's important. It's how your wife found out."

—*Joey Adams*

I t was in a coffee bar, of all places, that I was first picked up. I was ordering a half pound of espresso malted milk balls when I heard a voice behind me.

"Those are dangerous little spheres, those things—"

I turned to see an older man, head full of gray hair, in a loden jacket, wearing small gold glasses.

"Oh, yeah, tell that to my thighs," I joked, exhausted after a sleepless night and sprint to Miles's school for an early-morning mothers' breakfast, where once again I was floating alone as gaggles of preened yummy mummies discussed Thanksgiving plans and the price of the Printery at Oyster Bay versus Mrs. John L. Strong for engraving their holiday cards (I laughed remembering how, the year before, Mary sent her Christmas wishes engraved with a heart above the word "LOVE," and above the word "PEACE" was a Mercedes symbol instead of a peace sign— classic). I had zero appetite, so I simply ate some pieces of fruit as I waited for my cue to leave and then sprinted to Oren's Daily

Roast on Lex to have my daily candy fix and scratch that chocolate itch.

"You don't look like you have any problems," he said, still making eye contact. "I, on the other hand, am older than you, and those are deathly," he said with a wink.

After I paid and was headed for the door, he was a few steps ahead and held it for me. I thanked him and then found we were walking side by side, so we kept small talking: about the beautiful crisp fall day, the Christmas decorations that were going up earlier and earlier, and the crowd of people breakfasting at a nearby café.

"Who are these people who eat these long, leisurely lunches on a weekday?" he asked. "Don't you sometimes wish everyone had subtitles with what they do?"

"There are many people here who don't have to work, I suppose," I offered.

We both scanned the mostly Eurotrashy crowd covered in fashion logos, Bluetooth earpieces, and leather. "But I wouldn't want to be them," he said. "I need my work, you know?"

"What do you do?"

"I'm an artist. I paint."

"Oh, cool," I responded lamely. "I thought all the artists were downtown these days. Or in Brooklyn."

"Yes, well, I lived in SoHo forever, but now I like it up here. Quieter. I'm an old man now," he said, brown eyes gleaming. His light gray hair looked striking next to his dark Hershey's Kiss eyes, and as he sipped his coffee, looking at me, I suddenly realized there was a miniflirtation going on.

"No, you're not old . . . ," I said, scanning him, realizing he was prematurely gray, as his face was handsome and young. Ish. Maybe he was mid-forties? Okay, late. "So what do you paint?"

I asked. "Landscapes? Cut-up faces, Picasso style? Or 'abstract art'?" I added with finger quotes. Maybe it was Jackson Pollock–style splatters. Or Twombly-esque chalkboard art. I wondered what an almost-preppy-looking middle-age guy would paint. Turns out, I would soon find out.

"Why don't you come see? Any interest?" he said with a sip of his coffee.

"Sure . . ."

"Great, I have a new show at Lyle Spence Gallery in Chelsea. My name's John Taplett, by the way."

"Holly Talbott."

Even I knew that gargantuan gleaming space. That gallery was famous and the guy Lyle Spence had a recent spread in the art issue of *Vanity Fair* as one of the three top megagallerists in the game. He was always dating model-actress types and often got more press than the artists he repped. But the name John Taplett somehow rang a bell.

"Wow, that's major. . . . I've been there, to a Michael Bevilacqua show a few years ago."

"The opening is in two weeks, November twenty-third, from six to eight. You should come. I'll look for you."

"Okay. I'll be there."

He smiled, looked at me with a cool glimmer in his eye, and took my hand in his. "See you then, Holly Talbott." With that, he walked off toward the bare trees of Central Park.

22

"When I married Mr. Right, I didn't realize his first name was ALWAYS."

It was in front of Google, which found 12,342 hits with his name, that my jaw started to hit the floor. He'd had solo shows all over the world; I had met a quasi celeb! He was sexy, an artist (hot), and older, which would really freak Tim out. I could still be the younger cute minx and not the hag I had felt like in the last half year.

I started to get obsessed. Holly Talbott Taplett sounds ridiculous, yes, but he could be it, my next chapter. I called Kiki.

"Go, girl, that is GREAT! Snaggin' guys at the fucking coffee bar, what a buzz!"

"Come on, you make me sound like a trollop," I joked. "So, Kiki, promise me you'll come with me?"

"Ugh . . . you know I hate that pretentious contemporary art scene. I screwed an auctioneer at Sotheby's for a year and he talked about exceeded estimates in the sack; what a turnoff. The guy got boners for paintings with dead butterfly corpses glued on them."

"Pleeeease? Come on, Kiki, no one builds me up like you do.

And he's gonna be the center of the action, so it's not like he can really hang out with me! I need a cohort. Pretty please?"

"Okay. I must really love you if I'm going to hang out in one of those Sprockets-fests with a sea of black turtlenecks and white walls."

"Thank you! Thank you! I owe you one."

"You bet your ass you do."

A week later, Tim's assistant called to say that he would be returning from London and wanted to see Miles. Coincidentally, it was the night of the benefit I would be attending with Lars and Emma, so I didn't have to get a sitter. Even though I ended up semidreading the evening, it was kind of nice to get dolled up in black tie. When Miles came in as I was spraying my finishing spritz of perfume, the buzzer rang and my ex was on his way up.

"Wow, Holly? You look . . . great," Tim commented when I opened the door. Ha. Eat your heart out. Still, even on my best night I couldn't look twenty-frigging-five like Avery.

"Thanks. So you'll take him to school tomorrow?"

"Sure, will do."

"Okay, great, thanks! Bye—"

I leaned down to kiss Miles good-bye and could sense Tim looking me over. I knew he was wondering where I was going, but I didn't mention a thing, as if I always pranced around in tight gowns and spike heels, not schleppy bathrobes and spinster slippers. Little did he know the evening ahead of me would probably be a huge nightmarish bore and the event I was truly intrigued by was a week away at the Lyle Spence Gallery. But what he didn't know wouldn't hurt him. It was my turn to get out in the world, and I didn't owe him a thing.

23

"Love is a fire. But whether it's going to warm your heart or burn down your house, you can never tell."

—Joan Crawford

Lars and Emma's chauffeur-driven Cadillac Escalade was outside waiting for me, and though I was basically in an armored urban tank, I felt vulnerable. Not since I went stag with all my girlfriends to my junior prom was I so gussied up without a hand to hold. When we got to Cipriani on Forty-second Street, my heart started to pound as I entered the grand ballroom—a former bank with such exquisitely ornate architecture, it was truly a landmark treasure. Flashbulbs flew as many high-profile trustees of the charity—from Harvey Weinstein to the CEO of General Electric to the heads of every major investment bank and the hedge fund elite—swarmed in, seeking their calligraphied cards of table assignments.

I milled around the cocktail hour a bit awkwardly by my lonesome, but a delicious bellini took the edge off, as did some caviar (Kiki always called us "the Roe Hos"). As I happily sipped my peach-infused champagne, I noticed a pair of green eyes trained on me. They belonged to a familiar-looking guy, though I had no idea who he was. He was extremely attractive—but not in that pretty-boy, too-angular way where they're so hot that everyone notices; he had that special kind of gleam that made him appealing in a warm, cuddly way. A total grade-A nugget.

"Hi," I said, in sixth-grade mode.

"Hi there, Holland, right? I'm Elliot—"

"Yes, hi, how are you?" We shook hands. I knew we'd met, but I couldn't place him. His green eyes were so amazing, they looked quasi contacty, which would be scary were his smile not so nice.

"I met you very briefly. In the park, with your son?" he responded. "And your friend, Kiki?"

"Oh, yes—" I vaguely recalled Kiki trying to strike up conversation with him. He was very cute. But another 10021 guy? No way. Plus, if he was there, he was obviously in the banking world, which was too close for comfort. No matter what.

It was among my top three bullet points. If I actually went online to do a profile or something, my request for a non-banker would be as much in lights as one for a non-smoker.

"Holly!" I heard behind me. Emma. In full Oscar de la Renta beaded gown to the floor, as if it were the Oscars. But I guess for her it was, since she and her husband were the honorary chairs of the evening and Bill Cunningham from the *Times* was snapping away for Sunday's paper.

"Emma, Lars, hi! Thank you so much for having me—this is spectacular!"

As Elliot wandered away, I got caught up in introductions to their friends who would also be at our table, including a widower who was much older. Not my type, as I don't date dwarves. The poor guy didn't clear my boobs, so there was no way I'd Katie Holmes over him no matter what elevator shoes he procured from John Lobb. Great, I knew there was some ulterior motive to my being invited. Oh, well. We chatted through the appetizer and I could tell he was a kind man, but clearly we were ill suited. And that would probably be how it was from now on: Match Holly with anyone who can walk. She's single now, she has a kid, and she'd be lucky to get anyone in this ballroom! Nice.

The evening droned on and there were many speeches about all the good the money was doing, and at one point as I scanned the grand room, zombie-like, I saw a beautiful blonde shamelessly flirting with Elliot. Just as I was about to casually nudge Emma to ask who he was, the spotlight fell upon our table and she and Lars rose to go to the podium to accept a trophy for their generous philanthropic efforts around the city. *Le tout* Wall Street clapped in their honor and I looked around, noticing the same crew of bedecked wives. Emilia d'Angelo and Mary Grassweather, with glistening wrists covered in diamonds; Posey Smith, who was in Oscar, gave me a wave across the dance floor. I felt a bit of a sting that she had never followed up with me about that glass of wine—we used to spend time alone together as friends, but now I could see she'd moved on. It's funny, I knew that if I were to go home with and date and marry the geezer next to me, like that other divorcée at our school, I would instantly regain my social standing. My new armor of another wealthy (albeit older) husband would reinstate me as a worthy friend, committee chairperson, trustee of the school or museum or hospital. My haute couture and glittering jewels would be a wearable E-ZPass back into society. But lately, when I saw a huge diamond necklace from Fred Leighton, I wondered: Was it a Forgive Me present? My eyes settled on another neck, covered with canary yellow diamonds from Graff. Was that a Please Take Me Back gift? Was each woman committing to stay for these precious gems, tacitly agreeing to look the other way while their husbands had their cakes and fucked them, too? My mind was reeling when my cell phone beeped with a text message from Kiki, interrupting these musings.

"Does your robot party suck? Meet me at Marion's on the Bowery."

Since dessert was being served and I saw a few old fogies and young parents starting to thank their various hosts and bid adieu to their tables, I bolted.

The vibe couldn't have been more different at the downtown bar, with kitsch galore dangling from the ceiling, loud music, and strong gem-hued cocktails that rivaled those bellinis.

"Holleeeeeee!" Kiki yelled when I walked in, making me feel very much like I had entered Cheers. She had a table in the back with some of her girlfriends whom I'd met before, all very hip and wild, without edit buttons, à la Kiki.

"Holly! Girl, you look fierce!" Eliza, who worked for Vera Wang, so kindly said. "You look much younger, too!"

"Really?"

"That's 'cause I gave her a total makeover and we got rid of half her stuffy-ass closet," bragged Kiki, winking at me. "We filled her disgusting Vera Bradley tote with all her preppy crap and torched it. She's a fox now, right?"

"Total minx," replied Carrie. "And speak of the devil!" Out walked a nice-looking but younger, like, much younger, guy from the bathroom. "Nick! This is Holly, Kiki's BFF!" said Eliza.

"Hi, I'm Nick." He was adorable, but *hello*? Twenty-six? Twenty-seven?

Okay, so I soon discovered he was twenty-eight. But at thirty-four, that felt like waaay too tender an age for me.

"Holly, what can I get you?" he asked. He whipped his sweat-shirt off, revealing a white T-shirt and his forearms, which were sleeved in tattoos.

"Um, I'm, uh, not much of a drinker."

"Come on, don't make me drink alone—I'm gonna surprise you, how 'bout that?"

"Uh . . ." I looked at Kiki, whose eyes were widened as if to say, *Don't be an idiot, get a drink!* So I agreed, though I had to be up bright and early to give tours the next day at Miles's school.

The next thing I knew I was clinking glasses with Nick and his roommates, all three chefs at various restaurants I had never heard of. And I loved that.

NICK MATH

$$\frac{\pi(\text{Viggo Mortensen}) + \text{shower} + \text{ink} \div \text{truffle oil}}{\sin \text{danger}}$$

As my eye fell on his tats, he clearly saw me register that they were . . . well . . . in your face. But somehow weirdly appealing.

"This one's great, isn't it? My friend Scott Campbell in Williamsburg did it. He's a fucking artist, man."

I asked about his cooking, thinking how nice it would be to sit in his kitchen and have him whip up something delicious and have *Like Water for Chocolate* sex-through-food, minus the whole dying-in-a-fire thing.

I felt myself getting drunk. As in, hammered, old-school-style. I don't think I ever once lost control in my ten years with Tim—okay, maybe once in a blue moon a little too much champagne at a wedding, but not like this, in black tie, laughing with people in their twenties who didn't have children. But it felt refreshing. Freeing. I had turned back the clock. At least until my morning hangover, which felt light-years away in the current haze of neon, clinking glasses, and vintage Blondie.

24

"God gave us all a penis and a brain, but only enough blood to run one at one time."

—*Robin Williams*

As I lay, head throbbing, trying to get out of bed and don a pantsuit fit for touring prospective parents, I tried to piece together the prior evening, since I truly didn't remember getting home. Thank God I'd had a relatively quick divorce settlement or Sherry Von would have had PIs trailing me to see if I was some lush and unfit mom, not that I ever would have pounded like that were Miles not with Tim. Thirty-four is too old to be on the hooch like that, I thought, even if for one night in eons.

Then I remembered all of us stumbling outside onto the Bowery, Kiki kissing some chef boy, and Nick putting his arm around me. His motorcycle jacket felt tight around my shoulder and I felt protected. I remembered my speech wasn't that clear as I uttered something about there being no cabs and he said, "I have a ride." In Tim's world, that meant a chauffeur-driven car waiting outside. I said, "Great," and was then led by Nick through the cold air to a motorcycle in front of the old CBGBs. It was starting to come back to me: My mom would have spazzed. I stuttered something about this maybe not being such a good idea, picturing myself in a full-body cast peeing through a hole cut out of the plaster into a bedpan.

"Come on, Holly. Chill out. Live a little." At least he had a spare helmet so I wouldn't be some decapitated headless horsemom with brains scattered along Park Avenue. I am so not wired for risk. If I hadn't been drunk, it would be safe to say I would have gotten on that hog over my dead body.

But there I was. Flying up First Avenue. Though my thoughts were hazy, I remember thinking that if someone I knew could see me, they would probably faint in shock. Or at least thought I'd gone off the deep end. Holly Talbott with some guy on a motorcycle? Not a chance.

When we got to my neighborhood, the night doorman was already on duty (translation: asleep on the lobby couch), so there was no one to witness my very un-uptown chariot's arrival. Nick helped me off the seat, dress pulled up by my thighs. It was semi-undignified but, dare I say, badass?

"Holly. That was fun—"

The next thing I knew, he had kissed me, hard. He put his hands on my face and leaned me against his bike, grabbing my back as his mouth moved on mine forcefully. I finally had my own taste of a no-strings-attached kiss. It was a very rock-and-roll moment for me. I'd always been a prude, "saving it" for my first love. But I was now taking a page from Kiki's book—a little black book—and while making out was phenomenal, with the sound of Nick's leather arms moving around me as a sound track, it was also just a page from the book and not the whole book. In other words, I might have been able to engage in street-corner kissing, but I would not be sleeping with Nick. When I finally disentangled myself from his embrace and looked at him, he knew right away I would have to bid adieu and that he would not be scoring beyond this, but he was very cool and simply took my hand, gave it a squeeze, and got back on his bike.

After a long day of tours, I scooped up Miles and took him out for an early dinner in our favorite old-school diner, Three Guys, on Madison. He was so excited about some game Tim had scored tickets to, and I tried to just nod and be excited for him, but I knew this would mark the beginning in a grand game of one-upsmanship, where I was the Lame One because I wasn't ever going to be able to get backstage passes at concerts the way Tim could through his connections, or go to the Super Bowl or Olympics or God knows what else. While my ex provided LeBron James, I could only offer a grilled cheese.

It was cold on our walk home, but the twinkling Christmas lights that had sprung up everywhere somehow warmed us. Thanksgiving was a week away, and the vision of a majestic streaming row of glittering trees down Park Avenue soothed our bones despite the arctic chill in the air.

After some hot chocolate and homework, Miles was ready for stories and we climbed into his bed, piled among stuffed animals and fluffy pillows. He was in his favorite Spider-Man pajamas and leaned on my shoulder as we read *Rotten Ralph*, about a mischievous cat who did mean things like take a bite out of every cookie at a birthday party. But it had always made me smile since it mirrored the other side of childhood, the kooky one that is sick of the incessant litany of brush-your-teeth, wash-your-hands, manners manners manners. And somehow through the prism of my wild night before, I was happy to break free from my own locked-in rules of what was acceptable and go crazy. Maybe not rotten, per se, but definitely, and happily, a little less tame.

25

"The only time my wife and I had a simultaneous orgasm was when the judge signed the divorce papers."

—*Woody Allen*

Two nights later, after Miles went to bed, Kiki called to report that, third grade–style, Nick the chef had told his friend that he wanted to see me again. Just thinking about him, and the fact that he was a *Wrinkle in Time* doorway to the youth I'd never had in my married twenties, gave me a little spring in my step. The following Saturday night we'd all hang out again when he finished work at midnight. Tim took Miles every weekend he was in town, and so I'd be solo and able to sleep super-late Sunday, but before I could get ahead of myself, I remembered I had roped Kiki into coming with me Thursday to the Lyle Spence Gallery for that opening of the other suitor in the hopper. It was amusing to me that there were twenty years between the two men. Nick (a.k.a. Chef Boy to Kiki) and John (whom she'd dubbed "L'artiste") could not be more different. Both intrigued me. Both were NOTHING like Tim, so both were appealing just for that. I wondered which one I'd end up dating.

"You don't have to pick one," said Kiki over the phone on

the eve of John's opening. "You're *just* back out there! You have to have many irons in the fire."

"What does that mean?"

"It means keep a bunch of possibilities hot. Stay open. Date up a storm."

And while I loved stories and TV shows about women on the town juggling men, I never knew how they could sleep with all those different people. I'd gone off the market at twenty-four and was still frozen in the land of sexual baseball bases and hookups without full sex. But at thirty-four, no one was going up the shirt and stopping. It was kissing on a corner or pulling out the condom. After years on the pill I had forgotten I'd actually have to have someone bag it up for fear of diseases. Great.

"I don't think I'm an irons-in-the-fire kinda gal," I confessed.

"Come on, Holly. Guys do it all the time. There's such a double standard."

"But it's different. Women are more selective. It's like the egg and the sperm. We choose, and they spread their seed everywhere. I can't slut out and start sleeping with every guy."

"What's with the word 'slut'? Are you from the Stone Age? I feel like Sherry Von has entered your body like Patrick Swayze inhabiting Whoopi Goldberg in *Ghost*."

"I'm not Sherry Von. I don't judge people who do it," I said, shaking my head. "It's not that—it's just that I've personally never . . . slept around."

"How many guys have you slept with?"

I stopped for a sec to count. On my fingers. On one hand. Tim was the thumb on the next.

"Six."

"Holy shit," Kiki said, laughing and covering her mouth. "*Six?*"

"Sorry, what, is that too lame for you? I'm like some church choir girl?"

"No, but you'll definitely think I'm a road whore. Add a zero."

I was stunned. Even with Kiki's bold personality and various rolls in the hay with randoms since her split, I had no idea it would be that high.

"Sixty?!" I asked. "No way."

"Okay, not that many. Maybe forty. There were a lot of fun quickies, after only a few dates. Or none, like that 9/11 fire-fighter who had lost half the guys in his ladder. I truly thought I was doing something good for my country."

I decided to wear a plain black dress with silver buttons down the side, a gift Tim had bought me (probably out of guilt) from Barneys the previous year. I could only wear it in thin, non-period phases, and it zipped up perfectly. Miles was going to the Big Apple Circus with Sherry Von, and her chauffeur, Hubert, was in the lobby when I walked him downstairs and out to the awaiting Bentley.

Hubert looked at me and smiled as Miles piled into the car.

By the look on Sherry Von's face when she saw my spike heels and fur-collared coat, I could tell she was expecting my standard Theory black pants or Earnest Sewn jeans, Hollywould flats, and ponytail.

"Well, Holland, my, my, where are you off to?" she asked as if floored that I had access to someplace other than my apartment. She probably though it was covered in Kleenex from my tears. Which it had been certainly, but the white balls gathered at the foot of my bed from weeping were becoming less and less frequent. "Just a gallery downtown."

"Oh. How nice," she said, with acid, forcing a saccharine smile.

"With Kiki, actually!"

The corners of her smile slowly turned downward into a full-on grimace of Estée Lauder red lipstick. She said nothing, just flared her nostrils as if the two syllables of Kiki's name had somehow elicited an acrid odor out of the ether.

"Well, have fun!" I said, blowing a kiss to Miles. I could tell by her shocked face that she'd rather I'd said I was meeting my meth dealer.

"Miss Holland—" I heard Hubert whisper as he walked around the back of the car to his driver's seat. "You look divine."

26

"Is there a cure for a broken heart? Only time can heal a broken heart. Just as time will heal his arms and legs."

—Miss Piggy

Thank goodness Kiki, who is usually always a half hour late, was standing by the door when I arrived on West Twenty-seventh Street. It was frigid out and just the half block from Tenth Avenue was enough to make me want to crawl into a vat of lava and boil myself.

"Hi! You look . . . wow. I might turn lezzie," joked Kiki. "I just got here. Wait till you see these paintings."

I had been curious. My Google image search had turned up mostly still-lifes, renderings of objects such as a spoon, a pipe, and a half-eaten slice of pie. But the gallery's website said that this show contained John's first-ever group of self-portraits. So I was intrigued, but not prepared for what was on view in the packed, bustling space filled with shaven-headed art people and their fashionista muses.

In a word: Buck. Self-portraits, as in *stark-ass-naked* self-portraits. Oh, sorry. I think the arty term is *nudes*. I moved into the room, past a stenciled charcoal gray heading that read

"JOHN TAPLETT: SELF-PORTRAITURE," to see eight huge images of John *in full*.

JOHN MATH

The college professor you had a crush on
(Christopher Plummer c. 1967)
✕ worn-in hands + premature gray
÷ paint-stained jeans

The six-foot canvases reminded me of a softer Captain Von Trapp, but with sausage in my face. My jaw dropped. But the images were good, really good. Sexy. They were done in heated, frazzled, impetuous lines, like a sketchbook come to life in oiled color. They were life-size and sometimes headless, just the neck down to the calves, with each in a different pose. I felt myself getting guiltily aroused, like this was art porn. Every muscle in his ripped but not-too-ripped torso was there, every crease and line in his pelvis and, yes, WIENER. I could not believe it. Wasn't he so embarrassed? I was fascinated.

Naturally it took Kiki all of five seconds to start teasing me.

"You better shack up with this one, Holly. He's fucking hung like Seabiscuit."

"Kiki, shut up!" I said, blushing. "I don't even know him!"

She walked up close to the, ahem, intimate painting, looking back at me with a smirk. "I'd say ya do now."

"Holly, I'm so glad you made it," said John, taking my hand in his, then looking up to find me reddening into a pomegranate hue.

"Th-this is my friend, Kiki Talbott," I stuttered.

"Pleasure to meet you," he said, shaking her hand. She still had that huge Cheshire Cat grin on her face, no doubt thinking of measurements. And I'm not talking about canvases.

"Can you join us as well for the dinner afterward?" he asked.

Before I shot her a longing look begging her to come, she had already began her weasel out.

"Oh, I wish I could, but I'm seeing Interpol tonight at Hammerstein. So sorry!"

"Oh, well, I'm sorry to hear it, but hopefully we'll see each other again—"

Just then an attractive man with longish hair and bright green eyes approached. "Hello," he said, reaching out his hand. "I'm Lyle Spence."

"Hi, Holly Talbott, nice to meet you. This is such an amazing gallery," I said, recognizing him immediately from countless party pictures in magazines. "And congrats on the show! To both of you. I see some red dots already."

"We're very pleased," he said, while looking at Kiki. "And who is this beautiful creature?"

"Ugh, *creature*? Nice. That sounds like something from Animal Planet!" Kiki said, crossing her arms.

I almost spat out the white wine John had handed me. Here was the most powerful man in the art world and she blew him right off. In his own gallery, no less. While any girl in the joint would have her panties in a twist over a flirtation from Mr. Heartbreaker, she clearly didn't give a shit. And right away, Lyle Spence was intrigued.

"This is Kiki Talbott." I said, trying to pave over her diss.

"Any relation?" Lyle asked. "Same animal phylum perhaps?"

Kiki smiled, reluctantly.

"How about joining us for dinner afterward? I have Bottino rented out in honor of John."

"Oh, no thanks," Kiki said, looking at her watch. "I have concert tickets. Sorry!"

She managed to bolt, but not before Lyle begged her twice more to reconsider. She wouldn't, and instead pulled away from him to give me a kiss and head toward the coat check to retrieve her fur. I watched Lyle trace her every move until her exit.

"Kiki! Stay!" I whispered at the door. "Lyle Spence is staring at you."

"Yuck. Too good-looking. Too cocky. So not my type."

"Don't judge a book by its cover," I replied, watching him watch us.

"I don't read books. I read magazines." Kiki winked. "And you only judge magazines by their covers." And with that, she was gone.

At the dinner, John was seated next to Lyle and some mega-collector whose name I couldn't remember, a huge hedge funder from Greenwich, Connecticut. His wife, Missy, was familiar from the various charity circuits, and her boobs were literally defying gravity.

I almost started laughing in the poor woman's face because I remembered Kiki's comment at the gallery about her beaded beige number: "If you could weave vomit, it would be that dress," she said.

So there sat Missy in beige as her husband went on and on about futures markets and China. Word had it they'd met when she was a flight attendant on his NetJets charter, and with her bod, she gave new meaning to the word "liftoff."

"Excuse me, honey," George said, hailing a waitress. "But can I get some fresh cheese on the arugula, please? This Parmesan tastes like sawdust."

"Mine, too," chimed in Missy. "It's *inedible*."

Nice. Stifling a grimace, the waitress swiftly removed the offending plates from his and her majesty. I felt disgusting, remembering countless nights out with Tim's friends, who often spoke to waiters that way. Plus, Missy was once serving pretzels and peanuts herself, so why the turbulent 'tude?

The chair next to me remained empty during the salad course, until a man I instantly recognized pulled it out and sat down with profuse apologies. "The traffic was a disaster. The U.N. is a nightmare, I'm so sorry—"

"Is it Elliot? I just met you recently, right?" Super-green-eyes guy.

"Yes. And you're Holland."

"Good memory." I wondered what he was doing at the dinner. "Everyone calls me Holly, though."

"Elliot! Hello, dear," said Missy, rising to kiss him. Her massive, tanned boobs pressed against him as her husband talked with Lyle and John about acquiring a canvas for their Amagansett home.

When he sat back down, I inquired about his buxom friend. "What's Missy's last name again? I met them through my ex-husband once."

"Missy and George Miller."

"Is he in finance?"

"Yes. He has a hedge fund, Miller Ventures."

"Ahh, figures," I said. "Well, at least if their private jet crashes, her chest could get her across the Atlantic!"

I couldn't believe I'd said it out loud.

I was sponging Kiki's style of unleashing unsolicited brazen commentary. Shit.

But to my relief and surprise, Elliot was cackling. Guffawing, even.

"Yeah, you're right, no sinking there." He laughed, leaning in conspiratorially. "She's a character. I sat next to her at a dinner once and she went on about how she hired a surrogate for all three babies even though she could carry them," he said in disbelief. "She was too paranoid about George losing interest if she got stretch marks. I was floored."

Holy moly. You can't invent that!

"So you must be a hedge funder, too, no? I saw you at that nightmare event last week."

"Um, I—"

He paused, waving back to someone who had called to him, and then turned back to me. "I'm an art consultant."

Hmm, so I'd pegged him wrong. "Oh . . . so is this a good moment for you?"

"So-so."

"You must work for a ton of those awful hedge fund people. They all have too much money and decide they want to be collectors all of a sudden but have no taste, right? Let me guess: They just want the big names. Even if it's a crappy Picasso or Warhol, they're label whores, right?"

"You seem to know your stuff," Elliot said.

"That's a fun job," I pondered aloud. "Shopping with other people's money, very cool. I'd love to visit artists' studios and galleries all day."

"Well, let's do it sometime," he offered.

I looked down the table at John, who was deep in conversation with Lyle. But before I could even entertain the idea of juggling all my potential suitors, Elliot popped that idea bubble.

"Not a date, just . . . as friends," he added.

"Oh, okay, sure," I said. Maybe he wasn't single? I didn't see a ring. "I'd like that."

"Great!"

"Do you have a card or something?"

"No. No, I don't. Uh . . ." He fumbled for a piece of paper.

Luckily I had little cards, which I'd had printed after fishing out a pen from my bag too many times. I handed one to him.

Just then, John got up, walked over, and squatted beside me on the floor next to my chair.

"How about we get out of here?" he asked, in front of El-liot.

"Um, sure—" I said, gathering my coat.

"I'll see you soon, then," I said to Elliot, who rose to say good-bye.

But before John and I reached the door, there was a hand on my arm.

"Holly, I like that spitfire Kiki," said Lyle Spence, his eyes flashing. "How can I reach her?"

I smiled, knowing Cupid's arrow was lodged in his bum. After a parade of skeletal models and actresses and glamazons who perhaps rocked out at a photo op but bored him to tears the next morning, he was curious about Kiki, who had stormed into his gallery looking incredible in a Proenza Schouler satin dress and black Mendel coat with black leather high boots. It was clear to me that she had made her mark, like a constellation in that massive white loft, but in reverse: She was a bold, black-clad, fiery point of heat against the white sky of his cavernous space. I happily wrote down her number and walked out into the cold night with John holding my hand.

27

"When a man brings a woman flowers for no reason, there's a reason."

Ahhh, what to discuss on a date, post-divorce. The air between you is fertile ground for landmines of the past—baggage and children and exes. Should I plunge right in? Regale John with my whole history? With Nick there had been loud music, ambient bar noise, and no void to fill with intense conversation, but there I was with John, alone. I felt like talking points had to be structured, plotted out, almost, to avoid the elephant in the room: the Split. The demise of my marriage had been pervading my every thought and it seemed unnatural to be a tabula rasa now. I felt like a slalom skier expertly swerving to avoid the stakes of my last ten years looming down the hill. Or you can do what I did: Turn the spotlight on the man and make it all about him.

"Your work is . . . incredible, John. You have so much talent. I . . . loved the paintings." I couldn't make eye contact, though. Like a shy adolescent, I couldn't be up front about his up-front twig and berries.

"Thanks," he said, looking me right in the eye. "Were you surprised by the subject matter?" he asked boldly.

Clearly I wasn't too good at hiding my coy reaction.

"I was, uh, well, surprised at first, but I truly thought the pieces were truly amazing. Uh, the canvases, I mean."

"I'm glad to hear it. And I'm glad you came, Holly."

We walked and talked until we reached a clearing of buildings, revealing a full moon gleaming in the sky.

"God, look at that moon," I said in awe. "It's like a movie."

"Why is it like a movie?" he asked.

"I don't know; it's just so . . . perfect."

"Are you one of those girls who is obsessed with movies?" he asked.

"I don't know," I stammered. *Yes, you are, you liar.* "I guess, a little."

"Oh," he said. *Wrong answer, Holly!* "I'm not much of a film buff."

"Me neither: 'Buff' sounds all art house and indie, like I watch four-hour Korean films. I don't like films, I like movies. I like expensive Hollywood movies."

"Either way, it's a fantasy. I prefer real life to that. How could a movie capture *this*? Nature is perfect on its own. It doesn't have to be a faithful simulacra in art to be perfect."

Uh-oh, the artist thought I said something weird and childish. "I don't know, I just always do that I guess. A photograph or a movie can be kept forever and nature is fleeting. I am just saying the moon is so big and bloated, it's almost surreal. And tomorrow it will wane and be more real again."

"I'm not sure I understand," he said blankly.

"It's just that sometimes I see something like this and this sounds weird, but it's almost painful because it's *too* good. And it'll be over and there's no rewind button."

"I'd rather never go backward. Life should only be on the play button."

"Mm-hmm," I offered halfheartedly.

"Like . . . now, for example."

John stopped in his tracks and put his arm around my back, pulling me in and kissing me out of the blue. It wasn't some great jolt of mad love, but still, I felt buzzed. Like with Nick, a kiss beyond a decade-long marriage was still new, and I felt young and desirable. And scared. I was suddenly aware that he had raging hormones and his strength, holding and pressing me, was somewhat alarming. Tim's boyish face and hands were so different—John's sexily vein-defined hand grabbed me desperately, and while I was fully absorbed in our make-out-fest, my mind wandered to the paintings of his body, taut but worn. With younger guys, you know where they've been. But John, who had never married, probably had had a lot of experiences, and I could feel it in his body, all the women he had touched with those hands. And forget about silly "bases" and fooling around with a nearly fifty-year-old—non-shag hookups were clearly not happening at this phase of life. While I sometimes wanted to be Kiki-esque on a free and lust-spiked level, I'd never had sex without some sense of deep comfort. With thoughts of this entering my mind mid-kiss, I told John I was a bit tired and freezing and wanted to go home. I think he was surprised, but he kindly hailed a taxi. He offered to drop me off out of his way, and leaned in to kiss me again in the cab. It was nice, but I wasn't so blinded by frenetic passion that I didn't notice Mohammed the driver staring at us through the rearview, which semicreeped me out. But John didn't seem to see or care. His hand went down my neck to the top button of my coat, which he nimbly unfastened. He slid his hand down my back and grabbed me with those worn hands that gripped brushes all day. He kissed the side of my face and neck, which tickled in a sexy way that lit me up and made me feel warm and alluring, which is exactly what I needed. But then, in the heat of our encircled arms . . .

"I said, GO UP SIXTH! Comprende?"

Rude . . . John had totally snapped at the driver mid–neckbite. Who wasn't even Spanish. His snap was arresting, but then he turned his attention back to me and told me I was beautiful.

"Holly—" He lunged for me.

We kissed until we reached my building. I kissed him good night and went upstairs and crawled into bed, thoughts spinning dizzily through my head as I glanced at the cable box. Midnight. Maybe Kiki would be home by then? I hit her number on speed dial.

"YOU GAVE HIM MY NUMBER? ARE YOU ON CRACK?"

Caller ID.

"What? Wait, Lyle Spence? He called you already?"

"TWICE. What were you thinking? I know I give my number out to lots of guys, but I choose them based on good vibes. The guy could be a serial killer."

"No way. Serial dater, maybe. You struck a chord in him."

"So he said on my machine. Scumbag. He's hot as hell, sure, but I don't like 'em so pretty. How was your night?"

I turned *Letterman* on mute and regaled her with details about the breathless smooching, the flattering comments. But also that my gut said John Taplett, he of mammoth penis, was not The One.

"Who cares?" she said, almost laughing. "You don't need Mr. Wonderful, Holly. You need Mr. One-Nighter."

"I'm not good at that. I get attached. Not Glenn Close attached, but I'm emotional. Plus, I feel like if it's not going to be my husband, then why should I waste precious time?"

Kiki was quiet. "I seriously do not understand how you can

164

just get divorced and be talking about that prison of marriage again so blithely! Anyway, what makes you so sure he's not the next Mr. Holly?"

"I don't know. He's sexy and very confident, but I don't have the same comfort zone I did with Tim."

"Holly, news flash: It's apples and oranges! One was a husband you were with for years, and the other is one night so far. No one could compete with that—it's two totally different things! No one could be as close as Tim after one night."

As I lay in bed trying to fall asleep, I realized that she was right. I just prayed the ghost of my marriage wouldn't make it impossible for me to ever connect with someone again.

28

"Every woman should have four pets in her life: a mink in her closet, a jaguar in her garage, a tiger in her bed, and a jackass to pay for it all."

—Zsa Zsa Gabor

The next day after school, Miles's class had a gathering at the home of Teddy and Millicent Logan, he of Hexagon Capital. At the party, Millicent, Mary Grassweather, and Emilia d'Angelo came up as I was ladling some hot cider while Miles scampered around with some kind of Nerf sword.

"So, Holly. How're things?" Mary said, literally cornering me. "Any . . . dates?"

None of your business, I felt like saying, but bit my tongue. "Oh, not quite there yet—" I lied.

"Really? Well, time to get back on the horse, so to speak," Emilia teased in a singsongy voice.

"You want to act soon while you've still got it!" added Millicent with a wink. "The men today, they're going for the gals in their twenties!" Where was one of her stuffy husband's polo mallets when I needed it?

"I'm in no rush. Miles and I are doing great."

"Okay, well, don't wait too long!" Mary advised solemnly. "And we know plenty of nice guys Teddy works with at the fund we could set you up with." I loved how they assumed that the fund would be catnip to me when it was, in fact, potassium cyanide.

"Thanks—" No, thanks.

"You just say the word!" Never.

I extracted myself with complaints of my tiny bladder, heading for the bathroom. But before I got to the hand-stenciled hallway, Posey touched my arm.

"Holly, hi—" she said, looking a bit upset.

"Hi, Posey," I said stoically. I still was a bit wounded that as soon as Tim and I had split up, there was zero word from Posey.

"Listen, um, I feel really bad," she said, looking down. "I miss you and I've been unfair. . . ."

"What do you mean?" I asked casually.

"I just . . . I know we used to spend so much time together, and that this transition . . . you must be going through a hard time, and I kind of haven't been there."

Finally, an acknowledgment. "Posey, we're all busy, it's okay."

"It's not that. I just feel awful, but I told my husband I wanted to invite you to the theater with us and he said that, you know, he does a lot of business with Tim and your brother-in-law, or, uh, former, whatever—anyway, he said he felt uncomfortable with me kind of fraternizing with you when he is so . . . enmeshed financially with the Talbott brothers, and I just feel terrible."

Wow. A forbidden friendship! Just like me with Kiki. But, unlike Posey, I did what I had wanted to do, what my heart dictated rather than my husband.

"You have to do what you have to do, Posey. Don't worry . . ."

"Sorry about all this . . . if you ever need to talk—"

"Thanks so much," I said, forcing a smile. I loved how she didn't even finish her sentence. It was like *If you ever need to talk, don't call me 'cause my husband is so up your ex's ass and loves making dough off him that you are banished!* Nice.

She smiled back, squeezing my arm as I let her off the hook. I headed into the bathroom, closed the door, and exhaled. Just what I had suspected. I was an outcast! It's weird; you can know something in your gut but then just dismiss it as paranoia, but then when you're confronted with the cold hard fact that people see you as tainted goods, it stings all over again. It's like Sunny von Bülow knowing full well that Claus was banging that mistress but it was their love letters on her doorstep that sent her ballistic.

It suddenly, in that lavish powder room, became clear: Everyone in New York was either in business tangentially with Tim and Hal or wanted to be, so I would never be allowed to be back in that circle. Not that I wanted to be. But being a hedge fund wife did help me raise money, fill the ballroom at the St. Regis for my hospital benefit, and now I couldn't even do the charity work I used to! Well, so what. So I was booted out of the Wall Street elite. Truthfully, I was fine with it. These other women, on the other hand, would simply die. Without their money, fancy events, the life, they would wither on the vine! And that is why, whatever their husbands may or may not do "on the side," as Sherry Von said, they would always look the other way for fear of disrupting the delicate dreamy diorama of their lives.

I studied the Brunschwig & Fils paper and Hinsen sconces on

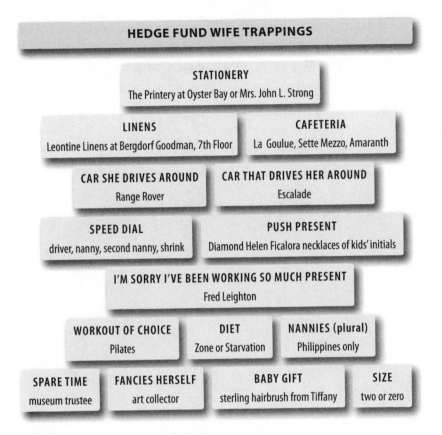

HEDGE FUND WIFE TRAPPINGS

STATIONERY
The Printery at Oyster Bay or Mrs. John L. Strong

LINENS	**CAFETERIA**
Leontine Linens at Bergdorf Goodman, 7th Floor	La Goulue, Sette Mezzo, Amaranth

CAR SHE DRIVES AROUND	**CAR THAT DRIVES HER AROUND**
Range Rover	Escalade

SPEED DIAL	**PUSH PRESENT**
driver, nanny, second nanny, shrink	Diamond Helen Ficalora necklaces of kids' initials

I'M SORRY I'VE BEEN WORKING SO MUCH PRESENT
Fred Leighton

WORKOUT OF CHOICE	**DIET**	**NANNIES (plural)**
Pilates	Zone or Starvation	Philippines only

SPARE TIME	**FANCIES HERSELF**	**BABY GIFT**	**SIZE**
museum trustee	art collector	sterling hairbrush from Tiffany	two or zero

the wall in front of me. Millicent's Vie Luxe Palm Beach–scented candle lingered in the air. I looked at the elaborately woven interlocking letters of her custom-monogrammed hand towels all lined up like little sergeants in a perfect row, not a crease on 'em. She really had the hedge fund wife loot down pat.

As I dried my hands I thought a bit about what Emilia had said. I did need to get a move on it, when I thought about it strategically, but on the flip side, shouldn't love not be sought out but rather fall in your path? My mom always said that if you make your life interesting, someone will want to join it. If I stayed on my own path, rather than chase someone else's, I'd be happier, anyway. I knew what I needed to do: get a job. And also: get out of this party ASAP. And at that moment, with all the stuffy banker wives in my midst, the bricks of my path were leading me back to Chef Boy.

29

"Alimony, a Latin term for removing a man's wallet through his genitals."

—Robin Williams

Kiki and I went for dinner at Il Buco on Bond Street the following night. I am certain I consumed a wheel of cheese. We had a cozy little table in the back and drank a delicious Bordeaux, laughing about one of Kiki's crazy clients, a lingerie store off Madison that sold $600 vibrators.

"You just see these hedgie wives walk in to survey the lace thongs and bras, and then their eyes fall on these megaschlongs and their baby blues just widen into saucers—it's fucking genius!" she squealed, banging the table. Just then, I felt my heart drop into my stomach. Oh, no, they were walking toward us.

"What's wrong?" Kiki asked, brow furrowed, looking up to find the unfortunate coincidence of the Logans and the Grassweathers heading for the table right next to us. Ugh. Our fun night and unedited conversations would now be shadowed by their presence.

"Oh, my goodness! Holly Talbott, what are you doing down here?" Little did they know I was downtown all the time. They were the ones who were fully trapped in 10021-land. This was clearly "steppin' out."

Teddy Logan looked at Kiki while Millicent glared. After a round of introductions, it became clear that our little table for two had now morphed into a larger table for six, much to the women's collective chagrin. The husbands, however, seemed visibly pleased about the new blood present, especially that coursing through the very hot veins of Kiki in her fishnets, extremely short minidress, and thigh-high boots.

"We're celebrating tonight!" said Millicent, all aglow. "Our daughter Penny won her horse show today! We're just ecstatic!" she said, hand on chest. "We've been in Millbrook all day, watching her jumping—she was just incredible."

"Congrats," I said meekly. I looked at her husband, who was totally tuned out and could clearly not give a rat's ass about Penny's ponies.

"Well, this horse is just spectacular. One of Penny's classmates at Spence actually helped us find him. We're flying down to Argentina next week for another horse auction."

"Wow, so how many horses do you guys have?" asked Kiki, kicking me under the table with the pointy winkle-picker toe of her black boot.

"Five, soon-to-be six. Diamond Horseshoe, Shining Star-burst, Gideon's Rainbow, Flaming Rubies, and Mike."

Kiki spat out her red wine. "MIKE?"

Millicent looked completely unfazed. "Yes. After Shining Starburst's late massage therapist."

I squirmed in my seat as I truly thought Kiki would lose it. *Please don't say anything. Please don't say anything. Please don't say anything.*

No such luck.

"I'm sorry, did you just say, your HORSE has a MASSAGE

THERAPIST?" Kiki blurted. She was hysterical. "No fucking way! Your *horse* gets massages?"

"Well, yes . . . they work very hard."

"Holy shit, Equus has a better life than me!" Kiki yelped, holding up her wine. "Go, Starburst Rainbow! Awesome."

Teddy Logan smiled, "That's what I tell Millie all the time!" he scoffed. "The bills for Diamond Horseshoe's rehabilitation alone are astronomical!"

"Rehab?" Kiki asked, laughing out loud. "For horses? What, was he addicted to horse tranquilizers?"

Great. Now Mr. Hedgie was in cahoots with Kiki to mock Millicent's posh Mr. Ed.

"It was *physical* rehabilitation after he tripped," corrected Millicent, aghast.

"Maybe we should order," said Mary, clearly trying to separate the two tables.

"Yes, let's," added Millicent. She opened the menu over her face.

"You should try the horse patties, they're sublime," said Kiki, revealing that she had drunk too much vino.

The husbands laughed, but I remained poker-faced, knowing I'd pay for this all when school started again next week.

I have never been happier to see a rodent. One scurried across the cobblestones on Bond Street, but I was too elated to finally exit the restaurant and our awkward accidental dinner partners to care.

"Kiki, how could you do that to me? I have to see these people every day!"

"Oh, come on, chill out," she said, laughing. "God, those pathetic women have such sticks up their butts! What lame-o's.

They act so old! They're what, like, late thirties? They look like they're collecting Social Security with all that St. John knitwear crap."

"It doesn't matter. I have to see those people, and they clearly weren't amused by your commentary."

"The husbands were," she said with a wink.

"Yeah, well, that's part of the problem."

"They totally couldn't hear what I was saying," she offered defensively.

"Kiki, I have news for you. Martians on the red planet can hear your so-called whisper."

"It's not like I even said anything bad!"

"Really? When you overheard Teddy Logan say he'd dropped out of University of Colorado at Boulder, I think his wife clearly heard you tell me how appropriate that was, considering he 'had the personality of a boulder.'"

"Well he does. Igneous rock is more interesting than he is."

Kiki. A handful, but I loved her. Sometimes I wished I had a designer muzzle for her like those Burberry SARS masks, but I knew her candor was a gift that enhanced my life, even though sometimes I wanted to press the pause button on her vociferous rantings.

We walked several blocks north, up to Mermaid Inn, in silence, where Nick was the sous chef. The place was empty except for some loud raucous party in the back, so we just sat at the bar to wait until they closed up shop.

"Sorry," said Kiki, putting her hand on my arm as we sat side by side on upholstered stools. "I guess I go off and you're the one who has to face the music later. The boring classical music, that is."

I smiled, forgiving her.

A waiter came up to us and offered us dessert.

"We have a special tonight, called Jamaican Me Crazy," he

said earnestly. "It's a pineapple custard with candied orange rind and coconut parfait."

"Uh, no, thank you," said Kiki. "We're all set." After the guy walked away, she said, "They should call that dessert Jamaican Me Sick."

Nick emerged looking beyond adorable in his white chef's jacket. "It'll just be one more minute," he said. "There's a table of drunk banker guys who are hassling our hostess and we just want to make sure she's okay to close up."

"Yuck," said Kiki, peeking around the corner to spy into the private room. She quickly darted back into the main dining room. Too late.

"No WAY! Kiki Talbott, was that you?" a voice bellowed out. Busted. Mark Webb staggered out of the room, shitfaced.

"And hey hey hey, it's Holly, too! Whoa, this is craaaazy."

"You know these guys?" Nick whispered.

"Sort of," I replied, wanting to bolt.

"I have to go to the bathroom," Kiki pronounced, heading away from Mark, who had been joined by two fellow Rolex-sporting revelers.

"Me, too—" I said, walking toward her.

But Mark grabbed my arm.

"What're you doing here, Hollllllllllly?"

I pulled my wrist out of his hand. "Just seeing some friends."

"Ahh, you doin' okay now? I miss you." He drunkenly leaned in, the smell of wine on his breath accosting my nose. But not just any wine, as he'd soon inform me.

"Come have a drink with us," he asked. "I have a bottle of Petrus, five thou a bottle," he bragged.

"No, thanks," I said, turning to the bathroom.

"Holly, you know I always kinda had a thing for you . . . ," he said with a sideways smile topped off with a wink.

"I thought my ex-husband was your best friend," I said, step-ping back. "Anyway, you have *a thing* for a lot of people."

"Ouch!" he said, in mock-wounded tone. Then "Rrrrear!" he purred, miming scratchy cat claws. Gross.

Kiki came out of the bathroom and took my hand.

"We're out of here."

Nick came out of the kitchen with his coat and followed us to the front door.

We went to Marion's to hang out for a bit, and then, amid the din, Nick leaned in. "What do you say we get out of here?"

Ah, the your-place-or-mine moment. My place, alas, felt off limits. At least for now; it was the apartment I had shared with Tim, the building with neighbors who would whisper, doormen who'd judge.

I ended up in Chinatown hiking to a sixth-floor walk-up above a restaurant that had dead Peking ducks dangling upside down by their webbed feet. I think I spied a dead suckling pig as well, but I had turned my head away from the neon-lit row of bodies too quickly to confirm snout sighting. The stench was disgusting beyond measure. *I'm not a snob. I'm not a snob.*

After I felt I'd merited a medal by my Everest-esque vertical hike behind Nick, with periodic breathless nods that I was, in fact, not going to drop dead (he asked if I was okay after every flight, as my panting clearly was that of a clinically obese person), we arrived at his door.

"My roommate's not here, so we have the joint to ourselves," he said, opening the door. When he flicked on the lights, I spied a roach running across the floor that was not unlike the size of a Honda Civic.

"AHHHHH!" I screamed, grabbing Nick.

"Oh, don't worry, it can't hurt you."

Ooooh. Not a good answer.

"I know it can't hurt me. But it can gross me out."

"Don't worry! It's more afraid of you than you are of it."

And with that, he stomped on it with his boot. I could hear the crunch of its exoskeleton under his sole. Vile. I scoured the living room for signs of others. With insects, if there was one, there were probably a million. But no sign. Just a Sex Pistols poster, Urban Outfitters-y chair and couch, TV set, empty wine bottle, and various scattered shoes.

"Come here," he said, reaching for me.

I kissed him as we fell onto the couch. His hands went through my hair and over my chest. As he moved on top of me, I fully sensed the six years that separated us. It felt cougar-iffic to have this younger guy moving over my body and groping for an older bod like mine with an urgency I'd thought would be re-served for some sexpot on the pole. He clearly seemed into it, though, I must admit, he hadn't yet spied the white stretch marks of childbirth on my upper thighs. Unlike Kiki, who had the sickest body this side of the Playboy Mansion, I was more worn out, not just by pregnancy but also by life. But the next thing I knew, my alice+olivia sweater was coming off over my head, so I'd be exposed in the Crate and Barrel lamplight.

Nick kissed my neck and chest. It tickled. I liked it. I laughed as he kissed my clavicle, my skin still so unused to the new man's style of foreplay. I felt another tickle across my chest—wow, he had a light touch!—and giggled as he kept kissing me, until . . . I realized the feeling felt . . . not like fingers. I opened my eyes and lifted my head back upward and glanced down. It wasn't delicate fingers on my left breast but A COCKROACH.

With shrieks so loud, you'd think a) the building was on fire, or b) one of the Peking ducks had resurrected from its greasy grave and started flying around the restaurant downstairs, I ran from the couch, seized by utter hysteria. I felt like they were crawling all over me. I kept swatting at my body, convinced one had wriggled down my bra, but my flailing limbs had apparently gotten rid of the multilegged creature, which was currently at large on the shag carpeting or in the crevices of the wooly couch.

"Calm down, calm down, it's okay—" said Nick, in a fashion so utterly calm, I understood at once that this was a frequent occurrence he met with the casual swagger of, say, a dust bunny that materialized from under a chair.

"It's not okay, I—I," I had to get out of there. "I really like you, I do, I just, have to go, I'm—sorry."

And with that, with the speed of mercury's winged feet, I pulled the sweater over my head (not before shaking it vigorously) and bolted into the freezing night, in search of a cab amid the smell of steamy soy sauce filling the night air.

30

"The only difference between marriage and prison is that a prisoner gets to finish a sentence."

For the next few days, Kiki had been MIA with work, and when I finally got ahold of her, I gave her the roach-on-boob play-by-play.

"So what you're saying is you broke up because of an insect."

"Multiple ones. And we weren't together, so we couldn't break up—"

"You know what I mean. So, when's Tim coming to get Miles?"

"An hour."

I was a wreck. They always say the holidays have the highest suicide rates. And while I wasn't planning on roping up a noose, the knowledge that my child and ex-husband would be spending Thanksgiving break together had resulted in a profound stomach pit. Not that I really wanted to be at Sherry Von's Locust Valley nightmare, with food prepared entirely by her staff, no soul, no warmth except that created by Hubert's beautiful votives and flower arrangements—but I wanted to be with my son, and that wasn't going to happen. I honestly couldn't even recall a time when I was on my own for Thanksgiving. My dad was on a cruise, my friends were all with their in-laws or extended families, and Kiki and I were going to go somewhere fun and do our own thing, until she threw me for a loop.

"So, about Thanksgiving . . . ," she said, in a funny tone I hadn't heard from her. "How about we do something different, spice up our plan of action?"

"Okay, like what?"

"Well . . . the other night I walk in from the office at, like, ten o'clock, and my phone's ringing. Lyle Spence."

"NO! What is he, like, a total stalker?"

"Actually, no. At first I tried to shake him while I flipped through the channels. But there was nothing on TV, not even Skinemax, so I just started talking to him. For three hours."

"What? Are you serious?"

"Holly: He's a riot. I couldn't believe it. He's really cool," she remarked in a coy, almost shy tone. (Kiki? Shy? Never!) "So we met up the next night and we had the best time. . . . I slept with him. It was amazing. And I really like him."

"No—"

"Yes! I'm as surprised as you are—I mean, he's a complete stranger and yet, I'm . . . into him. I asked him all about the crazy art world, his insane hedge fund clients, everything, it was . . . really fun."

She never spoke with such tenderness. "AND?"

"And he lives on Central Park West, right on the parade route—he says Garfield's nose bumps on his window, for Chrissake—and he has people over every year. He says it's a really fun group—friends, clients, about fifty people, and he invited us to come!"

"Really?" That could be fun, I mused. I did love watching the parade on TV with Miles every year. It would be depressing to watch Matt Lauer alone when I could have full view of the action in person. "Okay, let's do it."

I went into Miles's room and sat beside him to pack his bag. That morning we had made chocolate chip pancakes together and traced our hands on some construction paper to make turkeys. I hung his up on the fridge and, while he zoned out during his weekend dose of Nickelodeon, took mine and wrote on it:

My sweet Milesie,
I miss you already, but know you'll have a great Turkey Day. I love you so much and I'm so thankful for you, my little love. Xoxo Mom

I tucked it into his bag and zipped it up, and when I heard the buzzer from the lobby, we went downstairs so I could stay with Miles right up until he pulled away in Tim's car.

But when we got downstairs, I saw Tim looking surprised to see me. I wasn't quite sure why until I walked outside to load the duffel in the trunk. To my dismay, when said vehicle did approach our awning, there was someone in the passenger seat. Avery. Wrecker of homes. She quickly looked out the drizzle-covered windshield to avoid eye contact with the dreaded ex-wife, and I pretended not to notice her. While I knew she was very much in the picture, I guess I didn't realize she'd be there for such a family-oriented holiday. I was going to be off at some random party with strangers as Kiki's wingman, and poor Miles should at least be the focus of his father's attention, not her. Okay, breathe. I tried to stay calm.

"Hey, buddy!" Tim said, hugging Miles. "Ready for a great weekend?"

Miles turned to me. I knelt down beside him, fighting tears. "Be a good boy, sweets," I said, holding his face.

"I love you, Mom. Happy Thanksgiving." He bear-hugged me and I felt the tears begin to fry my retinas but blinked them back. As Miles turned to get in the car, Tim, who knew me so well, clearly saw my pink-hued eyes and leaned in.

"Holly, I am so sorry. I thought I would come up to get him."

"It's fine, whatever, honestly," I said, praying I could force back the cataracts with an emotional Hoover Dam.

"I know it must be hard. I feel . . . terrible seeing you hurt—"

Great. Of all the burdens I'd dealt with emotionally, his pity was like a backpack filled with shot-put balls, too heavy to bear.

"It's okay, Tim. What's done is done, right?" I could feel the waves mounting, pounding against the weakened resolve of my so-called dam. "Have a nice time," I offered, genuinely, as Tim gave me a small smile. His eyes looked guilty, but as I walked away, he hopped in the car, hit the gas, and drove my son off into the evening. That feeling of loss, of Miles being transported away from me, would now be a rough horse pill I would simply have to get used to swallowing.

I went back in the slow-as-molasses elevator. When I got upstairs, I staggered home and flopped on the couch.

A couple hours after I'd dozed off, the phone rang. It was John, wondering if I was free the following night. A random Tuesday, and as I had nothing planned, I agreed to see him. And after my roll in the hay-slash-roaches with Chef Boy, a grown-up man might be just what I needed: a mature antidote to my youthful dalliance.

31

"Many a man owes his success to his first wife and his second wife to success."

—Jim Backus

The next day was freakishly warm for the season, so Kiki coaxed me out to the park for one of our "psycho walks," which we used to take all the time when she lived uptown. Thrice around the reservoir or bridle path, followed by a lunch big enough to reinstall all the calories we'd burned off and more.

"So I have an idea," she said, face ablaze. "I think I found a job for you."

"Really?" I was happily surprised. "What is it?"

"Back writing about music. But not for magazines: working with my friend Randy, who's head of PR at Celestial Records, writing publicity stuff. You could do this in your sleep. And it's fun!"

"Whoa, Celestial Records. It's those two brothers, Noah and Sean Greene?"

"Totally. They're the Weinsteins of the record industry. They built this all from nothing in the last five years and have won, like, a trillion Grammys and stuff."

"Wait, didn't they have some, like, awful sexual harassment suit or something?"

"Yeah, they're gross, but they're geniuses. Anyway, Randy is awesome but can't write for shit. I told her about you and she needs someone part-time who can write the press releases, translate the sound into words."

"I could do that!"

"Hello? I know! Plus, it's only three days a week, so you could still do your tours for Miles's school, leading those hedge fund drones around the hallowed halls. . . ."

"Wow. That could really be just what I need," I said, imagining a career outside of mommyhood.

"So you have this hot date tonight?" Kiki asked, brow raised in mischievous sexpot glee.

When she reminded me, I got that nervous energy of an impending date with a guaranteed hookup. But I also had a queasy stomach, which made think that deep down, maybe I didn't want to go.

As we plopped at a small café on Seventy-third Street with our red cheeks and flyaway hair, I knew I needed some sexual advice from sexpert Kiki. I felt like *Fast Times at Ridgemont High*, a clueless Jennifer Jason Leigh learning how to fellate a carrot from Phoebe Cates.

"Kiki, do I . . . have to, like . . . bang John tonight?"

"No, of course not. Why?"

"It's getting weird to just kiss on street corners. I just feel this pressure like I haven't been 'out there' since the days of bases. I just feel so juvenile—what am I going to do, give this grown man a hand job?"

"Yeah. I think pulling log would be pretty weird at his age. You can't be yanking chain on a fifty-year-old."

"See? That's why I'm freaked out! He's forty-seven, by the way."

"Same thing. But I don't think you have to sleep together."

"You really don't?"

"Well, I always do, but I'm a big slut. You're . . . pure. Just kiss, you know, take it from there, play it by ear."

"Playing it by ear is what gets people pregnant and STD infested. I want to think about this. I have smooched the guy already, and isn't this what people do? I mean, they have sex! You do."

"That's me, but that doesn't mean *you* have to. Just tell him you want to take it slow."

"Ugh, that is so cheesy. I'll sound like a virgin in high school or a Bible beater who needs to be *held*. It's not like I have sex on such a high pedestal; I just don't know if I'm ready. I'm still wounded. Gosh, I sound so pathetic. The fact is, maybe I should get laid."

"Holly, you can't plan these things. Just surrender to the flow. You're so smart, you know yourself, feel it out. And don't analyze it, trust your instincts."

Kiki walked me home, kissed me good-bye, and wished me luck. It was strange being in my apartment alone. I was so accustomed to the sound track of Miles's clomping about and I missed the cacophony of his little feet and the sight of his light-up sneakers coming down the hall. To combat the loneliness, I blared Radiohead loud enough to overpower the hair dryer and I tried on multiple outfits. I felt a little more revved up post–music and makeup, but in the cab over to John's house, I started to think about the dangerous fantasy feud: Tim versus John. If I married John, I guess Sherry Von would be right: John's not "as good" as Tim. People would see us in the street holding hands and think I'd married a geriatric. But John was more creative and wasn't Krazy Glued to the NFL. Wait, what was I doing?! I wasn't going to marry John! Slow down, Holly.

Kiki was right: It was comparing apples and oranges. Tim was always threatened that I had such a fixation on older dudes. He had half joked that if I ever left him for someone else, it would be for an older guy, not a young buck, thanks to my outspoken obsessions over Jeremy Irons and Al Pacino. (And, P.S., I didn't have some weird Daddy complex, I just found the wisdom of age sexy, and the hot young studs were de facto himbos and dum-dums. Or had roachy apartments.)

As I arrived at the beautiful mansion that housed John's apartment-slash-studio, I started to get really paranoid. Being in his home felt suddenly intimate; the bed would be steps away. But walking up the stairs, I was calmed by the ambrosia of cooking smells and classical music. John leaned over the railing.

"Up here!"

"Hi! This is such a cool building!"

I reached him and we hugged, him clutching a wooden spoon covered in red sauce. John's apartment had huge twenty-foot ceilings and ornate original molding, and he explained that it was originally the Pulitzer family mansion, which had since been divvied up into many apartments. The Bach harpsichord floated through the dimly lit, loftlike space, as if it was a stage set. As sauce simmered on the stove, filling the air with herbs, we sat on stools by the big stainless island nearby.

"Do you like pasta puttanesca?"

"Yes. I love all Italian food. I could probably eat human flesh if it had marinara on it."

"That's appetizing," he said, sarcastically. "Spicy or no . . ."

Hello? I was joking. I ain't Hannibal Talbott.

"Spicy's fine."

The conversation was a bit stilted because we both knew we

were both sort of going through the motions until we would lock lips once more. But I needed to lay the emotional groundwork to get myself in the mood.

We moved the earthenware bowls of arugula and pappardelle to his Shaker table and ate his extremely tasty concoctions with a great red wine. He tried to verbally distill the libation for me ("oaky yet bold"), but it was making beds in a burning house: I don't know wines at all. I know I liked it, but I have zero tolerance and get hammered off a glass, so I stopped at that to stay sharp. We decided to save dessert (fallen chocolate cake) for later since we were so full, and I got the tour of the apartment, a cavernous two-bedroom with a full skylit studio for his paintings, where two more half-finished nudes sat on easels. His constant attention made me feel special, and his hand rested on the small of my back as he led me through each part of the house. I drank in the eclectic décor and tried to glean details of his life.

He seemed like kind of a loner—no photos of pals from school, no invitations leaning against the mirror, just books and books. And books. Every CD was classical or opera, which seemed hot in theory even if it was so not me. Although Bach can be great mood music. Who knew?

We meandered into the bedroom and I looked out the window at his view of the twinkling lights of the town house rooftops. I knew he'd soon be coming up from behind me to break the hour of no making out. I saw his reflection getting bigger in the window and soon enough he was wrapping his arms around my waist. He kissed the back of my neck, sending chills down my vertebrae, and my cashmere sweater against my stomach felt soft and tight through his strong grip. He turned me around and kissed me, the taste of wine mingling with the smell of his showered hair. We stumbled like a four-legged blind animal to the bed, and tumbled on the downy comforter, kissing madly. He pulled my shirt over my head, grabbed my chest feverishly, and freed me of my bra. This took the turn-on factor up a notch, but also made the border of my skirt and tights feel vulnerable as the next point of entry, and I knew at that moment, despite breathy sighs and flushed necks, that I did not want to have sex.

We messed around for another fifteen minutes as the stereo's harpsichord swelled sweetly. My mind was going a mile a minute. I do think physical intimacy can breed connection, get rid of inhibitions, and help two people feel more comfortable, but I somehow couldn't go the distance. What was my problem? And as he began to fumble with my skirt button, I interrupted.

"John, I—"

"Are you all right?" he asked.

"Yes, yes, I just—can we maybe not . . . go all . . . the way."

The second I said it out loud I was *horrified*. I sounded like an effing ninth grader. "I mean—I like you," I continued. "I just feel . . . not . . . ready. Yet."

"Oh, okay. Sure."

Crickets.

"Do you want to get some dessert or something?" he asked.

"Um, okay."

We walked like quiet mice back into the kitchen and I threw on my sweater sans bra. I followed him to the cake and put my arm around him as a signal that, hey, the party's not over because I won't hop in the sack. But he just continued serving the cake.

"Here you go."

"Thanks! This looks great, John." I took a large bite. "YUM! Move over, Betty Crocker, this is so amazing!"

"Thanks." I could tell my compliments to his baking skills were not going to make up for the fact that I had just put the brakes on our body lock.

"Listen, John, I am sorry if this is strange. I really like you

and, trust me, I . . . want to, you know, be with you and everything, I just want to feel ready. I hope you—"

"Sure, that's fine. I want you to feel ready."

"Great. Thank you so much. I'm so sorry. I just . . . well,
frankly it's been a while, and I want to feel secure."

"Fine, that's fine, of course."

"'kay."

"Do you want to watch a movie or something?"

"Sure . . ."

We went back into his room and flipped through the channels
until we found *Braveheart*, which I convinced him to watch, despite the punchline status of Mel in recent years. Extensions and
war paint, gotta love it; it always made me think that whatever I
was enduring, my life's dramas were small potatoes in agonizing
comparison to *prima nocta* rapes and bloody battlefields. We
watched the whole thing with some conversation throughout. I
was just about to fall asleep (when Robert the Bruce was ream-
ing his big-nosed diseased dad for betraying William Wallace)
when John tapped me gently.

"Shall I put you in a taxi? Or—you're welcome to stay
here. . . ."

I was frankly dreading going out in the cold, but I knew that
a morning together could be bizarre, so I motivated myself to
cab it home. Bra in bag, I walked to the door and he kissed me
good-bye as his hands went up the back of my sweater. I got a
jolt of lust and almost said, *Screw it, let's go back inside*, but instead
I smiled, waved adios, and went downstairs.

When I got home, I realized that he hadn't put me in a cab.
Tim would have always put me in a cab. You don't send a girl out
into the night like that! There are street toughs! Gang rapists
who travel in packs with switchblades and screwdrivers! Okay,
maybe not on the Upper East Side, but still.

Also: Why the hell did I apologize for not sleeping with him? What, was I supposed to be on my back for some pasta puttanesca? Didn't pasta puttanesca mean whore's pasta? I knew *puta* was "whore" in Spanish. He totally made me feel like I had to say sorry for not putting my ankles in two zip codes and doing him. I don't need to shag him rotten; he's a STRANGER. Maybe we are not built to love so many men, to have more than one serious bond where there is sexual intimacy. I started to feel like with each broken relationship, a little piece of me was taken, a slice of innocence. And now I was hardened, with pieces missing, and terrified of losing yet another chunk. Mine was only the second or third generation (minus the "bad girls" and whores and stuff) that had several or more sexual partners, and I wondered whether I was made to handle that.

I fell asleep, not waking until noon. I went out to the very coffee bar in which we had met, grabbed a vat of espresso, and meandered home to find a voice mail from John.

He said he had a lot of fun and that he wanted to see me again soon: "My brother has a farm in Connecticut. You mentioned that Miles will be with his dad this Saturday night, and if you're free, maybe we could go up there and hang out, relax. Let me know. . . . Bye." Click.

Hearing his voice so soon after made me feel a little less alone and somewhat comforted. I was such an impatient person that I wanted to feel all the togetherness and sparks and relaxed love that I'd had in my marriage so quickly. But I guess when you're older, things aren't as dramatic as they once seemed; people have to slowly get to know each other, right? And I was free that weekend. Kiki had mentioned a benefit for some hospital at South Street Seaport that sounded mildly fun, but maybe a night away with John could be better.

32

"My husband said he needed more space. So I locked him outside."

—Roseanne Barr

Thanksgiving morning was so frigid, I wanted desperately to bail on Kiki's brunch on the West Side. But she called not only to wake me up, but also again twenty minutes later to confirm that I was shower-bound. I phoned Miles on my cell, which I'd lent him for the weekend (it felt too weird buying a six-year-old his own cell, even though half his class had them).

"Happy Turkey Day, sweetie," I said, trying to stay strong and squash to the back of my brain all impulses to cry. It was like trying to hold down vomit.

"I love you, Mommy. Happy turkey. Are you making turkey for yourself?"

"No, honey, I'm going out with Aunt Kiki. We'll be thinking of you. I can't wait to see you Sunday morning!"

I got ready, throwing on a cozy soft sweater dress and boots, shoved a brush through my hair, and made my way to the West Side on foot since I knew it would be a total zoo. When I got to the gorgeous building on the park, I prayed Kiki would be there, and luckily hers was the first face I saw when I walked into the warm, bustling apartment.

The second belonged to Elliot Smith.

"Holland! Hi, nice to see you," he said, kissing me hello.

"You, too! Ugh, I'm frozen solid."

"Here. I have a mug of scalding cider here with your name on it."

He handed it to me with a warm smile and I just stared right into his mammoth green eyes, wondering again if they were color contact lenses.

"It's so funny your name is Elliot Smith. I loved his music—"

"It's the best. Sharing a name with a celebrity can have drawbacks, but one benefit is that I am un-Google-able—all the pages are his music fan sites."

"Ahhh, interesting. Well, at least you share a name with a genius, and not, say, Michael Bolton,"

"Right, like in *Office Space*—" he added.

One of my favorite movies. "Okay, I just watched that again—so brilliant. But being in the art world, you probably never slaved away like a faceless drone in some sad cubicle, right?"

He shrugged. "You'd be surprised."

"Holl! C'mere, you look hot!" Kiki said, looking me over. "Talk about MILF! Foxy mama!"

"Oh, thanks." I looked bashfully at Elliot.

"Are you okay?" Kiki asked, sipping her hot spiced wine. "You're all red!"

I put my hands on my cheeks, "No, I'm okay. Just wind-whipped a little."

"Let's go get some food," said Elliot. "The spread is amazing."

He led me into a huge dining room overlooking the park, and a humongous Blue's Clues dog bumped his nose on the giant window. The room was packed with various art folk, very downtown leggy wives of collectors, an editor from *Artforum*, a Serbian sculptor Lyle repped, and some big-fish hedge fund collectors I recognized from the circuit.

Lyle came running over and gave me a kiss.

"Holly, thanks so much for coming," he said, while rubbing Kiki's back tenderly. "Otherwise, I knew this one would never show."

"My pleasure, thank you so much for having me. Your apartment is amazing."

"Thanks. Enjoy, please make yourself at home. . . ."

Lyle took Kiki's hand, and she followed him through the crowd to another room, and then I spied them disappearing through a door into what I guessed was a bedroom. So my supposed wingman was over 'n' out, headed for some holiday hay rolls. Roger that.

Thank goodness for Elliot, who became my new wingman. We stuffed ourselves on a tower of bagels, smoked whitefish salad, turkey, mashed yams, and finally pumpkin pie while watching every float, marching band, and Shania.

Overheard background conversation involved the painter Lisa Yuskavage, where people were staying for the Basel art fair in Miami, and the runs the market had taken in subprime mortgages.

"I feel like the hedge fund world fully feeds the art world right now. This place is hopping with these guys," I said, craning my neck to see a new hotshot wunderkind who had opened his own shop at thirty-one and supposedly already had a billion under management.

"Yeah, they're definitely linked; that's for sure," Elliot attested. "Art is a big statement when you walk into these guys' offices."

"It's so funny how you confirmed that these guys want the hot name-brand painters. If it's not recognizable, it's not worth it. The same way their wives want all the right labels from the big fashion houses."

"Pretty much."

"They want their pieces to be recognizable, right? It's not worth it unless everyone knows what it is."

Elliot smiled. "You got it."

"Like Shania just sang, *that don't impress me much*."

"What does impress you, then?" He smiled, looking at me.

"Oh, gosh, I don't know. Humor. Honesty. Generally not being a dick. I used to think nice guys were so boring and I was drawn more to the life-of-the-party types. My friend Jeannie and I used to say "Easy Math: Nice+a MetroCard=a Seat on the Subway. I.e., Nice counts for nothing." I shook my head at my own stupidity. "But now I've grown up a bit and realize there's something to be said for simple *Sesame Street* values."

"I hear you."

He grinned and looked out the window, coincidentally at a Cookie Monster balloon, as two prepster guys moved next to us.

"So, you traveling a lot these days?" asked one to the other.

"Yeah, well, it's all about the BRICs right now; you know how it goes."

I leaned into Elliot conspiratorially. "That means Brazil, Russia, India, and China," I told him. Emerging markets. Tim spent a lot of time flying to the BRICs, though in retrospect, I couldn't be sure. Though maybe he was there to visit BRIC brothels, getting *special* massages.

"Hey," said Elliot, smiling. "You do know your stuff."

"Well, after a decade married to a hedge funder, I am down with the lingo."

"Why'd you split up?" he asked gently.

"Our divorce papers say irreconcilable differences. That *difference* was a catalog model in a pencil skirt." Darn! My stupid mouth. Bitter much? Uh-oh, I hoped this poor guy wasn't going to be bored to tears by my baggage. "How about you?"

"Yeah, my ex-wife and I just kind of woke up one day and realized we were incompatible. I was a Sagittarius and she was a cheating bitch."

I spat out my cider, guffawing. He was really funny.

"Sorry. That sounds mean," he caught himself. "I actually bear no ill will against her . . . just her Pilates instructor."

"Oh, please, don't worry!" I said. "My ex-husband speaks Assholese fluently."

Elliot smiled. "Funny, I think my wife took that course at Berlitz." He laughed. "That's why I'm down with your *Sesame Street* values."

"Glad to hear it."

Elliot pointed out the window. "Check it out!"

We looked out the window at an approaching humongous hot-air Kermit and Miss Piggy side by side.

"It's us!" I said. "Though those guys are technically *Muppet Show* and not *Sesame Street*."

"Still Henson, though," he remarked correctly. "But you are so not Miss Piggy."

"Are you kidding? After this brunch?"

"Okay, well, you might have her appetite, but you have a much better metabolism."

"Great," I said sarcastically.

"That's a good thing," he said. "There's nothing worse than a woman who eats a lettuce leaf and drinks Diet Coke."

"Thanks, Kermit."

"So what's your son's name? I remember when I saw you guys in the park that time he seemed like a sweet kid."

It was a relief to talk to a guy and not have to drop the mom-bomb.

"Miles. He's six."

"Great name."

"You have kids?"

"Nope, sadly."

We talked about our respective splits and Miles's shuttling back and forth, but it all felt cathartic; we were in the double-divorce safety zone of talking freely. Nearly two hours passed as the crush of the parade slowed to a meek trickle and finally the police barrier came down and Central Park West's regular traffic resumed in lieu of giant Snoopy. I realized we'd been sitting there forever—and that Kiki had not emerged for a while. I looked around the apartment.

"Did Lyle do this all himself? It's unreal."

"No, he had this decorator, Sheila Davis. She does every-thing, stem to stern. And, uh . . . well. Never mind."

"No, what?"

"She gets very close with her clients, let's just say," he replied diplomatically. I raised my eyebrow. "Okay," he continued. "She doesn't just install your bed. She climbs in it."

"Aha, I get it. Daryl Hannah in *Wall Street*."

"You got it."

"So are your art collector clients mostly Gordon Gekko types?"

He paused. Maybe he wasn't supposed to talk about his cli-ents? Whoops, I hated to pry. "Some," he said simply, with a cute knowing smirk. He stood up to go get a glass of hot spiced wine, and the door to the bedroom opened. Lyle and Kiki emerged looking shamelessly un–put together, all mussed hair, wrinkled clothes, and halogen smiles.

They put the "bed" in "bedraggled." I shot Kiki an *Oh, no, you di-in* look and she did something I'd never seen her do: blush. To a rose hue. My ass-kicking, full-of-chutzpah, big-talkin' pal was suddenly this Jane Austen maiden, radiant with joy, emitting contagious waves of besotted, girlish love.

"Holly, hon, I'm gonna stay here for a while, is that okay?"

"Sure!" I said, leaning in closer. "Enjoy," I added teasingly. I thanked Lyle for a wonderful Thanksgiving, one that felt festive and fun at a crucial time.

"I'm headed out, too—I can put you in a cab," Elliot offered.

"I'm on the East Side, just across the park; where are you going?"

"I have a grand commute," he said. Meaning Staten Island? "Two blocks away."

"Oh, I love the West Side," I said. "All these creepy buildings with gargoyles and fancy names," I added. "Like 'the San Kenilthorp or whatever.'"

"Yes, it's all very *Ghostbusters*," he said.

We exited the grand lobby and went into the chilly air.

"These clouds look kind of ominous," I said, noticing the dark gray that had eclipsed the sun of a few hours before.

"I know, I think it's going to pour. But I'll get you in a cab hopefully before it starts."

No such luck. The second we stepped onto the curb from under the canopy, torrential rain began to pour.

The day had started so beautifully, neither of us had brought umbrellas. After a few minutes and zero cabs, I was starting to feel bad about his chivalrous gesture.

"Oh, no, you're drenched," I said, noticing his hair dripping with rain.

"I feel like Dan Aykroyd in *Trading Places* in the wet Santa suit!" said a soaked Elliot.

I paused. He likes movies. "I was thinking John Cusack in *The Sure Thing* when they're stranded on the side of the road," I said.

"Good one." He smiled. His wet hair flopped on his face and his eyes looked bright against his rain-splattered red cheeks.

"You go, Elliot, please. I'm totally okay—"

"No, no, I'll find you one."

Sweet.

A few minutes later, sure enough, one cab's lit-up medallion number was visible through the thick mist, and Elliot ran up a block to snag it just in time. He opened the door for me and I slid in, drenching the pleather seat. "Thank you so much!"

"It was Kermit's pleasure. Happy Thanksgiving."

33

"When two divorced people marry, four get into bed."

—Jewish Proverb

After an afternoon braving midtown during the biggest shopping day of the year, I climbed into bed at 8:00, which I hadn't done since *The Muppet Show* was on air in the eighties. I would pack in the morning for my minitrip to John's house. I woke up refreshed and renewed, but as I lay in bed, the thought that flashed through my head was not about my upcoming weekend companion in Connecticut, but rather about Elliot. It had been fun talking to him. He didn't exactly show interest in me, but I didn't care. I felt 100 percent comfortable yapping beside him, which was new. The dating thing was so awkward and forced at times. But hey, if you don't throw yourself in traffic, you won't get hit.

The next afternoon John pulled up to my building and we began our drive to the country, two virtual strangers heading out of familiar territory of buildings and bustle. The noises petered out; the clogged streets were replaced by mellow meadows and stark trees set against an electric blue Tim Burton sky that darkened on our drive of twisting turns. John tuned the radio to WQXR, where classical music was punctuated by a soothing DJ whose voice was so relaxing, I thought he was born to read bedtime stories. With the icy air making the windows opaque with frost, it felt even cozier inside the car, a beat-up Volvo with piles of brushes and books shifting in the back, where I was used to having a car seat for Miles. I wondered if he would be able to relate to Miles if they ever met. After an hour or so, we pulled into a driveway set between two old stone pillars covered with frozen moss.

The place was beautiful but kind of run-down, in a shabby-chic, worn-in-by-love way. We settled in and unloaded the groceries John had fetched from Eli's to make a nice dinner, and since there was no TV (for shame!), it was just us, the food, and the fire for entertainment. We were just in time; the second we unpacked the car, I heard an ear-piercing thunderclap and sheets of sleetlike rain started to hail down, making our warm indoor nest even cozier.

After a scrumptious mozzarella and tomato salad, we took the roasted chicken out of the oven and while I started to cut it, John turned me around and grabbed me for a kiss. I kissed him back but was kind of startled by the mid-dinner action and dislodged myself from his grasp to return to the bird.

"John—"

He took the knife out of my hand and threw it on the floor. I was shocked, but definitely turned on by his animalistic need to prey and chuck a sharp knife. I guess the pounds I'd gained from my Thanksgiving inhalation of a massive buffet were not a problem. We stumbled into the living room mid-make-out, fell onto the dusty couch. He grabbed me and ripped open my cardigan, making the buttons fly off, scattering in all directions, hitting walls and the coffee table in a pitter-patter of falling plastic disks. Damn J.Crew. Though I supposed button-down sweaters were not exactly designed to be torn open.

"John—whoa, down, boy," I said, laughing. But I was a tad weirded out. He didn't smile. He grabbed me and kissed me harder, then bit my neck hard. Ow! Holy LeStat!

I was turned on, but was somewhat alarmed by his heated fervor and quasi-violent sexual aggression. I must admit, it's great to feel so enticing that a man is drawn to animalistic pouncing, but it's sort of another thing to be hickey-marked. I could feel him now, hard through his pants as he moved on top of me. I tried to calm him down with more soothing affectionate moves, my hand through his hair, my fingers slowly moving up and down his back as we kissed, but he was grunting with stormy anticipation, echoing the deluge outside. Lightning sizzled the sky as thunder clapped while he reached between my thighs. I was heated from the fevered kiss and caught in the spell of the moment, his fingers inside me as he unbuckled his belt with feverish intensity. He whipped his belt out of the loops and hurled it across the room. He took off his pants and lunged back toward the couch on top of me, and then he grabbed me so hard, it hurt my arms, and flipped me over, facedown. This was weird. I mean, doggie-style for our first time? Hot, sure, sometimes, but not now—not exactly romantic for our special intimate premiere. No, this was odd. Suddenly, I got a wave of awkwardness mingled with disgust; I felt that I could have been a blow-up doll, or Pam Anderson, or, as Andrew Dice Clay so eloquently said in the eighties, "two tits, a hole, and a heartbeat." I did not want to have him inside me.

"John, you know what? I'm so sorry, I—let's slow down—"

He didn't. I felt him trying to go ahead as if he'd been given the green light, when I was clearly flashing yellow.

"John, c'mon. Stop."

He didn't listen. He was pushing harder, ignoring me. And then I got scared, really scared.

"STOP! STOP IT!"

Red light. As in, get the hell off me.

I got up and pushed him off.

"John, what the hell? I'm sorry, but this isn't feeling right. I'm not ready! Why did you keep going?"

"Why did you come up here this weekend?" he said, enraged, eyes ablaze.

"What, I can't come up and get to know you? I have to spread 'em before dinner?"

"You don't go away with someone if you're not going to get comfortable with them."

"I'm sorry, is this getting comfy, being thrown onto your couch facedown and having my sweater ruined?"

I bent down to pick up the buttons that had flown off.

And then, I saw it: sheer, unbridled ire. He looked like he wanted to kill me. In fact, for a nanosecond, I thought he might. I'd be a headline. Miles would be motherless. The guy in Italy had turned out to be nice, but maybe John was the one who painted his canvases with blood. Holy shit.

"GET OUT!" he screamed venomously.

"What?" I said. Okay, maybe I wouldn't be decapitated. But did he mean *get out*, like, leave?

"I SAID GET THE FUCK OUT!"

I shook with fear and ran to grab my bag.

"GET OUT, YOU DICK TEASE! YOU BITCH! YOU WOMEN ARE ALL THE SAME!"

I was terrified and held back shocked tears as I ran to get my stuff in the kitchen. I had no idea what to say; he just kept yelling, red-faced and red-peckered, from the living room. I stuffed my boots back on, threw my weekend bag over my shoulder, and bolted out.

Into the torrential and freezing rain.

34

"Adam & Eve had the ideal marriage. He didn't have to hear about all the men she'd been with, and she didn't have to hear about how his mother cooked."

The word "boonies" was an understatement. I was in the middle of nowhere. Some twisting route without double yellow lines. I'm talking back roads. Like the kind where a ski-masked maniac descends from the trees wielding a chainsaw. I was a dead woman. I could not have been more drenched. Even my bones were wet. Now I knew why everyone said I should get Miles his own cell phone; it was so I didn't have to be in the Dark Ages without one. You've heard of up shit's creek without a paddle? That was me. No boat, either. Just mired in shit. This SUCKED. Okay, Holly, calm down. *Braveheart, Braveheart, Braveheart.* This was no biggie. Sugar, yes it was. My veins were frozen. My blood must have had ice chips in it. There were no cars to be seen, it was 7:30 at night and I was a wet rat on the road's shoulder, quivering with chills. Honestly, it was so hellaciously awful, it was almost funny. Except it wasn't. A car came by and I tried to wave it down, but they kept going, exactly as I would have if a deranged-looking, drenched lady was hitchhiking, no doubt with a machete in her T. Anthony weekend tote.

I started panicking after ten minutes walking along the road.
I didn't think I could deal with this. I looked up at the dark gray
clouds as if to beckon, "What else ya got for me?" Were it not for
Miles, I would have prayed to be struck by lightning and just put
out of my misery. Two more cars passed, their white lights turning red as I saw them from behind, driving away into the soak-
ing night. A few minutes later a truck approached and slowed
alongside me. Wait: What was I doing? This grizzled, flannel-
shirt-wearing driver could be a headshot from Central Casting
for a serial rapist or murderer. Not that John the supposedly sensitive artist was any better. I looked up into the trucker's cab at
the man's weathered face. His beard was messy, his trucker hat
askew. He was something out of *Fargo*. But I was freezing and
soaked and desperate, so I smiled up at him.

"Hi, sir, I need to get back to the city. Do you have a phone
I could use?"

"Hop in, Sunshine."

And then boom-chicka-bow-wow porno music came on and
I banged him in exchange for his help. Just lying.

His name was Mo (I swear) and he wasn't going my way, but
he kindly drove me to the train station, for free, where I found a
pay phone. I must say, it's always refreshing when someone is just
plain nice for no reason. I was lucky; who knows what he could
have done, and let's just say after John, the Bach-blaring painter,
clearly wanted to throttle me, I wasn't exactly wise hopping into
a tractor trailer with grizzled Mo. Thank God he didn't beat me
and hack me to pieces and then rape the pieces. My near-frostbitten
finger dialed 1-800-COLLECT.

"Kiki?" I bleated through my hoarse throat.

"*Holl?* Where are you? I thought you were in Connecticut."

I burst into tears and told her the whole series of events.

"Holy shit. Fuck that psycho asshole. I'm going to tell Lyle never to show him again. That guy is insane! Okay, stay there, I'm coming to get you."

"No, Kiki, it's fine, I think a train's coming soon, so I'll just go to Grand Central. Can I come over, though? What are you doing? Oh NO, you have your event tonight!"

"Of COURSE, you're coming right over. It's that benefit at South Street Seaport tonight. I was getting ready to go meet Lyle there, but fuck that, my girls are all there taking care of everything. Let's just hang here! I'll put you in a hot bath and pj's and we'll watch Molly Ringwald movies. You're going to be fine. I'll be here waiting."

"No, Kiki, do not cancel your date."

"Hey. I'm not Dicks over Chicks. Especially not you, Chiquita."

She was the best. All I wanted to do was boil myself to warmth and pound hot chocolate. Luckily, the train pulled in minutes later and of course it was freezing and I got all kinds of looks from young suburban revelers cruising via Metro-North into the big city. I cried on the train about the mess my weekend had become, the mess my life had become. What had I done? Maybe I should have listened to Sherry Von and just stayed in my marriage so I wouldn't have to be alone. Tim had his issues, sure (workaholic, an evil mom, sometimes getting a tad too hammered for our age, too-intense reverence for sports, extra-marital bangings) but he had no *skeletons* like John-esque psychotic breaks. I was starting to realize it really *was* a jungle out there. And with Tim, I didn't have it so bad, minus the him-leading-a-double-life thing. I didn't know if I could make it now. My whole body was so ice cold that the only thing that warmed me were hot tears as they fell down my cheeks. I closed my eyes and let the side-to-side rumble of the train lull me into a sad daze.

I got to Grand Central an hour later, my hair and clothes damply matted to my face, and when I arrived at Kiki's, she opened the door holding a glass of red wine. Because I looked not unlike a sewer rodent, she started laughing when she saw me, but it quickly turned into a pity laugh as she relieved me of my drenched coat.

"Oh, come here, sweetie!" She hugged me and I had to smile, it was all too over-the-top awful and pathetic.

"Listen, Holly, this was all a heinous dream—you are going to be fine," said Kiki. "Go in the bathroom, I have a relaxation tank for you."

"Huh?"

"Get in the bath; just looking at you is making me fucking cold," she ordered. I went into the large marble bathroom that Kiki called her "hotel bathroom" and was happily surprised. Kiki had drawn me a scalding bubble bath and surprised me with a candlelit tub. I was touched beyond measure.

"Take your time," said Kiki, sipping her wine. "There's a glass of pinot for you on the side of the tub. See how you feel when you get out."

"I can't believe this. Thank you!"

It was the first time since I'd lost my mom that I'd felt so mothered. I was so worried about Tim and Miles all these years, I'd barely ever stopped to pamper myself and was run ragged. In the burning hot lavender-and-lanolin pool, I washed away the last few hours' debacle and enjoyed the simple, oft-taken-for-granted good fortune of searing hot water. The therapeutic heat made everything melt away, and aside from the soothing *agua*, I thought about how the best blessing was the girl outside.

While I kind of wanted to just be quiet and chow in front of Andrew McCarthy and the gang on TV, I also knew Kiki had worked her ass off on this benefit and my minivisit to hell shouldn't stop her from going. At about 10:30 I emerged, ready.

"So—" I said, resolved. "Let's go to the Seaport thing. I want to."

"No WAY," said Kiki, shaking her head of perfectly blown-out shiny locks, chandelier earrings (or as she called them, "chande-learrings") clinking. "You have been through the ringer tonight, and we are zoning here on the couch."

I told her I wanted to go to the party, no popcorn-and-eighties-flicks healing process needed. We'd dance up a storm to "I Will Survive" or some grrrrl-power anthem, and I'd feel better. Why feel sorry for yourself when you can shimmy your ills away?

I began raiding her incredible, packed closet full of way-too-short-for-me hemlines that would make Paris Hilton blush, and we blared some vintage Duran Duran as I dried my hair and put on makeup. For a moment there during "Rio," I actually felt okay, worlds away from where my night began. Kiki had made me feel safe again.

We cabbed it down to the Seaport and walked down the rickety wood slats to get to what I could already tell was a raging success. Lyle was standing just inside with Elliot.

"Hey, Holly! What are you doing here? I thought you had some romantic weekend." Lyle asked, while kissing Kiki hello on the cheek and wrapping his arms around her tiny waist. I noticed their fingers were intertwined, which was very lovey-dovey for Kiki. She was very much the PDA type, but I'd usually spied hands way up thighs, not tender hand-holding.

"Long story," said Kiki, "but we're going to have a blast."

"Nightmare afternoon," I confessed to Elliot as Kiki and Lyle walked ahead, arm in arm. "But nothing a large beverage can't eclipse!"

"What can I get you then? A vat of absinthe perhaps?" he asked, smiling. He looked very Harrison Ford in *The Mosquito Coast*.

"Hmmm. You know what I'd love?" I think he was expecting some fancy bubble-gum-colored chick drink with an umbrella. "A Coca-Cola."

"Two Cokes, please!"

We clinked fizzy brown glasses and Kiki waved us through the VIP checkpoint and into the cavernous tented outdoor space on the waterfront, which was filled with heat lamps, Christmas trees, glass bars, and a DJ booth twenty feet up. People were dancing on every surface, the bar, tables, chairs, even the ottomans.

Kiki and Lyle came up with two green drinks that looked like antifreeze.

"Wow, Keeks, congrats, this is huge!" I marveled.

"Holly, take this—"

"What is this concoction?"

"It's a green apple martini. So yummy." She slammed back a gulp, then offered me a sip, which I tried with trepidation for fear of poison taste, but it was more like Sour Patch Kids liquefied in the Cuisinart. *No, gracias.* "OH! Holly! This is my friend Randy, from Celestial Records!"

I turned to see a smiling woman with thick black glasses. "Hey there!" she said, shaking my hand firmly. We gabbed about my years in magazines and even a summer at Arista in college and she handed me her card, telling me to e-mail her some clips of my work. I was embarrassed to explain that I hadn't exactly been in the workforce for some time.

"I've kind of been in Mommyland for the last few years," I said, hoping she'd still think of me as hip versus culturally put-out-to-pasture. Which I had been. But now that Miles was in elementary school, I'd felt myself starting to reenter the world of pop culture. I was finally more attuned to new bands, trendy writers, and hot films.

"I'll tell you what," she yelled over blaring Joy Division. "I'll get your address from Kiki and messenger you the CD and bio for our new band, Candygram, that Noah just signed. See if you can write a kick-ass release for them and e-mail it to me."

"Done!" I said confidently, hoping I remembered how to do that. It had been five years. She seemed like she'd be a chill boss, even if she had a tough-cookie vibe; my gut was that she was a straight shooter.

"Looking forward to it," she said, and saluted me, army-style.

As Randy walked away, I looked around for Kiki, who was on the dance floor with Lyle, dancing-slash-making out. She twirled effortlessly in her Louboutins, looking like the *Dancing with the Stars* people, but not B-listy. The next thing I knew, I felt a hand take my wrist. Elliot spun me around, then led me next to Kiki and Lyle, who at this point were practically entangled in a Lambada-esque coil of limbs that would make Patrick Swayze and a pre-nose-job Jennifer Grey blush. Elliot rolled his eyes at them, and we both shrugged, laughed off their PDL (public display of lust), and danced nonstop for an hour. To hit after 1980s hit we laughed and sang along. As Elliot recited every lyric perfectly, I knew that while those older-man Al Pacino fantasies would always be alive and well, I loved being with someone my own age—a common thread, a childhood of the eighties, and a shared knowledge of that time in music. "Come On, Eileen," "Karma Chameleon," "Too Shy, Shy," all played in a row as we danced. When "Hungry Like the Wolf" came on, Kiki grabbed me and whispered, "This is John's song!" I died laughing and was thrilled to be in such a radically different environment than a few hours before.

Elliot excused himself to go to the bathroom, so I third-wheel danced with Kiki and Lyle to Blondie. I was sweaty and vibrant, thighs shaking from the rare workout, now two hours of solid jumping. My throat hurt from belting the tunes and I knew I'd wake up with a sore throat, though making your voice box raw by singing your heart out was worth it. I looked around at Kiki, who waved to me as Lyle kissed her neck, his arms around her waist.

Then Kiki's face suddenly dropped, her eyes widening. I knew something was wrong when she inhaled sharply.

"What?" I looked at her, then looked at what she was looking at behind me.

It was Tim.

Sucking face with his slag. Kiki grabbed my arm in support, but it was too late. I couldn't believe he was a) back in the city and b) so PDA-ish with his relationship. I was a deer in the head-lights. Specifically, Avery's massive, tanned, protruding headlights. She was a blond stick with boobs in a dress so tight, it looked as if it had been sprayed on. He was my teddy bear, kissing her with his eyes closed. I stared at them in a grief-induced trance, until finally, she broke the suction-cup kiss and he opened his eyes and saw me.

He gave me a meek "Hi there," with a tight grin, and I turned and ran. Kiki ran after me out the door and down the board-walk, where my heel caught in a gap between the planks and I bit it. Splat! I lay in a big X like mowed roadkill on the walkway, my knee bleeding. I peeled myself up, sobbing, and limped up to a cab area.

"Holly, wait—" she called.

"I'm going home, I'll call you tomorrow."

I grabbed a cab, dove in, and we screeched off. I looked out the back window and saw Kiki, with Lyle running up behind her, looking nervously at me. As we pulled off toward the FDR, I felt myself fall into an abyss of jealousy, regret, and panic, trapped in an elevator, the coffin of a life I'd chosen, and I wanted to get off.

I saw visions of my happy times with Tim projected on the screen of my brain, like hazy flickers of black-and-white old home movies: long walks holding hands, cheers at football games in the cold, dancing at parties, and New Year's embraces. I saw sunlit afternoons and breakfasts in bed, the exchanged smiles when Miles was a baby. But it all vanished, all those perfect memories evaporating into thin winter air. Caught off guard by seeing him, the sobs choked me so much that I felt a stabbing pain in my neck. I wanted him back. More than I had ever wanted anything before in my life, I wanted a time machine to go back. Maybe I could pay more attention to his needs. Or look the other way. Or confront it but say we had to try and make it work. Couples counseling. Anything. Where had we gone wrong? I sighed, wiping a tear. Too late. He was gone, kissing a slut-rag in Lycra.

Drunk on black anguish, I got in bed and wept into the pillow, hoping this was rock bottom and that it was only up from here. The pit was so deep now, and the worst part of it was that in all my fantasies of running back to him and begging for him back, now it was truly too late. Too much had happened in our now three seasons apart—we probably didn't even know each other anymore. There's so much healing and rebuilding after a catastrophic breakup that you grow back new parts where the wounds were, and they are stronger and more impenetrable. And that's what scared me. I had a bulletproof vest around my heart. Maybe I could never fall in love again. I was too jaded, too tired, and too sick at the thought of teaching the long course of Holly 101 all over again. It was so exhausting. Friends, hobbies, favorite foods, movies, stories of childhood. There was too much to teach. I wanted someone to just download my history and know me, implant their brain with Matrix-style file on my life so I wouldn't have to always start over. How exhausting.

I wanted to shake the Etch A Sketch of my life and erase the messy mistakes I'd made. I wanted a clean slate, to turn the white knobs in different directions this time.

I couldn't sleep. I watched the outside light fade into midnight blue and black, tinted with the orange glow of Manhattan's electric veil. I thought of ex-boyfriends I could call for a dose of nostalgia, for someone to say I was special in their eyes. That was all I wanted: to be wanted again, and also to want them just as much, to feel like we fit together, like I wasn't alone in the world. I remembered a line from *Our Town*: "People are meant to live two by two." It sounded very Noah's ark, as if we were hippos or geese or something, but it felt true that night. I was desperate in my pain to find that other half—not just to have one, because I'd had that before, and two cobbled-together halves don't make a whole. Deep down, I knew that anyone at that moment would feel stapled on as an artificial half; I needed to be whole on my own first.

I did what I always did in moments like this: popped in my shrink, Woody Allen, for a post-midnight screening. This time, I chose my all-time number-one fave, *Hannah and Her Sisters*. It was the perfect spoonful of sugar to my heinous medicine of the present. I laughed my ass off, sat in therapy with Michael Caine, got the autumn chill right alongside a confused Barbara Hershey, and realized, in the last moments of the movie, the ultimate truth to Woody Allen's final line. His brilliant character goes from near death to vibrantly alive to suicidally depressed and finally back to blissfully happy. He marvels, kissing his new wife's neck after a year of despair, that "the heart is a very resilient little muscle." I sure hoped he was right.

35

A man tells his wife of fifteen years that it feels like they've only been married five minutes. "That's so sweet," the wife says. The husband replies, "Five minutes underwater."

The next day, Tim came to drop off Miles, who ran into my arms for the best hug ever, momentarily drawing my attention away from the previous evening's liplock betwixt ex-husband and urchin in a seemingly sprayed-on dress.

"I thought you all were in Locust Valley for the whole weekend. I didn't expect to see you in the city last night," I said quietly.

"Yeah, we were, and then Avery's friend was involved with that charity. . . ."

"Mm-hmm." I knelt down and unzipped Miles's bag.

"Mommy, can we make Rice Krispie Treats? Pleeease?"

"Sure, lovie."

"Okay, well, bye, then—" I said curtly. Shoot. I shouldn't have let him see that it got to me. But it did.

"Holly, for what it's worth . . . ," he said softly. "I'm sorry."

I could tell that he really felt bad. Good. Asswipe. But while all along I thought that was what I wanted, pure regret and atonement on his part, it didn't help.

I shrugged, smiled, and quietly said good-bye as Miles skipped into the kitchen.

"Yay, there's a prize in this one!" Miles ripped open the box top and tore open the airtight bag, sending Snap, Crackle, and Pop flying onto the floor. He started digging through the cereal, in desperation, as if the SpongeBob pencil topper was the lost ark. "Got it!" The collateral damage was the Krispies all over the place, but his smile made scooping it all up worth it.

"You're too much, sweetie." I laughed, hugging him so hard. "I love how you treasure complete junk."

"Mom, can I tell you something?" he said, smiling. "I love you. More than Avery. Don't worry."

I giggled. "Well, I should hope so! Seeing as how you're my little nugget I carried around for nine months!" I teased, giving him a squeeze.

"Mom?"

"Yes, Milesie."

"You're a good person."

I laughed out loud but almost wanted to cry. Maybe I would put a pin in my dating life for now. How could I want another man in my life, when I was raising this one?

"Thanks, honey," I said, kissing his forehead. "You are, too."

That night, after a feast of our chewy squares, an hour of stories, and tuck-in, I closed Miles's door and went to scope the TiVo. As I reached for the remote, the doorman's buzzer rang.

"Yes, Tony?"

"Hi, Ms. Talbott. Delivery from Zabar's."

"Huh? Oh, I wasn't expecting anything. I didn't shop there—are you sure it's for me?"

"Let me double-check," he replied, putting down the receiver momentarily. "Yup, it's for you."

"Oh, weird. Okay, then."

Maybe it was from my dad, who had called to check in on me? Or maybe Kiki. A few minutes later, I opened the back door and a man walked in with a huge bag loaded up with loot. There were pink peonies sticking out, tied with brown ribbon, and the bag was packed with soups—butternut squash apple, wild mushroom bisque, cream of broccoli, and chicken noodle, which Kiki called Jewish penicillin.

Then I saw the card, which I opened.

I was flabbergasted. It wasn't from Dad or Kiki.

Dear Holland,

I'm so sorry your night headed even further south than the Seaport—Kiki said you weren't feeling well and I wanted to send over some things to make you feel a bit better. Let me know if you ever want to meet up for some Coke. A Cola, that is.

Elliot

What a mensch. He seemed close to Lyle, but I couldn't get a read on him. I knew his divorce had been recent like mine, so he was probably gun-shy about any relationship, but as a friend he was clearly in the Kiki stratosphere of thoughtfulness.

Later that night I called Kiki to download the details of the delivery.

"Wow, Zabar's, he's my kind of guy," Kiki said. "That's pretty amazing. Guys never do shit like that."

"Should I call him to thank him? Can you get his number?"

Kiki rolled over and nudged Lyle to get the digits and I didn't miss a beat dialing them; that's what you do when someone does something nice. But then as I heard the ringing, I suddenly got inexplicably nervous. Why? We were friends! There was no sign of romantic tension . . . what was my problem?

"Elliot, hi! It's Holland. *Holly* Talbott."

"I don't know any other Hollands," he said with a little laugh.

"I can't even begin to thank you enough—this is the sweetest thing ever—the soups—I'm just so touched; that was so thoughtful."

"Yeah, well I had gone to the bathroom and when I got back, you were gone and Kiki said you went home sick—"

"I wasn't, actually. Well, sick to my stomach, yes. Bumped into the ex at the party. I saw him across the dance floor with a girl half my age and kind of flipped out."

"I'm so sorry. That's rough—"

"Yeah. Good times."

He recounted how his ex had stunned him by appearing at a party a few months ago, immersed in a massive kiss and wearing a massive rock.

"So that's how I found out she was engaged: I just saw this ring in my face. It was kind of crazy."

"Oh, my gosh." I felt lucky that at least Tim wasn't getting remarried. Maybe he would marry Avery at some point, but I had a feeling from those CDs about cavemen kicking the cavewoman out of the cave that he wouldn't be tethering himself to anyone anytime soon.

"So I have to go to Milwaukee for two days this week, but maybe when I get back we can hang out?"

"Milwaukee? Random. What's there, a client?"

"Uh . . . yeah," he said. "A collector. I don't visit the red states that often, not since my cross-country drive in college."

"You know, I always wished I had done that and really gotten to know America," I mused. "I have a very *Beavis and Butt-head* vision of what lies between the coasts."

"It's amazing," Elliot marveled. "I felt this John Cougar Mellencamp heartland happiness the whole drive."

"That sounds so cool. I've always wanted to do a *Thelma & Louise*–type road warrior blitz like that. Minus going off the cliff. Though some days I don't blame them," I joked.

"No, you wouldn't want to do that," he chided. "It would be quite a loss."

"Well, honestly, Elliot, the last few months have brought me pretty close to 'pedal to the metal' at the mouth of a canyon. . . ."

"I'm sorry—"

"Divorce is no picnic, as you know." I sighed. "It's been . . . an unpleasant time."

"I know. Even though you can have so many problems in a marriage, after a split you get this gnawing regret whenever you're lonely."

"EXACTLY!" I exclaimed. He got it.

"You kind of have to remind yourself that there were real reasons that compelled you to question things," he said.

"Oh, my God, verbatim my thoughts, verbatim," I responded. He fully understood my plight and the schizo nature of a divorce, where you may have anger but still replay the film stills of the good times.

We ended up talking relationship shop for almost two hours. I unloaded the entire Tim saga, including every hideous detail and describing a sobfest during which Kiki had suggested I buy stock in Kleenex.

He didn't know whether to laugh or hunt down my ex-mother-in-law when I regaled him with tales of her insanity, including her boarding her four standard poodles in obedience school in rural Lichtenstein for two months the summer before.

"Isn't that redundant? Is there anything other than rural Lichtenstein?" he mused. "I never heard of some booming urban metropolis over there."

"Unclear. But I know what you're saying. Maybe it's all fancy poodle obedience schools all over the whole country."

"That Sherry Von person sounds like a bitch, pardon my language," he apologized.

"Please, I curse twenty-four/seven now. I never used to, but Kiki's mouth has been a bad influence on me! I hope you don't think that's un-ladylike or something. Since you're Mister Heartland and all."

"You're very feminine."

"I am trying to edit out the bad words. I always used to ream Kiki, who has a vocabulary that would rival Webster's, and yet she uses *fuck* to qualify everything. It's contagious, I'm afraid."

"No censoring needed."

"So, I know you said you're going away, but maybe when you're back we can go check out some galleries," I ventured. Maybe he would teach me how to appreciate some of the "emerging artists" whose prices fetched more than old masters, which I found somehow incomprehensible.

"Um, sure. . . ." He didn't sound so sure. Maybe he didn't want to spend time in galleries when he had to do that every day.

"Or if that's too close to work and feels like a pain, we can do something else—"

"No, no, that's fine. I would love that."

We made a plan for a few days later.

"Can't wait," he said. "Feel better."

"Thanks, Elliot."

"Okay, girl across the park. Sleep well."

"You, too."

36

"Marriage is a great institution, but only if you like being institutionalized."

Now that it was officially countdown to Christmas, and twinkling lights, pine, and red and white tinsel had exploded all over New York, the big hot topic of discussion on the Upper East Side was on everyone's lips. It was the only thing anyone was talking about the next day at school. No, not politics, or the latest Hollywood gossip scandal.

"So Holly, where are you guys going for vacation?" Mary Grassweather probed.

Every year, the instant the first garland was hung in the first window on Madison, the Inquisition began. Everyone was afire with shared itineraries, comparing Aman resorts, or headed straight from school to Scandinavian Ski Shop.

"Um, not sure yet," I responded to Mary. "Tim and I agreed to split up the time, but I'm not sure how it's going to work just yet."

Oooh, too tricky an answer.

"Well, we're going to Nairobi to an elephant orphanage!" exclaimed Emilia d'Angelo. "It's called the Arnold

Slutsky-Rosenblatt Trust and each of the kids will select a baby elephant to adopt and they send you pictures and stuff, isn't that so exciting?"

"Oh, fabulous!" cooed Mary. "But I bet it's not eighty-nine cents a day like the kids on TV!"

"Yeah, try three thousand a month! But these pooooor elephants are endangered!" Emilia said, making an exaggerated sad face like a little kid or a drama tragedy mask. "So," she said brightening suddenly. "Mary, where are you off to?"

"We're off to Lyford. Sooo looking forward to getting the hell out of here!" she said it as if New York were some seething lava pit she needed to be airlifted from. "The NetJets people have been great. We've changed the date so many times, but finally said, let's just pull the kids from school a few days early and get down there!"

This I never understood, either. My parents always saw the school calendar as a locked-in grid that would dictate our lives, not some malleable list they could chuck on a whim depending on urges for sand and surf. I never missed school days unless I was on fire with fever. But Miles's class always thinned out to a skeleton crew in the days before a vacation, as kids jetted off to resorts around the globe for a head start on fun in the sun.

If the exotic locales to be visited by Miles's class alone were drawn in red lines on a map, it would certainly encircle the earth, with the most concentration in the Caribbean islands and Western ski resorts.

It bugged me how everyone I knew would simply ask *where* we were going versus *if* we were going anywhere; it was simply assumed everyone went jetting off in all directions. I'd love to just respond "Abu Dhabi" or something random just for a reaction. And yes, this was a group of the privileged Wall Street offspring,

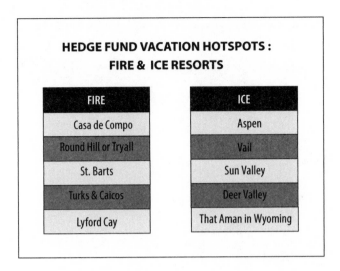

so yes, most people did travel, but some didn't. There were kids who couldn't afford to globe-trot or parents who couldn't take off work. Either way, I knew I'd be having the first Christmas alone in my life. My dad was going to stop by for dinner on his way to his annual trip with his golf buddies, but Miles would be off with Tim, and on New Year's I would be watching Dick Clark solo with a bag of microwave popcorn. But deep down, I was starting to feel weirdly independent versus lonely. I wasn't sure whether it was Kiki's influence, my new pattern of trying to go out more, or just alone time to think and pull myself together, but I was slowly changing into someone less stressed. I didn't carry around as much nervous energy as I had; I was bolder. Stronger, more daring—like when the CIA recruits spies who are not tethered to anyone; not that I'd be sleeping with a sheik to get international secrets—I just felt free and empowered with possibility. A new year always psychologically felt like a corner was being turned instead of just another day in a chain of days but with a new numeral; it felt like a cliff and a fresh jump across that chasm of 11:59, where I'd land on another cliff and start my next run. I just hoped I could stay strong for the holiday season. But something inside me was gearing up for that moment, as not only would the gleaming megawatt ball be dropping, but hopefully my inhibitions as well.

37

"I was married by a judge. I should have asked for a jury."

—*Groucho Marx*

I pressed play on my machine. BEEP! "Hi, Holly, it's Tristin Archer from Randy Simmons's office at Celestial Records Publicity; how are ya? So, I'm calling because Randy read the Candygram release you e-mailed her and she loves loves loves your writing. So Randy would love love love to schedule a time for you to come in for an interview. Call me back!" This chick was probably the friendliest girl around. Or she was on major uppers. I scrambled to get a pen to write the number down. Celestial was a cool label and I was very intrigued. They had just been half bought by Warner Music. The Greene brothers, Sean and Noah, always seemed to sign the best bands, from new wave to hard rocker boys that were ubiquitous on MTV2 to star rappers, all minting money. Plus, their offices were a palatial renovated chocolate factory on the Lower East Side, and they had their own studios and hip interiors. It was establishment cool, but still up-and-coming, like Sub Pop records in Seattle circa 1990. And this position could meld my love of music and writing.

———

Two days later, heart pounding, I went down to the legendary offices, which had been designed by starchitects 4Team, design gurus who had done the hottest restaurants, galleries, and offices around. I knew of them not only because their work had been published and hailed in virtually every shelter mag, but also because Tim had interviewed them when he redid Talbott Capital (he went with Gehry instead). Music played in the waiting room, and everyone who walked by looked interesting and original.

"She'll be right with you," cooed the stylish receptionist-slash-vixen as I plopped down on the Corbusier couch and perused the newest *Billboard*. A few moments later, out walked Randy in head-to-toe black. Her black glasses, black T-shirt, and black leggings were punctuated only by a red stripe down the sides and (yikes) shoe-boots with spikes on them.

I followed her into a massive loftlike corner office as she spoke about the artists on the label. She was a fast talker and clearly took zero bullshit from anyone, but I liked her. As we talked about the industry, I could tell she was definitely going to be a ballbuster.

"So. Holly. Let me be straight with you. I like you. I have always liked Kiki, so I read your piece and really liked your writing and your pizzazz. But you worry me." As Shaggy from Scooby Doo would say: Zoinks. *What's wrong with me?* Before I could ask why, she steamrollered on.

"I have a fear that you are creative and want to be creative, and while this position has its creative sides, including writing, what I really need is a salesperson. You would be *selling* the bands to the press. You have to be convincing. You need to be brash. Basically, you need to be like Kiki. You need to be in-your-face. You seem very poised and uptown to me. But what you need to be is a pain in the ass. You need to be a never-say-die, rubber-cockroach publicist, and I'm not sure you want to be that."

I sat silent for a minute because I knew she had totally called my bluff—I didn't want to be a rubber cockroach. But I wanted to work, and knew I could definitely sell. I also knew from the moment I walked into the stunning offices that I felt exhilarated. That this was a place I could go to every day, meet new people, and begin a new chapter. This was, in essence, the perfect day job.

"I can sell. Trust me, I may seem polite, but I can be a hustler," I said.

"Really?" she said, leaning in, incredulously. I felt like Sandy in *Grease* when Rizzo says to the gals, "She's too pure to be pink."

Clearly I needed to convince her I could hawk the acts to the editors or she'd send me packing.

"I can sell anything. I've always been great at convincing people of things. I think it's because I'm a very enthusiastic person," I offered with a big smile that was met with a frown. "Sometimes enthusiasm can be very contagious."

"Or very annoying, depending on how it's served up," she retorted.

I looked at my lap. Uh-oh. I shouldn't have worn my charm bracelet. It definitely looked too mom-ish and un-edgy, with letters spelling M-I-L-E-S dangling from my wrist. Randy looked at me, squinting her eyes, and reached into an Andy Warhol–signed Campbell soup can filled with writing utensils. She took out a single yellow number–two pencil and placed it in front of me at the edge of her desk.

"Okay, Holly. Let's give you a shot," she said, leaning back in her swivel chair, and crossing her arms. "Sell me this pencil."

I looked at it for a second and tried to come up with sassy copy: Mellow yellow! Rock it old school! Forget your snazzy pens, retro is in! A crossword puzzler's best friend! S.A.T. tool extraordinaire! But instead of my quirky little sales pitch, something came over me, something that had to do, I think, with not giving a shit. I wanted this job, yes, but I had already hit rock bottom and was strong enough to cope if I didn't get it. So I did take a page out of Kiki's book. Ripped it out, more accurately. I finally summoned my newfound indie streak and used my impulse to get a bit of backbone.

I picked up the pencil and held it in my hands.

And then I snapped it in half, to Randy's shock. Then I placed the two pieces gently back on her desk.

"Now you need a new pencil."

Silent pause.

Then, blue ribbon moment: As the corners of Randy's mouth slowly turned up, I knew I had scored like Dustin Hoffman's aggressive audition in *Tootsie*. Her hand extended across the desk and I shook it.

I'd start two weeks from Monday.

38

"My wife was a great housekeeper. When we divorced, she kept the house."

Kiki shrieked with joy that I had managed to finagle the job, and howled over my bold move with the pencil.

"You are balls out, girl," she said, practically beaming with pride as my coach to "have more fuck-you," as she called it. "Okay, so I have some news, too . . . ," she teased.

"Tell!"

We were getting coffees in Via Quadronno, and she gestured to a nearby table that was suddenly freed up by two ladies who lunch.

"Sit down," commanded Kiki. I obeyed, curiosity mounting. She took a deep breath and looked at me, eyes sparkling. "Lyle asked me to go to Paris with him!"

"No . . ."

"*OUI!*" she squealed with glee.

I was elated. I couldn't believe Kiki was falling so hard, but sure enough she was giggling like a nervous schoolgirl.

"Holl, we were in bed last night and he goes, 'I've never felt this way about anyone. I don't want to be without you,' and he asked me to come! And we're going to Miami this weekend for ArtBasel."

"Oh, Elliot must be going to that—"

"Yeah, I think he is. Lyle said you guys have plans to go out soon?"

"Yes, gallery-hopping. Wait, Kiki, I'm sooo excited for you! Traveling is major. But international traveling is even more major."

"I know, bonding right? Having passports stamped together cements you as a couple. Crossing border equals crossing over into boyfriend/girlfriend territory. I didn't even want a boyfriend! But Holly . . . I think I'm in love with Lyle."

"LOVE? *Love* love?"

"Yes," she said, soberly. "He's brilliant, and kind, and funny. And goddamn it, what can I say? He worships me!"

"As well he should!"

And what I experienced was the mark of true friendship: butterflies in my stomach on Kiki's behalf. Her giddiness was my giddiness. Even when I selfishly realized that I couldn't hang with her over the holidays, as she would be jetting off into a glistening dreamy wonderland of twinkling lights and Parisian love in the air, I was ecstatic.

39

"Scientists have discovered a food that lowers sex drive by ninety percent. It's called wedding cake."

Two days later, I met Elliot for a day of walking around town. We wandered into nearly twenty galleries, and his knowledge of the artists was beyond extensive, although we did the quickie *Reader's Digest* version of gallery-hopping with quick whizzes through each. In a few he exchanged speedy greetings with a couple of gallerists, but for the most part it didn't seem like he either knew many of them or wanted to strike up conversation. I wasn't sure why he seemed so shy but I thought perhaps he didn't want any of these professional colleagues to think this could possibly be a date. Not that it was.

One show featured a young artist named Atlas Jones, whose vibrant canvases of giant eyes started to make me feel very paranoid.

"I mean, who could live with these?" I asked. "I couldn't walk naked in front of them; it's like being stared at."

"I see your point. I do think he's very original, though," he mused.

"His name just sounds like an artist," I said.

"Really? I thought porn star," said Elliot.

"Atlas Jones, yeah." True. "Atlas is kind of a cool name. You don't hear it often."

"No, it's way too much pressure," he said, shaking his head. "That's like naming your kid Hercules or something. With my schnook name, I could only go uphill—"

"Oh, stop it. I love the name Elliot," I countered.

". . . but with Hercules it's all about disappointing people."

He had a point. The kids at school might have a teasing field day.

"Yeah, you're right. Plus, it would be too weird if he was a toothpick."

"Hey! Don't knock toothpicks," he chided, gesturing to his own lanky frame.

"Trust me, I'm not. I love tall and thin."

"You do?"

"Sure."

It was true; Tim's robust build and six-pack abs were truly not my "type" pre-marriage—all my previous boyfriends had had that thin, nerdy build that I found sexier than some buff hunk. In fact, my high school best friend, Lisa, and I always made up phrases about our love for thinner, more approachable guys, like Toothpick or Take It Elsewhere, Nerd or Need Not Apply, Dork or Don't Bother.

I had to smile looking at Elliot in that way—he definitely fit the mold of my pre-Tim type. As I looked at his green eyes, I remembered that rare feature was on my laundry list of dream characteristics when I was a teenager, dreaming of Prince Charming.

The last gallery we entered contained not one, not two, but twenty paintings of clowns. As I drew breath to gasp in horror, Elliot said, "I hate clowns. Who could look at those every day?"

"I know!" I said, laughing. "Everyone makes fun of me because I'm freaked out by clowns, but I would be so paranoid it would jump down from the canvas and strangle me in my sleep!"

"Let's get out of here."

After our legs got tired and we warmed up with hot chocolates, we headed uptown in a taxi, and as soon as he confidently said, "Hi, we're making two stops," I felt foolish for even entertaining the thought that anything would go down. The problem was this: Now I liked him. A lot. As we were driving, he got a call on his cell and immediately said he'd call back when he got home. He was so polite and never talked on the phone in front of me; his charm and manners weren't canned ye olde chivalry-style, with dramatic coats thrown on puddles, just heartfelt and sincere like someone who could be a true friend. It was the tiniest gestures that made me feel somehow, not to sound so anti-feminist 1950s, but, taken care of. A light hand on the small of my back. Asking if I was too chilly or tired. A breezy comment about my outfit, how I looked "very Parisian." All of them made me see the quiet magic of a male companion—platonic or nay; it was nice to get some positive attention and have that companionship where you can feel feminine and spend time at least imagining what it would be like to be in a couple again.

That night Miles and I decided we would go out for dinner, since he was leaving soon for Aspen with Tim and I would be putting my nose to the grindstone at my new job soon enough and wanted to celebrate. We settled on Swifty's, which was slightly too nice for a child, but he was an only child and accustomed to rising to the occasion and being a mini-adult. In his brown corduroy jacket and navy pants and coat, out we walked, arm in arm into the cold. It was a delightful but bittersweet time, as I knew very soon he would be gone for a whole ten days. Tim's jet would be flying him, along with Sherry Von and Hal, to Aspen, where he'd be in Powder Pandas ski school, along with countless other hedgie offspring, dropped off by moms who hit not the slopes, but the designer boutiques, clad in Dennis Basso sable coats and toting Chanel bags. In Colorado. It was like New York and L.A. but with snow. I could just see Sherry Von holding court in the Caribou Club, where we ate dinner several nights between party-hopping at various mansions of the financial elite, complete with troughs of caviar you could do a swan dive into, insane artwork, and high-tech security systems that rivaled Quantico. I had been going to the same annual Christmas parties for ten years strong, and every year the hosts would give everyone a tour of that year's additions—the new office complete with five flat-screen computers, à la *Swordfish,* that looked like a Dr. Evil–style lair from which they could launch a nuclear assault. There were military de-accessioned night-vision suits for paintball, state-of-the-art snowmobiles manufactured and custom ordered from the Ukraine, and custom skis with the latest in experimental design and laser-etched monograms.

Going to the same place for the holidays is a touchstone you measure your year by—a yardstick of where you've been in the last twelve months. How different my life had become since my last opening of presents under Sherry Von's majestic fifteen-foot tree, which was decorated not by herself and her family by a roaring fire, but by her staff, guided by Hubert and the floral artisans of The Aspen Branch. The house was bedecked with flowers, wreaths, and garlands, all adorned with hand-blown or silver ornaments from Cartier, Baccarat, and Tiffany. Hubert teetered annually on a vertiginous ladder to hand place each trinket with love all the way up to the ceiling. Our smaller spruce was always covered in popcorn I'd threaded together and Miles's papier-mâché and cut-out ornaments from nursery school like my mom did with mine. She'd literally saved my lovingly patched-up three-year-old creations for decades; those crayoned lines and googley eyes were what made our tree soulful and unique. Anyone with an AmEx Black could swipe their way into crystal globes and sterling snowflakes but ours had a colorful innocent twinkle way more magical. As always, Kiki stood by helping; she was thrilled to be part of a tree-trimming experience.

"Oh my God, this is so American, I love it!" she squealed, the first Christmas after she and Hal were married. She cut a star out of the snowflake-embossed foil I'd bought at Kate's Paperie. "Okay, here it is! Should I put it on top?"

I smiled as she proudly held her six-pointed Star of David. Miles and I still put it on our treetop to this day. I asked Miles if he was excited for the various parties in Aspen.

"The Mitchells' snowman contest is the best! I'm gonna win this year!"

Rob and Sugar Mitchell (he of Parallelogram Capital) were insane billionaires who were based in London but flew all over the planet, James Bond–style. Their son, August, was Miles's age and had a twin sister, Hazel. Last year their contest featured assistants to help the kids (defeating the creative purpose, in my opinion), with props to fashion snowman facial features: Chanel buttons that had fallen off Sugar's various coats for eyes, Hermès scarves for their snow necks, and Cohiba cigars for noses. I was mildly horrified by the excess of in-home cinemas and staffs of twelve, Dom Perignon at brunch, and hundreds of jets all lined up in a row at the airport. I wouldn't miss it, though I would miss my son so terribly, my entire body ached. Especially because

I was sending him, via jet no less, to Sherry Von's nest of over-the-top spending and opaque values.

The next morning, we packed up his suitcase with snow-suits, hats, Turtle Fur gators, and mittens, and zipped it up to go downstairs. With a heavy heart, I sat beside him in the lobby until Hubert pulled up the car as Tim hopped out.

"I love you, honey," I stammered, trying to force back tears.

"I love you, Mom. Merry Christmas." He kissed me on the cheek. And then a cry of "DADDY!" and he ran into Tim's arms. Over Miles's shoulder, Tim looked at me and smiled.

"Merry Christmas, Holly."

"You, too."

So there I was: solo. I caught up on my TNT movies and even walked around the city by myself doing hokey stuff like scoping Christmas windows and visiting the Rockefeller Center tree along with all of Kansas.

The next night my dad came in to see me and we sat for a lovely dinner at La Goulue, which normally was buzzing with the beautiful ladies who lunch but this time had a warm, cozy aura since most regulars were off under a palm tree. In fact, with the mahogany walls, drinking red wine and going for the cheese platter, I felt so happy to see my dad.

"Hanging in there?" he asked me after we toasted his visit. "It's a tough time. Mom always made the house so beautiful. That's why I always travel this time of year with the guys. It's too hard to be home and know there would have been stockings and lights and her food."

"I know. I always try to make our apartment like she did. Whenever I'm sad I always go back to missing her. Missing my whole young life."

"I know what you mean, kiddo. I can't even believe I'm going to be seventy. It's surreal. I bumped into an old friend the
other day—a guy I hadn't seen in fifty years. Half a century!"

"Well, I'm a girl half your age who has been put out to pasture!"

"Nonsense. You're young, you're bright, you'll find someone,
Holland. I know it."

I sat silently and smiled a sly smile.

"You met someone nice?" he probed.

"Maybe. I hope."

He reached over and squeezed my hand. "He'd be a lucky
guy, sweetheart."

I came home and checked my machine. Nada. I wondered when
I'd hear from Elliot. Was I supposed to call him? The man should
really call. Not to be some anti-feminist type, but given my
emotional vulnerability I didn't feel like I could boldly dial the
digits, even though we were only friends. But I knew he was
always busy at work . . . I should try him. There would be no
games this time: a) we were just pals, and b) I'm not the kind of
girl who sits by the phone.

A day of frequently checking voice mail later, I dialed his
number.

"Holly Talbott, I was just going to call you!"

"Really?"

"Really. On the off chance you're free tonight . . ."

"Yes. Whatever it is, yes."

"Terrific. So what have you been up to?"

"It's been hard, you know, my first holidays without my son,
so it's been . . . a bit lonely. But I've been doing all the tacky
New York tourist stuff."

"Like what?"

"I've been to two Broadway shows, all the holiday windows, eating like a pig, the tree, museums."

"You ate a tree and a museum?"

"Ha-ha. Almost," I said, smiling at his weirdness. "Seriously, though, I've done more visitor stuff than regular New Yorker stuff. Everything but a horse and carriage and the Empire State Building."

"So when can I come pick you up for tonight?"

We agreed he'd come by at 8:00, leaving me just enough time to take a bubble bath and get ready without being rushed. Something about hearing his voice put me totally at ease and I felt a little less alone in the wake of Miles's and Kiki's simultaneous departures.

When the doorman buzzed, I wondered if I should invite Elliot up, but my apartment still felt like a family apartment. I even still had a wedding photo up, and snapshots of family vacations I didn't have the heart to suddenly replace with Mommy & Me versions post divorce. So I opted to just go downstairs. Which ended up being a good call, because Elliot would have had to pay waiting time to . . . the horse and carriage that were sitting there when I arrived.

"What is this?" I asked, beaming and in shock.

"Your chariot," Elliot said, climbing out to walk to me. "I know you had a theme going with the tourist stuff."

"Oh, my gosh. I haven't done this since I visited with my parents as a kid!" I wasn't sure if I should hug him or play it cool. Luckily I didn't have to decide. He hugged me immediately and almost picked me up.

"Sheesh, don't lift me, I'll give you a herniated disk."

"You are just right. Guys don't dig toothpicks."

"Oh, yeah? Then why do all guys drool over models all the

time? Your friend Lyle included, I might add," I teased with a wink. "I've seen him with many a cover girl in the press over the years."

"Yeah, and he wasn't into them. He's more attached to Kiki than I've ever seen him with one of those girls."

We climbed into the carriage and Elliot put a blanket over our laps to shield us from the frigid but delicious air. We rode down Fifth Avenue along the park, then by the Plaza and then past all the twinkling lights of the boutiques, gussied up for the holidays. It was heaven. Every time I had to trek through midtown it felt like such a crush of bodies and I always had somewhere to go, rushing off this way or that, attempting to do errands against the force of thousands of people. When you're hurrying somewhere you can never pause to drink in the moment, but that carriage ride gave me the chance to savor all the sights and also to let me know that Elliot, through his bold and romantic gesture, definitely could be more than a friend. The suspicion was confirmed when we pulled up to the NBC building and climbed out.

"The Empire State Building doesn't serve dinner," he said. "But the best view of it is right up here at the Rainbow Room."

I was euphoric. "I haven't been here in ages!" I exclaimed as he led me through the doors to the grand lobby of 30 Rock. When we walked in, two guys were carrying a full-length mirror—presumably for one of the many sets in the NBC studios. Elliot stopped walking and put me in front of the mirror, standing behind me and putting his hands on my shoulders.

"See? Look at yourself. You look like you just swallowed a vat of radium and you're glowing from within."

I caught myself blushing in the mirror and looked down bashfully. I had that excited sense that we were on the same plane in terms of our connection and I couldn't have been more relaxed and at ease about it. The bellinis upstairs were delicious and the view from our window table beyond intoxicating, and I kept thinking that because he made me feel beautiful, confident, and generally happy, I was suddenly smitten, and this time, felt that I could finally picture myself sleeping with him. I wasn't frigid! I wasn't scared or nervous or shaky. I was calm and whole. I felt known and understood and it was so new a sensation that I almost felt reborn.

Weirdly, the more he said, the more I felt like Elliot was more similar to me than any guy I'd ever met. For one, it was as if his taste buds were grafted onto my own. Same tastes, same dislikes. He loved mushrooms, hated fennel, and was a coffee addict. We ate a delicious dinner of grilled artichokes with lemon, light fluffy gnocchi with vodka sauce, and coffee gelato. After he paid the check, Elliot asked the maître d' if the private party room was available for a sneak peek. He let us in to the grand room, dark and majestic. The massive Empire State Building looming in the giant floor-to-ceiling windows, and the whole city was before us, an ocean of glitter.

"This is the most gorgeous thing ever," I said, absolutely mesmerized.

"No," Elliot replied, taking my hand and kissing it. "Second most."

With that, I was, as they say, a goner.

Elliot moved the hair out my face, then caressed my neck down to my shoulder. He leaned in and kissed me so passionately, I felt as electrified as the countless skyscrapers that peppered our majestic view.

We grasped each other as he kissed my neck and ear, jolting shivers down my back as our fingers interlaced, our breathing growing heavier.

Suddenly a dude burst in and switched on the lights—the

definition of buzz kill. We looked like busted teens in the basement rec room, all guiltily disheveled and rosy. Elliot took my hand. "Let's go."

We hailed a cab and this time I felt perfectly fine having him come to my place, and we kissed excitedly the entire ride home. When we pulled up to my awning the driver had to turn around and announce that we had arrived. I didn't make eye contact with our doorman, who I was certain would report the sighting to the whole staff. Inside the apartment, we jumped on the bed and as we kissed I realized I was turned on by Elliot the person, not just the newness of him. It felt safe being in his arms, not loaded with shades of the past or elevated on a pedestal, just real and comfortable. And just when I thought I couldn't like him any more, he awed me with each passing moment, a cute smile here or a dopey gesture there. In our blissful downy vacuum he was more forceful than I first realized; he pulled me to him with such confidence, like a man who goes after what he wants. I felt oddly protected by his strength despite his thin frame. He pulled me down to him and we kissed for what seemed like hours. But whereas John had gone immediately for my bra, Elliot just had his hands in my hair and down my back, under my sweater. Was he not turned on by me? Why no going for the gold? The make out continued and I started to really want him. I put my hands under his shirt to feel the skin underneath. His stomach and torso felt like perfection and I moved my hands up his chest as I climbed on top of him, pants on. We kept kissing but I sensed him tense up a little bit.

"Are you okay? What's wrong?" I asked.

"Nothing at all. I just . . ." He put his hands on my waist and rubbed my sides. "I thought we maybe should take it slow, you know."

Oh.

"Oh . . . okay," I said.

"Trust me, I want to sleep with you. I really want to, I just thought—"

"Cool, sure, fine, whatever."

This whole not-wanting-to-rip-my-clothes-off-and-nail-me thing begged the question: *What the fuck?* I thought all men were little horndogs. I wanted to be begged for it! I didn't want to feel like some dirty ho who's craving it from him. Am I some estrogen-dripping predator? Should I be playing it more coy? Oh, my God, it suddenly dawned on me: Men are the new women.

Lost in my thought about changing sexual tides and the androgynizing of the world, Elliot pulled me back to him and kissed me.

"Sweetie, I see the wheels turning."

"No, I just, I don't know." He did call me sweetie. But why no pouncing, lion-style? Eff it, why not be frank? "I just have never had a guy stop me, that's all. I usually am the one to put on the brakes. But I guess you want to take it slow, so . . ."

"I just wanted to let it happen and not speed it up for *you*."

"What do you mean for *me*? Can't you see I'm pawing you?" I was semi-embarrassed by my odd situation.

"Listen, Holly," he said, putting his arms around me. "All I want to do right now is sleep with you, trust me."

Okay . . . "So . . . why? . . ."

He put his hand on my face. "I just wanted you to know that it's not like that with you. From the day I first saw you, I was smitten. Then after we met again, I really liked you."

All right, how could I not be into that response? "I hear you, I guess. Me, too."

"Come here—" He grabbed me and we kissed even more intensely. I felt so open and able to talk with him, which enhanced my yearning. I didn't want any barriers between us, because the more I knew him, the more I liked him. Boldly, I pulled my sweater over my head. He kissed my neck and chest and I could tell he was changing his mind. Panting like teens, we rolled over the comforter, melding into each other until he really was trying to undress me and reached for my skirt. This time, I stopped him.

"No, you're right, let's just wait . . . ," I said flirtily.

"Now you want to wait?" He smiled.

"Maybe you were on to something. Plus we've already talked so much about it, it's awky now."

"Awky? I'm not awky, are you awky?"

"No, not really."

"So?"

"I just think you were maybe right. Let's wait. Until tomorrow."

"Tomorrow night, eh?"

"Yeah, I promise. Sex date. I haven't done that since I lost my virginity."

"Me neither." He smiled.

"Really? How did you lose it?" I asked. Maybe I was plunging too fast into his young romantic life. "Is that too personal?"

"There's nothing too personal for me. No skeletons."

"Okay, I just wasn't sure if I could quote unquote 'go there' yet."

He wrapped his arms around me and squeezed me. "Sweetie, you can go anywhere with me." I loved how he called me sweetie. I felt like the happiest, most comfortable me there ever was. "It was my high school girlfriend. She insisted we play 'In Your Eyes' by Peter Gabriel, and there weren't remote controls back then, you know, so I had to get up and walk across the room to press play on the stereo since she wanted to lose it to that song."

"I lost mine with the Rolling Stones playing."

"Hmm. That gives new meaning to 'Start Me Up'.

"Yeah, more like 'Let It Bleed'."

"Nice!"

"See, Elliot, I must be comfortable with you if I'm telling you about First Time gore. Hope it's not an overshare."

He kissed my forehead, putting his hand on my shoulder and running it down my arm. "No such thing."

I smiled and kissed him.

"Listen, though . . . ," he started, his forehead crinkling with seriousness. "There's something I wanted to—"

The phone rang. I gave him a look to say hold that thought as I reached for the phone, perplexed about who would be calling at midnight. Miles.

"Hi, Mommy, it's me."

"Hi, lovie! I'm so happy to hear your voice!"

"I know, I missed you, too . . ."

"But Milesie, it's so late, even with the time change, how come you're up?"

"I'm supposed to be in bed, but I couldn't sleep. I wanted to say hi. Dad and Avery went out, so I'm just here with Grandma. She's in her room watching Nick at Nite. I went in, but she said I had to get back in bed, so I wanted to call you."

Elliot got up and I signaled one minute, but he smiled and mouthed out that I should take my time. He went into the kitchen while I talked to Miles, sang him a lullaby, and tucked him in over the phone.

"Okay, pull up the covers," I instructed.

"I did it!" he seemed to like this.

"Twinkle, twinkle, little star . . ."

I sang to him, and when I was done, he quietly said, "Good night, Mom."

"Good night, sweetie, I love you."

While I didn't want him to be a total mama's boy, I did love that he needed me and thought of me all the way out in snowy Colorado. Thank goodness Elliot and I had ended up at my place. He came back in with some hot chocolate I didn't even know I had, and in T-shirts and underwear, we cuddled like married people.

"This is good," he said. "But you know what's even better?"

"What?"

"Machine hot chocolate. It is the best thing."

I couldn't believe it. "TOTALLY! I love machine hot chocolate! All my friends teased me in college because I'd make them go to the Cumberland Farms to get some everyday!"

"Same. My friend and I were so addicted that we made friends with a guy in the kitchen and during the summer he smuggled us a machine and we had it in our house."

"Oh, my God, that's my dream! Except I'd probably drink myself into a Roseanne Barr state."

"Then there'd be more of you to love."

He turned out the light and kissed me good night. Once he fell asleep, I was dying to surprise him by climbing on him naked, but we had our sex date for the following night. I lay there watching him (thank God he didn't snore) and thought about Tim. Of course I knew Tim so much better than Elliot—I had been with him for so many years. But looking at Elliot's cute face, and knowing how much I loved kissing him and how much I wanted to know him more, I realized that I was a truly different person now. The biggest shock is when you look back on a relationship and understand for the first time that even if you did try and go back to each other, it wouldn't be like before, because you're completely changed. The agonizing first months apart and the suffering and the heartbreak sculpt you into a new person, and that was the Holly that Elliot was curled up next to.

40

"It's not true that married people live longer than single people . . . it only seems longer."

The next morning we woke up at around noon and I immediately snuck to the bathroom to degrease my face. Looking in the mirror, I could have sworn you could fry an egg on my T-zone. While I was brushing my teeth I felt a hunger pain in my stomach; I was dying for anything, and I had nothing in the fridge since Miles was away. I came back to bed (hair brushed, teeth minty) and flopped on Elliot, who smiled and hugged me like a little bear cub. I felt so happy and needed and couldn't believe how easy it was to wake up with him or that it was our first time waking up together. It felt so normal.

"I'm hungry," he said.

"Feed me, Seymour, feel me AWL night long," I sang from *Little Shop of Horrors*.

He laughed and looked up at me and patted my face.

"Do you want to go out for a big yummy brunch?" I asked him.

"No."

"Well, I hate to tell you this, but I'm not some pancake-flipping Betty Crocker type."

"That's okay. I am."

"Really?"

"Yeah. Do you have pancake mix?"

"No. I have nothing. I have mustard."

"Mustard, huh. Looks we're going to order in."

"I have a single girl's fridge."

"I don't think you're a single girl anymore." Did that mean he was my . . . boyfriend? I thought so. My heart did a Nadia Comaneci. I excitedly scampered to get my little pail of menus. There were hundreds.

"Holy shit, what did you do, go through Zagats and demand menus from every place in town?"

"Kind of."

"You are very organized."

"I know: Martha Junior."

"This looks good to me," he said, producing a big one with a sun. "The smiley yellow guy is telling me this is our place."

I dialed and Elliot kept yelling out more stuff to add until finally I put my hand over the receiver and said, "Yo, this could feed a family of four!"

By the time I had hung up, we had ordered a quasi buffet. We smooched in front of cartoons for a while (Miles had left my TV on Nickelodeon), and I learned that Elliot was a massive SpongeBob fan even though he had no kids. Odd-slash-cute. We smooched and watched until my buzzer rang.

I spread out all the goods for us, which made me feel like I was preparing something for him by peeling off the tinfoil on his egg and cheese on toast and flopping it onto a plate. So domestic! Mrs. Brady, dream wife. Okay, maybe not. But at least I made everything look nice. I even found a tray my mom gave me and laid everything on it with OJ poured into glasses and coffee in mugs and brought it to him in bed.

"Wow, lucky me; look at this spread you made!"

We ate and watched the screen, a trance of dancing starfish and choruses of underwater weeds, corals, and bubbles. The funny voices made him smile and I saw in his zone-out that he was still like a little kid in there, which I loved. Just as long as he didn't start hanging with the Culkin brothers and buying an amusement park and elephant-man bones. After an hour more of lounging, I hauled out of bed to draw the blinds. I gasped.

"Come look at this!'

Sometime between midnight and noon, the city had been covered in a blanket of sparkling snow. There was a full-scale blizzard in progress, with wind and flakes whipping the window, making our bedside perch even more romantic. We basically spent the whole day in bed, as one eighties movie rolled into another, and the next thing we knew, it was dark again around 4:00 p.m.

I went to hop in the shower, and as the hot water fell on me, I secretly fantasized that he'd surprise me by coming in and join-ing me. But he didn't, so I got dressed in a soft cashmere sweater and skirt and plopped beside him and asked what he wanted to do.

He didn't say anything; he just looked at me. He sat up and reached for me, kissing me gently at first, then more and more intensely as we got lost in each other's embrace to the point of dizziness. He calmly unbuttoned the cardigan I'd thrown on; his slow, methodical motions made me practically swoon. He kissed my chest above my bra and back to my mouth with vigor. But just as he'd ratchet up the hotness factor, he'd slow down and be calmly doting again. He delicately pulled one bra strap down, kissing my shoulder where the strap had been. He kissed across my collarbone to the other bra strap, which fell beside my elbow as he kissed my shoulder and unhooked my bra. The surge of need for him pulled through my entire body as he slid a hand under my skirt, up my thigh. I gasped when he touched me, feeling at once total freedom and unbridled anticipation. While he had the appetite and fervor that John had, I saw something more in Elliot, like an emotional need, like he really was deeply into the moment, body and soul, as opposed to just trying to get off. I took his T-shirt off over his head and rubbed my hands along his chest and stomach, kissing him as we lay against each other. Having sex with him at this point was something I was even more excited for because he had prolonged my cravings. Although I have to admit, I oscillated between a) wanting him to want me so badly that he couldn't help but throw me across the bed and climb on me, and b) wanting to keep the wait going so that we'd relish it all even more.

I knew this time would be it, and while my heart was racing, my mind was calm. He stopped kissing me and took the rubber band out of my hair and ran his hand through it, bringing his lips to mine again. I could feel chills down my arms and back, and as he unzipped my skirt I felt like the perfect combination of a swooning schoolgirl and a complete va-va-voom woman being seduced. He slid off my panties and looked into my eyes.

"It's not quite evening yet but I figured you'd give me a green light," he said, holding my hands.

"Green."

I laughed, and when he kissed me again, I knew this was as right as anything was ever going to be. He seemed to carry me in one of his arms as he moved my comforter down with the other, always making me feel like a total goddess. But he wasn't some too-gentle "lover" type that was all about snail-paced makin' love—he started out slow and lovingly, but then the sex parabola spiked and he grabbed me harder so I knew he had his own needs, which gave me even more of a kick. I put my arms around him, and he looked into my eyes, then kissed me as we moved together in a perfect rhythm as my hands moved down his back. As he moved, he held me in one of his strong arms and wasn't scared to show he was enjoying it; he was quiet but breathy, and as his inhalation quickened he held my hand in his and squeezed it hard. I was so turned on by his being turned on that I thought I would melt into the sheets.

I could feel my orgasm coming in the distance, like waiting on a platform and seeing the train approaching from far away. It grew closer and closer and rose until I knew it would roar next to me, and when it did, after all I'd been through, it felt like a miracle. Elliot was beyond hot in bed. But it was way more than that. I felt bound to him like we were the same unit, those conjoined twins attached at the heart. Except not tragic. We had taken such different paths but somehow gotten to this moment together, our parallel roads finally converging. It was a big emotional salad of pleasure and relief and love and wanting to squeeze him just short of bruising his skin, Angelina and Billy Bob–style, minus vials of blood.

Even some of the most satisfying "thunder under the covers," as Sir Elton put it, can lead to nervous post-coital interaction, but luckily we shared no heinous silent pauses post-rumpus. Instead, Elliot grabbed me and kissed me quickly several times on the lips, and then my cheeks and forehead. It was crazy but it almost felt like he was already family. I was so into him that I was afraid I was getting ahead of him in my vision of us as a couple—it took every fiber of my being not to yell out "I love you!" I truly wanted to scream it out, though obviously I would never. I beat down the urge with a reach for the glass of water on my bedside table and swallowed away the need to confess that I was head over heels, besotted, utterly smitten. I stared at his flushed, gorgeous face and could not believe this perfect creature was somehow with me. Then came the inevitable question that I tended to ask out of fear of post-first-sex silence, which instantly made me into every woman in New York.

"What are you thinking about?"

Loser. Bad. Dumb.

"I'm thinking . . . that you are very . . ." He paused.

Gorgeous? Sexy? Fabulous? ". . . Yes . . ."

"Familiar."

I smiled.

"Seriously, you feel like . . . I've known you all my life or something. It's weird," he said. I looked at him and rubbed his side. "In a good way, weird," he added. He moved a strand of hair out of my eyes and looked at me before kissing me again.

My alarm clock sounded the next morning for my first day of work; Randy wanted me to get my feet wet during the crickets period of the holidays, when no one was around and I could ease in, and Elliot and I could barely move we were so wearied from the mad passion of the weekend. The sheets were in a tightly knotted ball and there was raw mattress beneath me.

"Wow, we must have really done some damage; there's exposed mattress." He smiled and, shocker of all shockers, started to make the bed. As IF Tim would have ever lifted a finger; it was always me running around to the other side and back again, flattening out every last crease so you could bounce a quarter off it. With two pairs of hands, it was so much easier! And really having two people, not just feigning couplehood and then truly feeling alone. As the white sheet billowed above the bed before we matted it down, I had to blink back tears in my eyes. Sherry Von was wrong—I did find someone. Someone who seemed perfect for me. And even if he dumped me, he was proof that I was capable of falling in love again. I just hoped he wouldn't shatter my heart into a trillion tiny shards.

41

"Why is divorce so expensive? Because it's worth every penny."

A
fter we got dressed in a hurried frenzy and walked out onto Fifth Avenue, Elliot's pager started going off.

"Jeez, I thought the art folk don't rise until noon! Kiki said Lyle's always still asleep when she leaves his apartment at ten!" I stuck my arm out, praying I'd get lucky enough to find a taxi.

"Holly, wait one sec—I have to talk to you about something—"

Suddenly a cab pulled up next to a mound of snow and a woman hopped out. I thanked her, which I always did, and then wondered why I always thanked people when they were simply getting out at their destination.

"Yay! Free cab! That was easy." I turned to kiss Elliot good-bye. "Wait, did you want to tell me something?"

"Come on, lady!" shouted the driver in a thick Middle Eastern accent. He followed his command by leaning on his horn. Nice.

"Go ahead," Elliot said, kissing me on the cheek. "We'll talk later."

On the ride downtown I was so elated from the magical blur

of the last forty-eight hours that I wasn't even nervous about beginning work.

When I arrived I did get a sudden minisurge of anxiety about the unknown new chapter and hoped my audition press release for the job wasn't the only good one I could pull out. Tristin came out to greet me, wearing a Band-Aid for a skirt, then gave me the grand tour, including the coffee machine, which was very key due to the weekend with Elliot, which had netted me probably four hours of sleep a night. That's the thing about dating: you're trying to not snore, not even breathe, or God forbid fart. I drank three cups to get out of my comatose state. Half the people weren't even there, and as I walked by Randy's office, my wave to her was greeted with a brisk smile while she talked on the phone.

We arrived at my desk, which was against a huge window and right next to Tristin's. My giant clear iMac was such a vision of joy, I almost hugged it—I almost didn't trust people who preferred PCs. After I pounded the java, we hit the supply room. Move over, Staples. I got excited just looking at the reams of colored paper, notebooks, pens galore, tape, even Magic Markers. I got so much loot, it took three trips up the aluminum staircase to get it to my desk. And on the last journey, I could not fit by the guy who was heading down as I headed up.

"You must be Holly Talbott," he said in a serious tone, all business. "Sean Greene."

"Yes, hi, nice to meet you," I said, managing to shake his hand, despite the piles of stuff in my arms. "I'm so sorry, I'm raiding your supply closet, it's like the first day of school."

"Let me help you," he said, relieving me of three boxes of rainbow paper clips, fluorescent Post-Its, and a desk calendar.

"Thank you so much, you are such a rock star," I said, suddenly feeling dumb. "I guess I have to stop saying that as a substitute for 'you're the best' now, since you actually know real rock stars."

We landed at my desk and plopped my loot on the table. He smiled at me, said, "See you around," and walked down the hall.

"Holly, we have our staff meeting now and you're gonna get all your artists including The Saints, that new hot hot hot Brooklyn band," said Tristin. "You are gonna love love love them."

After the meeting, which seemed to last an eternity, I left with the files and stacks of demos for my three new bands and hit the phones, calling all the managers to introduce myself and make appointments to meet them for lunch. I also phoned all the tour managers to get dates for New York shows so I could invite all my editor friends and get the ball rolling.

Just then, Noah Greene, *el presidente* and cofounder of the label with Sean, walked by me and stopped to look me over.

"Soooo, you're the new Dartmouth chick we hired. I thought it was a barnyard up there in New Hampshire! Who knew a smartypants could be so cute?" He walked off before I could say a word. I was in a state of shock. I think that was some form of un-kosher sexual harassment or at the very least extremely unprofessional behavior, but since I hadn't heard talk of a pube in his Coke or whatever Clarence Thomas did, I went back to work, semi-weirded out, but also flattered. I drafted a release for The Saints, whose album was "dropping" in three months but who already had a rising hit leaked on the Internet, making my job cake. The day flew by and I called my friend Maggie, who had been in production with me at *Paper* and was now at *Spin*.

"Mag-dogs!"

"Holland? Holy shit, how are you?"

"I'm in PR for Celestial."

"No way!"

"Way. I switched to the other side. I know it's like D.A.s who sell out and go defend rapists. But not."

"No, I meant no way that you're working at all. Didn't you marry some hedge fund dude?"

"Um . . . yeah, well, we actually split up. My son's in school, so I thought I'd get back to work. It's just three days, so it's really great."

"Awesome! But wait—how are the creepy Greene brothers?"

"They may be slimeballs, but they have a killer ear."

We ended up talking for thirty minutes, and by the wrap-up, she had agreed to run a piece. Success!

I came home exhausted to find gorgeous flowers waiting.

"I miss you already. I'll call you when I'm back from the red state. Dinner on Friday? Or Saturday? Or both? Elliot."

I smiled, elated. Despite my insanely busy day, whenever I had a nanosecond of downtime, I'd think of him and get that incredible jolt all over again. It was so much fun to remember and re-remember those moments, drawing from a memory bank of something better than gold bars. I was so enamored I couldn't wait to refill my stash of Elliot memories by making new ones that weekend.

Before bed, Miles called again for a chat, long-distance tuck-in, and songs.

"You sound happy, Mom!" I was amazed he could notice a change in me through the phone wire. Maybe I'd been too mopey before.

"I do? Well, I am happy."

The next day I was swamped again and the morning flew. I hadn't even thought of lunch the day before, and I couldn't be-lieve a chowhound like *moi* had become one of those losers who claimed they "forgot to eat," but I did. But the first-day nerves had subsided by the second day, and by 2:00 p.m. I was starving. I walked by Randy's office; she was eating a cheese danish (I rarely saw her without one), sitting with Tristin reviewing album cover photography for Rotting Corpses, a Brazilian death-metal act whose single was called "Dig Up (My Grave)." I nervously crept in the doorway and they both looked up as if to say *What?*

"Um, Randy, could I ever, do you mind if I um, just . . . dash across the street and grab a sandwich?" Their brows furrowed as if I were speaking Farsi. I felt stupid or, as Kiki used to write, stoopid.

"Uh, why don't you just take your lunch hour?" said Randy.

I'd been out of the workforce for so long, that I only remembered my assistant days when I'd been forced to eat at my keyboard or starve. But even though I'd been doing nothing but mommying for six years, my position was high level enough to merit a real lunch. I grabbed a falafel and walked the streets, wandering into cool little shops I'd never seen before. Thinking of Elliot and his cute note, the harsh pavement beneath my boots might as well have been clouds.

At work the next day Noah Greene came in and put his hand on my shoulder.

"Hey you—come in my office."

I nervously followed him up to the third floor to the brothers' lair, which I hadn't seen yet.

"Wow, this is amazing," I said, scanning the Warhols and Lichtensteins on the wall. "Your art is fantastic."

"Thanks. We hired a top consultant. She gets us the best

shit," he bragged, gesturing to an amazing Motherwell behind his couch. Then he walked to his bathroom door and opened it. "Check it out, I got a Jasper Johns over the pot." Nice.

Back in his office, he flopped onto a big Eames lounge chair, his crocodile boots up on the matching ottoman.

"I know this great art adviser, Elliot Smith. Do you know him?" I asked.

"Like the singer? No. And I know everyone in the biz."

"Really? I know he works with Lyle Spence a lot."

"I've bought tons and tons of shit from Lyle. But never heard of Smith."

Oh, well. I thought I could score Elliot a new fat-cat client. But before I could butter him up further, Noah changed the subject.

"So, good job with this *Spin* piece. How'd you pull that off? I had some broad here two years who barely got what you got in three days."

"I know this guy Matt Sevin and suspected he'd like the album, and he did." While there clearly weren't fireworks love-wise with the golden sneaker–clad hipster, I had definitely still felt comfortable sending him the tunes. "It's a small world, you know."

"I like you. You can write, too—the press release is terrific. The chick in the marketing department copied parts of it verbatim for the sales force."

"I saw. I'm flattered."

"They like you, these people. Editors, people around here. I want you to take on another act. We're signing this young broad, she'll be our Britney, but not a fucking thing like her—she's like an anti-Britney. Thinking chick. Like you. She's called Casey Sinclair, and she's a beauty. Hot little body on her. You're gonna help us make her a star."

"Wow, that is great, thank you so much."

"You better kick ass for me."

"I will, Noah, I swear. I will kick ass."

The following day Noah gave me the still-unfinished demo; he was grasping it in his little pig-in-a-blanket-sized fingers and slid it conspicuously across my desk and walked off.

42

Q. Why do married people gain weight?
A. Because single people go to the fridge, don't see anything they
want, and go to bed. Married people go to bed, don't see anything
they want, and then go to the fridge.

I celebrated New Year's Eve solo, as Elliot was seeing his family upstate, but truth be told, I never liked it anyway; all the forced merriment and drunkenness always felt like too much pressure. It was kind of like Saturday nights; I always had more fun on an unexpected Tuesday than when everyone else was geared up for paaartay!

Miles came home the next day, and I was so excited to see him, I was pacing by the window.

"Mom!" He ran to me and we stayed up way past his bedtime, talking about ski school and looking at all the Christmas gifts his dad and grandma had gotten him, a sea of Spider-Man everything. We popped popcorn and played the match game with his new special set printed with pairs of Marvel comics characters. I always played to win and yet he beat me three games in a row. Either my brain was going to mush or my kiddo was darn smart.

"How is your new job?" he asked.

"I love it," I responded truthfully. Being at Celestial really gave me a sense of purpose, and I had fun being down there. I paused for a second, wondering whether or not to share the news of Elliot with him. On the one hand I wanted to protect him, but on the flipside as an only child, and a mature one at that, I wanted to share with him my excitement.

"There is something else new, honey," I ventured slowly. "Some*one* new, actually: my new friend, Elliot."

"Can I meet him?" he asked without missing a beat. Phew. I figured Avery was on frigging family vacation with him so I could at least have him meet Elliot.

"Sure. I'd love that! I have our *Nutcracker* tickets for January fourth. Would you want him to join us?"

"Yeah! I want Elliot to come, too."

Elliot called me when he got back and I downloaded all the work news, including Miles's request.

"I'm honored," said Elliot. "And excited—I haven't been since I was a kid."

"See? Tim said he never went and that it's very 'fanook' to take my son to the ballet. He doesn't want him pirouetting down the soccer field. Please."

"Fanook?"

"It's what they called that dead gay guy on *The Sopranos*."

"Oh, come on."

"I know! He's living in the Triassic Period like Sherry Von."

Elliot came across the park to pick us up and then go back to Lincoln Center. He wanted time to chat with Miles before the curtain, so we gabbed in the car (Elliot was surprisingly well versed in the various Power Rangers) and shared a quick mozzarella and tomato sandwich from the designer concession stand before taking our seats. We whispered as the lights dimmed and I almost melted when Miles wanted Elliot to sit in the middle. The vast room was dark, except for a spotlight on the orchestra conductor on the stand. Elliot and I held hands as Tchaikovsky's overture began against a curtain of a snowy landscape shining with glittery whiteness. I leaned down to look at Miles's face, which was transfixed.

The little girls and boys danced the party scene with the parents. The creepy cloaked uncle came in with the Nutcracker, and the scene with the rats had all the well-dressed children in the audience giggling with joy. Next was my favorite part, the snowflakes. The delicate pointed toes lightly leaped and patted the floor silently as the almost-real snow fell from the staged sky, making a sparkly blanket of shimmering white across the New York State Theater stage. The precision and synchronicity of Balanchine's steps never ceased to give me chills, and when I looked at both Elliot and Miles, they had matched rapt eyes focused on the leaps and twirls before them. Next to them, taking in the glistening blue-white glow and fairy-light prances, I was in heaven.

At intermission, we walked out onto the promenade to score some M&M'S for Miles, who spied a classmate from St. Sebastian's.

"Wylie!" he yelled, and sprinted to his pal. They talked about their vacations (Wylie was on safari, La Singhita) as Elliot and I held our place in line for snacks nearby. I had been bursting because we hadn't had the chance to maul each other in a week but obviously had to restrain myself affection-wise in front of my son.

"He's a special kid," Elliot said of Miles. "Amazing."

"He likes you, too."

"Amazing mom, as well," he added.

"I missed you," I said, and he stroked my arm the way he had the weekend before.

"I missed you, too."

We both sighed simultaneously, in echoed desire to beam, *Star Trek*–style, into the same bed.

"*Holly* . . ." The way he said my name, in an almost whisper, made me feel so emotional about the excited newness of this, of how this man walked into my life and helped me rebuild myself, that I got caught up in a tidal wave of the moment.

"Elliot, I love you."

Shhhhit.

So awash with blinding adoration was I that I fumbled big-time. I made the worst mistake possible. I committed the dater's cardinal sin: I blurted out the words that send men running and screaming. It hung in the air, and as soon as it was out I wanted it to be carried away by the spinning whoosh of a gliding tutu, but it wasn't. And the worst part was the reaction: Elliot leaned in and kissed my cheek. I felt a sinking pit of utter humiliation and embarrassment, suddenly wondering if this whole thing may have all been a fantasia construction in my head. Maybe we were just having sex like regular grown-ups. Maybe I was living this whole overactive imagination–spun lie. I pretended to be totally fine and blasé about my verbal diarrhea. We were next in line, and with a smile on my face, I ordered our candy and sodas. I was nonchalant and normal, but it was all a total Meryl Streep blocking the pounding fear that shook my whole body.

We said good night by the fountain outside, where throngs of people were rushing for cabs. I spied one and we split pronto. As soon as we got home and I finished Miles's bedtime stories, I dialed Kiki, fingers shaking.

"Hi, it's Holly. I know you just got back from France tonight and you're totally jet-lagged 'cause it's 3:00 a.m. Paris time, but I am freaking out."

I relayed, in a state of panic, the details of my royal screwup.

"No! You didn't."

"Yes, Kiki, I did. Please don't freak me out even more. Jesus."

"I told you never to do that!" she admonished.

"KIKI! I know, okay? I effed up hugely, I'm aware. I'm just asking what the hell do I do now?"

"Okay okay okay. Damage control. Let's think. . . . Okay, I've got it: Maybe, you can show him you say that to a lot of people all the time, like how British people say 'darling' and stuff like that. Why don't you say 'I love you' to, like, the cab driver."

"Great, thanks," I muttered, rolling my eyes, with even deeper alarm at my goof.

"Or—to me, you know, when you talk to us, just always say 'I love you' or 'loveya.' Throw it around and stuff so he knows it doesn't really pack that big a punch for you."

"Do I have Tourette's? What was I THINKING? I am losing my mind. It was like I was out of it for a second. On drugs. I can't believe this. See? He is drugs to me! My mind is MUSH."

"Honestly, it's not that bad."

I was mute.

"You know what? It's not, Holly, think about it: You were just honest, and frankly, if he can't take that or wigs about it, then he's not the one. He's not. If he can't deal with a little Hallmark-style confessional, then fuck him."

"But I really like him," I said, starting to cry. "I think I do love him."

"Honey, he's so fucking into you," Kiki assured me. "I saw him looking at you at that Seaport party when you said that you hate mimes—his face was lit up like a Christmas tree, he was so enraptured."

"I don't know. . . ."

"The guy is enamored."

"*I'm* enamored. I can't think about anything else. I'm writing my work stuff and I drift off."

"That's normal—"

"People always say the beginning is so amazing and exciting, but I feel ill. Not when I'm with him, but all the time we're apart I'm spazzing about *will this last? Does he miss me? Does he love me? Will he be my husband?*"

"He'll say it. Soon. Trust me, his 'I love you' is in the mail. It's on its way."

"You think so?"

"Oh, yeah. For sure."

"Why is 'I'm crazy about you' just not the same? He said that in bed the other night."

"Because it's not. Be patient. It's in the mail."

43

"Men marry women with the hope they'll never change. Women marry men with the hope they will change. Invariably they are both disappointed."

—*Albert Einstein*

The postman was delayed.

After a day of agonizing pacing, Elliot left a voice mail.

"Hi, sweetie, it's me. I just found out I have to go to Geneva for a few days. But when I come back I really want to go out together. Maybe that new Broadway show they gushed about in the *Times*. Okay, I miss you a lot already and also I . . . have something I want to tell you. Have a good night—"

Though *sweetie* sounded promising, I was still a wreck. Kiki came over for Chinese order-in and to play with Miles. She had brought back a bag of French loot for us from Bonpoint and Collette. After ripping open our presents, we sat around a big puzzle of the United States and attempted to forge sections of our great nation but only managed to piece together chunks of each time zone, floating in an ocean of carpet beneath.

"So what do you think it means?" I asked Kiki, who had just listened to my saved voice mail. "I need analysis."

"Oh, look, Miles, this one goes with Kentucky," said Kiki, expertly snapping the jigsaw pieces together, *Rain Man*-style. "Okay, so cute he's into Broadway like you. You practically had to drag Tim. And helloooo, I think we both know what he's going to 'tell you.' You have nothing to worry about!"

"Really?" I wasn't so sure. "I think the axe is going to fall. I totally flipped him out."

"Nah. Clearly he wants to confess his undying *amore*."

The phone rang. Maybe it was him?

I went to screen but the caller ID was blocked.

"Hello?"

"Hi, Holland Talbott, please?" a man's voice asked.

"This is she," I responded, wanting to shoot all telemarketers.

"Hi, this Dan Allen from *Law & Order*. You bid on a cameo a while ago from Lancelot?"

"Oh! Yes!" I looked at Kiki with a huge smile. I had totally forgotten.

"Is that Elliot?" she asked.

I shook my head as I fumbled for a pencil to scribble down the details of my call time. It was a night shoot right by the Staten Island Ferry, one of the ripped-from-the-headlines episodes based on the ferry crashing and killing all those people 'cause the captain guy was on crack and heroin. I would be one of the said victims. And, he added, while gushing blood and screaming in horror, I would even get a line: "Where is my husband! I can't find my husband!" Gee, how fitting.

I hung up the phone, floored. "Remember the lot Tim bid on for the Lancelot event ages ago? That was the *Law & Order* people! I'm shooting this the day after tomorrow! I can go after work, so can you hang here with Miles?"

"What do you say, kiddo? How bout a pizza party with Aunt Kiki? We can watch *Spider-Man*."

"Yaaaaay!"

Flushing nervous thoughts about Elliot from my head, I plunged into work, which ended up being a great equalizer in terms of putting myself together about my blunder. If a gal's not working, she could be subsumed by second thoughts on every date comment or gesture, a slave to the mental rewind button, ending up a Monday morning quarterback replaying every move, wondering where she'd fumbled. But Celestial was so crazed all day, I didn't have the luxury of worrying about my love life.

I was jamming away at my computer with my headphones on, listening to Casey Sinclair, who may have had the bod of Britney, but she taught me something about first impressions, as her throaty wail was more Fiona Apple than bubble-gum pop. I positioned her more as a clever songwriter, playing down her looks, and put the finishing touches on her bio and press release while carefully studying the clock. It was well after 5:00 and I was the last breathing soul in the building. Or so I thought.

"Hey you, Dartmouth," I faintly heard over the track I suggested to be the single. I took off my earphones and looked up to find Noah standing there. "What're you doing still working? Everyone else here is out the door at 4:59."

"Oh, I just had some stuff I wanted to wrap up for Miss Casey. She's really good. I'm sending all this to her manager tonight."

"Randy cc'd me on the new stuff on the Saints CD," he said slyly. "Not bad. Not bad at all." He winked. I gave him a tight smile and turned back to my keyboard. I felt a strong satsisfaction that I was getting positive feedback and knew deep down I was back in my groove with writing about music and that my absence hadn't made me even remotely out of the loop. For this professional go-round, motherhood offered me perspective; I never stressed like a crazy person the way I had in my early twenties. Miles centered me far more than anything else could, and now with work on top of that and possibly a boyfriend I was nuts about, finally the dots of my life seemed to start to fall back in a line that made sense again.

After finishing, I reported to my location farther downtown. It all seemed very glamorous—there were trailers lined up, huge floodlights, people with headsets everywhere, and a craft services catering tent with a smorgasbord of my kind of food.

I called Kiki to check in on her and Miles; they were in the kitchen waiting for the microwave to finish popping the popcorn.

"Have fun!" Kiki wished me. "Be a good dead body! I guess that means: don't move."

"Okay, I won't. But I'm not dead; I have a line, remember? I'm in the big time."

"Don't start scripting your Emmy speech just yet."

"Ha. Can I talk to Miles?"

I wished him good night and he promised to go straight to bed after *Spider-Man*. I felt so happy that the two people I loved most were together; I just prayed Elliot could stay part of our little family.

I walked to the corner of Whitehall and Pearl, where I was instructed to knock on the trailer door marked "MAKEUP," which I found instantly. Inside were two gorgeous gay guys, who had me step into their ministudio.

"We're gonna make you a beautiful wound, my dear," said one laughing, who had spikey platinum hair and about ten leather bracelets. "Sit down." He pounded the back of a chair, which I plopped into as instructed and sat quietly as he began to clean my face. Only to add blood to it. I would have thought someone could just spray me with that fake vampire red stuff or even ketchup, but it was a painstaking process that took more than an hour.

"You're all set, Holly!" He turned me around to the mirror and I started laughing—but it was nervous laughter.

"You're . . . oh my gosh, you're an artist. This is amazing!" I beheld the scarily realistic gash on my forehead, red liquid oozing down my face.

"We'll refresh that blood before the shoot."

I hung out marveling at my battered visage for a few more minutes until a team of people came in, all with fake blood, for retouches before their close-ups. A sweet-faced production assistant led me to Wardrobe, where I was given a pre-splattered beige coat to throw over my outfit.

I was walked down to the set, which was blindingly bright despite the nighttime shoot, with high-wattage lights everywhere; it was surreal and exciting and everything I'd hoped it would be. I was introduced to the director, who placed me with a bunch of extras, who, like me, would be staggering in pain toward ambulances after our ferry crashed.

"Okay, people, let's do this!" he shouted through a speaker.

I would be panicked, shouting and sobbing, then wrapped up by the blanket of an EMT worker. Got it. We rehearsed only once and then were instructed to take our places.

"And . . . action!"

"Where is my husband!" I wailed in distress, turning my head in all directions in desperation. "I can't find my husband!"

The medic threw a blanket around me and helped me into the ambulance.

"And . . . cut!" yelled the director. "Great. Let's try it again."

"Was that okay?"

"Sure. We just want to get a few takes. Love the panic."

"Okay." Yay. This was the most exciting thing ever.

"Action!"

We did it two more times with various technical pauses between each, and somehow being part of my favorite show was so exciting to me. I tapped into my emotional well and got more and more worked up for each take. I was amazed at the irony that here I was, bruised and blood splattered, a physical echo of my year from hell, all because Tim had gotten me this gift. It was incredible, really, especially considering my line. Finally, on the fifth and final one, I seriously delivered.

"Where is my husband! I can't find my husband!"

I even produced real tears! Where's that Emmy?

"Cut! Terrific."

"Thank you so much, this was so much fun!"

I was "wrapped," as they say, bid adieu to the nice people I'd spent the last few hours with, and started to walk north in hopes of finding a cab. Forgetting that I looked like I'd been bludgeoned by several blunt objects, I was at first alarmed when the rare pedestrian looked at me aghast with terror. The streets were empty since the financial district is abuzz only during the day, but almost every window in the looming buildings was lit. Worker bees inside were still toiling away for their various investment banks.

As I paused for a moment, looking skyward at the glass tops of the vertical structures that seemed to puncture the clouds, I heard something. A voice. A very familiar voice.

"So, Tracy, let me know, okay—"

"Okay, Elliot . . ."

I thought I had just been struck by lightning. Or was in cardiac arrest. Or got in a Staten Island Ferry crash. I ducked behind a humongous work of public art, a gargantuan sculpture to shield me.

No.

No! Not again. My breathing mounted and surged into a full-on hyperventilation. I stood there motionless, like a squirrel in the road knowing a Hummer would run it over in seconds. But I would not be some mowed rodent. Maybe I didn't save 10 percent for myself. Maybe I threw in everything, every fiber of my being, prematurely professing love and physically expressing my unedited adoration in every doting squeeze and dewy-eyed glance. That's what I do. But unlike my Brooklyn beholding of Tim and Avery's encircled limbs, I was stronger this time. I wasn't going to cower behind the sculpture and sneak home this time. Instead I stormed out from behind the behemoth.

"Geneva, huh?" I stood, eyes ablaze, choking back tears.

"Tracy" looked at me like I was insane and walked away, as I stood quivering. Elliot took a step closer to me.

"Holly? Oh my God, are you okay?"

"I thought you were on a business trip—"

"I was. I got back early. I was just going to call you—are you hurt?"

"What are you doing here, Elliot?" I yelled, volume rising.

For a moment, he said nothing. Great. Busted.

He took a deep breath. He looked crushed and reached out to me, but I backed away. "Holly, I tried to tell you but we kept getting interrupted and then there was never a good time. Do we need to get you to a doctor?"

"No. It's fake blood. I was just on *Law & Order*. It's a long story."

"What? What are you talking about?"

"Let me ask the questions," I said, trying to force back tears. "As you know, after everything I've been through, I really, really can't abide lies. Now, what is going on?"

Elliot exhaled and looked at his feet. "Holly, I have been in agony over this—"

I started to cry. Just drop the bomb, Elliot. Was he not really divorced? Did he have a kid with a supermodel? What?

"I'm not an art consultant," he said, soberly. "I work for a hedge fund."

You could have knocked me over with a *BusinessWeek*.

"What?"

"I wanted to tell you. I swear. I was only at the gallery that night because Lyle is my brother. Everything I know about art is from him."

"LYLE IS YOUR BROTHER?" Now I was in surreal overdrive. "Are you kidding me?"

"No, I—we have different fathers but grew up together in the same home. We have the same mom, he's my brother. And in this crazy coincidence, when I met you in the park that time, I never thought I'd see you again but I'd noticed you and how you were with your son and it made an impression on me. I had been on my phone but was put on hold, and I couldn't help but overhear your conversation about how you would never ever date anyone in finance ever again and I thought to myself, wow, that might be the only woman in this city who thinks that," he said, breathlessly. "Then, astonishingly, you guys turned up at my brother's gallery, and once I started talking to you, I liked you. A lot. I remembered you'd said that and so without even thinking I just blurted out that I was in the art world."

"I can't even believe this. You're not an art consultant? You're a goddamn hedgie?"

"Listen, Holly, I really don't want to lose you. I—"

"Forget it. How could I ever trust you again?" I spied a taxi driving by. "You're way too good a liar. You deserve an Emmy for that performance, Elliot. You should be on *Law & Order*!"

And with that, I hailed the cab and screeched uptown.

44

"Marriage is not a word, it's a sentence."

O f course my strong front dissolved like aspirin the moment we turned the corner. I began to sob so convulsively, I seriously thought the driver was going to take me straight to the ER.

"Miss, you hurt? You want to go hospital?"

"Oh, no, no, it's just makeup," I said, bawling.

"But, miss, why you cry? You hurt?"

"I'm fine, really, thank you—"

I looked out the window on the FDR Drive, watching the boats along the East River against the night sky, then the creepy former insane asylum on its own island, abandoned and crumbling. The pain of yet another heartbreak, raw and crushing, pushed its way up my chest into my throat, where what felt like a Wilson tennis ball was lodged in my esophageal passage. I had truly thought Elliot was everything I'd ever wanted:

ELLIOT MATH
NetFlix junkie
+Colin Firth accent
π(little gold glasses)
/identical taste buds
=male me

When I got home, my red face and full head wound struck a sound of alarm in my doorman, whom I quietly assured I was fine. I landed on my floor and opened the door. I just hoped and prayed that Kiki, the only person I felt I could turn to, was not in on this.

"I had no idea. NONE," swore Kiki. She was shaking her head in shock. "Jesus Christ, are you okay?"

"It's the makeup from the show," I said, wiping a tear and sitting down.

"Lyle just called and said Elliot is despondent and said he never told me because Elliot made him cover for him and then it just dragged out. I'm so pissed. I ripped him a new one, if you want to know the truth. I'm ripshit."

"I don't know what the truth is anymore," I sputtered in a sad daze.

"Listen, Holly," Kiki said, kneeling down next to me. "It was a shitty thing to do. Elliot lied, they both lied. But . . . the feelings that were there are true."

"I have to go to bed. This is, was between me and Elliot, so I don't want you and Lyle mired in this—"

"Hey, I've got news for you: I am mired in it. You are like my sister, and if you want me to never see him again—"

"No, that's ridiculous, we're adults here. I don't need high school–style solidarity."

Kiki followed me to my room, where I put on my pajamas and climbed into bed. She sat beside me on the comforter. "Holly. It was an assholic thing for him to do. Lying is always bad. But in his defense, you wouldn't have even given him a chance if he'd told the truth, right?"

"I don't know. I don't know. I'm just tired. Of dating. Of men. Everything. I have to go to sleep."

Kiki leaned down and gave me a hug. "Call me in the morning."

After dropping Miles off at school, I took the train, zombie-like, downtown to work. I was amused that all the craziness of the awful previous night had played out with wounds all over my face. How perfect: an outward manifestation of what was now bleeding on the inside.

At work, Randy and Tristin immediately asked me if I was okay due to my sullen demeanor, but I shrugged everything off and just said I was tired and hit my desk, where I jammed in a trance for hours straight without a break. The one silver lining was that I was in a deep groove with the writing, and every e-mail I got back from Noah and Randy was a cyber thumbs-up.

I felt distant not only from the world I'd been in as Tim's wife, but also from the new self I'd forged in my time alone. The only thing I could do was throw myself into quality time with Miles and kicking absolute ass at work, which I did, arriving early, right after Miles's school started, and staying late when he had soccer after school. When I saw Elliot's number on the called ID, I blew it off. When I got a voice mail from him, I deleted it before I could even hear what he had to say. I couldn't let myself be open to heartbreak again. I was almost a robot; that's how much my grief and surprise about his revelation rocked me. I couldn't imagine that someone I had bonded with that deeply had a whole other life than the one presented to me.

I stayed home and made dinner for Miles every night, or took him ice-skating or to a museum. I did everything that I had been meaning to do, and got into a good solid routine with work, Miles, and his school. One night I came home and found a delivery at my doorstep. It was a Kermit the Frog felt muppet with a little sign that simply said, "I miss you." I took the sign off, threw it in the trash, gave the toy to Miles, and flushed thoughts of Elliot out of my mind as hard as I could.

I tried to focus on myself. I did things I loved. I finally made a dent in the leaning-tower-of-Pisa-style stack of books to be read on my bedside table. The more I disappeared into the stories of other people in other eras, the more I melted in dreams of faraway lives not my own. I watched countless movies, took long walks to and from Miles's school, and worked up a storm. I was fully immersed in the writing and the music. Sometimes, when I heard an amazing song, it would trigger thoughts of Elliot. But even though I was subdued as the weeks passed, I felt that eventually things would all be okay. I wasn't ready to get back out there just yet, but when the time came, I knew I'd be all right. My defenses would be up this time.

About two months after the fateful night in the financial district, Kiki came over to cook dinner with Miles and me. I had seen her for lunch two weeks before, and she had attempted to make a plea on Elliot's behalf, but I shut her down so quickly, she knew not to mention his name. So when she walked in and said she had to tell me something, I swiftly replied, "It better not have to do with Elliot."

"It doesn't. It has to do with his brother," she said, smiling as she took my hand. "Lyle proposed to me last night," she said, clearly trying to hold back her excitement. "We're getting married."

"Oh my gosh!" I screamed, getting up to hug her, despite my utter and complete shock. "Are you sure?! You've only known each other five months. . . ."

"I know. If I were you, I'd tell me not to. It's crazy, but Holly,

I've never been so sure of anything. This guy is . . . everything to me. With you and Miles and my family, of course. I just love him so much."

"I've never seen you so happy."

We hugged again and cried.

"Can you believe it?" she asked, wiping a tear. "Me? The one who never wanted to remarry. And now I can't imagine not being with Lyle forever. It's so weird."

"I'm elated for you, really."

"Will you be my maid of honor?"

"I'd be honored."

45

"I just got back from the best trip. I drove my husband to the air-port."

The small wedding was set for two months away. Between total work immersion and spending all my free time with Miles, I helped Kiki gear up for her intimate nup-tials. While she regularly planned events for a living, her own wedding was much more of a challenge to be original. Plus, she was so busy with her clients that I decided to repay the favor of her being my social quarterback by taking over some elements of the wedding, for example, all the paper: invitations, table cards, place cards, and menus. I'd found a hundred-year-old letterpress by South Street Seaport years back during my jury duty break, and when I showed Kiki the proofs, she ran her finger over the delicate grooves of the embossed lettering and got dewy-eyed.

"Holly, this is beyond anything I could have imagined. I re-member when Sherry Von insisted on her Dempsey & Carroll engraving and the invitation looked like everyone else, and this is so . . . me."

Next she enlisted me to be the sole judge and jury on her dress.

"I'm thinking Vera is so omni," she said as we hit the Seventy-eighth Street salon last after a tour of every other bridal atelier in town. And yet, the second we walked upstairs and Kiki saw what would be The Dress, she knew she had to have it. She disappeared into the dressing room, and I almost burst into tears when the bride emerged. She was so transcendently beautiful in her ethereal lace gown, I thought she'd float away. I knew that Lyle would melt into a Wicked Witch of the West–style puddle on the floor when he saw her.

I just hoped I could hold it together seeing Elliot, whom I hadn't laid eyes on since confronting him. Whenever I thought of him, I got a pressing sadness in my chest, but I strongly forced it all out of my mind. Only when I was straightening up Miles's room and caught a glimpse of that smiling green froggie did I occasionally wonder if maybe he was truly a good person despite that lie.

"Holl, you okay?" she asked, looking concerned. I nodded; I didn't want to ruin the sparkling moment with glum selfish thoughts on her big night, mixing my blue state with her shining white.

"You're stressed about seeing Elliot, aren't you?"

As usual, she nailed it, but we were adults and I had to suck it up and be strong. I'd gotten over a marriage, I could get through this. Or so I thought . . . why was it so hard to flush thoughts of our time together out of my mind when it had all been such a brief whirlwind? Well, I figured, a real tornado takes only a few seconds too and ravages all those homes, taking eons to rebuild.

"Okay, I know I said we wouldn't talk about this," Kiki said, taking my hand. "But he's a great guy, like heart of fucking gold, he feels awful about lying to you, but he knew you wouldn't give him the time of day after your monologues against the Wall Street Boys Club."

I looked down, comforted at least that he felt guilt, something Tim was lacking during our demise.

"Holly, listen to me: Elliot's *amazing*. You were onto something. Remember when you told me he felt so familiar to you? Well, that was the tip of the iceberg: He *is* you."

"How do you know he's me?"

"Where do I start?" Kiki laughed. "He uses red felt-tip pens just like you. He quotes Woody Allen. He bounds up a flight of stairs two at a time. At the movies, he holds up the Jujubes against the screen to see the color and then chucks the black ones."

"Oh my God, I do that!" I marveled. "I never trusted anyone who liked licorice."

"Give him another chance," begged Kiki, squeezing my hand.

"And I guess I climb stairs like that?" I thought aloud.

"Holl: he is your mirror."

I was just so gun-shy after Tim that I was too freaked out; I'd sealed myself off emotionally and wasn't sure I could feel vulnerable again for a while.

A few weeks later, I connected with Kiki's closest friend from college, Eliza, to throw her an over-the-top girls' bachelorette party, per Kiki's request. It would be tiny: Me, Eliza, Kiki's awesome cousins Marina and Lauren from L.A., and her two gay best friends, Stan and Andy, whom Kiki called "Standy." Eliza and I labored to get the itinerary just right, and the night before the wedding, in lieu of a rehearsal dinner, we gathered in Kiki's apartment (which had basically become just a clothes locker since she'd met Lyle) to kick off our friend's last twenty-four hours as a single gal. I couldn't believe she was getting remarried. She'd been split from Hal for two years and yet the whole unraveling all seemed so recent. But because her marriage to my ex-brother-in-law had been so difficult and so dead for so long, I knew she was ready for the real thing, despite her original claims to have wanted sexy romps with young studs.

Just then, the gang burst in the door and Stan shrieked.

"Girl, are you trying to have guys try and do you tonight?" he asked. "'Cause they will be all over you like hair on a weasel."

"Hey, I'll be married, not dead! Ain't no crime to turn some heads while I'm still unattached, right?" Kiki joked, excited for her romp on the town. "So what's on the naughty agenda?" she asked, her eyes sparkling with mischief.

"Well," said Eliza, shooting me a look, "First we thought we'd have some COCKtails . . ."

We went in the kitchen and I almost dropped the tray I was laughing so hard. It was filled with Andy's attempt to knock off Rosa Mexicano's orgasmic frozen pomegranate margarita. But in each was a straw with a penis head at the top with a hole that you suck through.

"AHHHH!" screamed Kiki when we emerged with the cock-topped cocktails. "NO WAY!"

We all died laughing, Stan turned up some vintage Madonna, and Andy took out a shopping bag from Ricky's filled with X-rated adornments.

"Okay, girls," said Andy. "As we all know, any good virgin bride must have a veil . . ."

He produced a long white tulle veil with flowers at the top. It looked like any other veil except that it had about fifty little plastic penises sewn all over it.

"That is hy-fucking-sterical," Kiki snorted between sips of her indecent beverage.

Kiki's cousins could not contain themselves; they were riotous hyenas, though the dick veil may have thrown semiprim Marina for a loop. We gathered the gang and headed downstairs where our vehicle awaited us; we had booked the Party Hen—a mobile trailer that was covered entirely in feathers with a giant chicken head on the front. It was a rager on wheels. We climbed in and the interior had a disco globe, couches, and a full bar.

"We can just drive around and pick up cuties as we go!" screamed Andy, blissing out.

"Talk about Mobile Party Unit!" said Stan. "I feel like we're rappers. This is awesome."

We all piled in and took off, cruising downtown to Tortilla Flats, a restaurant where everyone got hammered and chowed quesadillas, and then rolled on to karaoke at Winnie's in Chinatown. Everywhere we went people howled laughing as Kiki walked by with her dick-covered tulle. Between drunken Koreans singing unintelligible lyrics, we took turns belting out vintage Bon Jovi and Springsteen, and Stan made us do shots, which I never have been able to do. At about 11:00, we went to Culture Club, the eighties cheesefest. It was packed with hordes including two rival bachelorette bashes, and we all danced up a storm. In the middle of "Safety Dance" I noticed wasted Kiki start to cry.

"What's wrong, Keeks?" I yelled over the music.

"I just—"

Everyone else started to notice her welling eyes.

"I just love you guys so much!" she cried. We all encircled her and hugged and then danced as a gang of football players in a group huddle, faces to the floor, loving our bride and loving the night.

At 12:45, the Hen lay us all home like eggs dropped all over the city, and I got in bed and stared at the ceiling. Despite my fun twentysomething-esque night on the town, over the disco ball and mobile party there hung a little shadow. It grew to a gray little cloud that didn't rain, but certainly hung ominously over my yelps of "Cheers!" Over my best Pat Benatar pipes, it cast a subtle pall of fear. I couldn't believe I would have to summon the strength to see Elliot again, but it was upon me the next day and I'd have to armor up. As I'd sung into the crowded bar, *Love is a battlefield*. I hugged the pillow, remembering when it was him beside me in that very bed, and drifted off to sleep.

46

Husband: I was a fool when I married you!
Wife: Yes, dear, but I was in love and didn't notice.

The next morning was a frenzy of getting ready, putting Miles in his new little suit, and speeding downtown to the venue, the restaurant Chanterelle, where Lyle had taken Kiki to dinner on their first formal date. As we pulled up I felt happy to have Miles as my little coat of armor, but was so nervous I could hardly move as we stepped into the restaurant and looked around at the gathering group of friends and family. I saw a beautiful older woman with incredible green eyes hug Lyle—clearly his mom. I gulped as I surveyed the room. Standy came up and gave me huge hugs. The beauty of the bachelorette party—aside from seeing how ecstatic Kiki was to have her posse together—was to bond with her gang. I felt like I had comrades in the trenches of seeing Elliot again.

Kiki stepped into the room and walked up to the front, where Stan, who was a top florist Kiki had worked with for a gazillion years on all her events, had fashioned a chuppah out of cherry blossoms, with small flickering votives embedded among the branches. As I stared at the beautiful little arch meant to symbolize the new home Kiki and Lyle would build together, out of the corner of my eye, I saw Elliot hug his mom and look over at me. I took a deep breath as acid scorched my tummy, and walked beside Kiki as Elliot followed and stood beside his brother.

It was very casual; everyone took their seats in three small rows that formed a horseshoe shape around the couple, who held hands facing each other in front of the group, with Kiki's rabbi standing in the center.

After the solemn, lovely traditional vows (none of that Brad-and-Jennifer "I swear to give you back massages and make you banana soy milkshakes" nonsense), the two kissed. The rabbi blessed them: "Always follow your bliss. . . ."

Elliot looked at me. I kept staring at the rabbi.

"Always love each other and make every day magical and un-wrap it as the gift that it is. . . ."

I tried to keep facing the rabbi, but my eyes defied me and wandered to Elliot's face. His eyes were transfixed on me in the same gaze that bound me to him in our very short but very intense time together. In that millisecond, I was transported back to those sublime wintery nights, not the gun-shy, scared ones of recent memory. I swallowed hard and looked down, trying with all my might not to cry. I looked back at the rabbi as the tears burned my retinas. I blinked, sending a warm tear down my cheek.

"I now pronounce you man and wife!"

Lyle stomped on the glass and then kissed Kiki, as the guests applauded wildly. After her first kiss as Mrs. Spence, Kiki turned to me. "Thank you for everything, Holly. I love you!"

I hugged her and saw her husband hugging his brother and best man. As we parted and Kiki's mom and Miles came to hug her, I turned to find Elliot beside me.

"Hi—," he said quietly.

"Hi."

"Can you come with me for a second?" he asked.

My chest was pounding. "Um . . ." I looked over and saw Miles taking pictures with the bride. "Okay."

Elliot started walking through the restaurant. I followed him, nervously, to what I supposed would be outside. But he walked me all the way into the back, where I saw a small wooden door. Was this another exit to the street?

It was not.

It was a bathroom.

"Step inside, please," he said, in all seriousness.

"Elliot, what is this? You want me to go in the bathroom?"

"Yes. Please."

Weirded out, I walked past him into the bathroom and he closed the door behind me. There we were: Me. Him. The toilet.

"Can you please explain why you have led me, on my best friend's wedding day, into the crapper?" I asked, arms crossed.

"Yes," he said, and took my hand. "I can. In fact, I have a lot of explaining to do." He walked closer to me and looked at me with those insane eyes. I prayed I could hold together my steely front.

"Holly, I didn't want to say it in some field of flowers or in bed like everyone else. I wanted to take you to the most unromantic room around to tell you: I love you. I am beyond in love you. Anyone can feel in love after incredible sex in bed in a snowstorm. But I feel it now, even after you not speaking to me for months. Even with this horrible vanilla candle here. I can love you in this john. I can love you anywhere. Just let me."

My eyes were so glassy, I could barely see by the aromatherapy candlelight. I was blind and mute.

"Holly. I love you," he said again.

"You do?" I started to tremble as he took a step closer. "Still?"

"Still," he said. "More than ever."

I blinked and more tears rolled down my cheeks. "But you didn't say it back when I—"

"I didn't say it back when you said it because I was caught off guard. I still hadn't told you the truth about my job and I felt awful about lying to you. And . . ." He cleared his throat and looked at me. "I also have never said it to anyone in my life but my ex-wife."

I was stunned. I had said it many times. "You haven't?"

"No. And then when you said it, I thought I did, too, but—"

"I couldn't help it, it just came out in the moment—" I fumbled, still embarrassed.

"I know. But it wasn't just a moment for me. From the moment I saw you and Miles in the park, I knew you were different from anyone I'd met. I feel so bad about what happened and I've been miserable ever since. Could you give me another chance?"

My emotional shield disintegrated instantly. I reached for him, putting his arms around my waist. He hugged me and then put his hands on my cheeks. He leaned in and gave me the number one best kiss in my life: there, by the dripping sink of a restaurant bathroom, I felt home again. And no saccharine, petal-strewn, Mozart-filled oasis could touch our weird and rustic haunt.

When we finally emerged and rejoined the group, flushed and aglow, Kiki and Lyle took a break from pictures and ran to hug us. Elliot saw Miles with Kiki's cousins and went up to him, and Miles gave him a big hug and showed him his new pocket Power Ranger. The food was amazing, the champagne flowed, but more than anything there was a soul and warmth that filled the cherry blossom–filled room. As I looked at Kiki laughing across the table next to Lyle, I was overcome by emotion. Elliot squeezed my hand as I nervously rose to propose a toast.

"I'd like to talk about my friend and sister, Mrs. Kiki Spence,"

I started. The three tables cheered and clapped. "Where can I start? I owe you my life, for one. I've heard men talk about their army buddies and how in the trenches they are cemented to these guys forever. Now, I'm not saying that being a divorcée in New York City is akin to warfare but . . . wait, yes I am. Kiki, you have been with me through everything and are the most loyal, most giving, most accessible—including 3:00 a.m. phone calls—most nurturing person I know. You've been beyond an amazing friend to me, you've been a mother." I blinked back tears, missing my mom, and saw Kiki crying, too. "Lyle, if she takes half as good care of you as she has of me, you will have a life filled with so much laughter, so much happiness, and so much comfort. Kiki, you are like a big warm blanket."

"Cashmere!" she yelled out.

"Yes, cashmere. You calm, and soothe, and warm. We all hear so many jokes about marriage—skeptical quotes and inferences of balls and chains—but I think when it's right, it's the greatest thing in the world. Kiki, I don't know if you remember this, but you sent me a small book after my divorce, with all these funny quotes from Robin Williams and Woody Allen and all these comedians making fun of marriage. They were hilarious, and definitely made me smile during a very difficult time, but I think we both know—as do those comedians, since they both got remarried—that if it's great, it's not an 'institution' but a luxurious resort. You don't marry someone you can live with; you marry the person you can't live without. And you are inseparable for a reason. Instead of a ball and chain, you two are each other's wings. May you two be a team to face the world, armor for those trenches, and beyond the passion we all know you two share, may you always remain best friends. Lyle, I also know what it's like to be best friends with Kiki. And it's a gift that I treasure." My voice broke as I thought about all we had been through together and how strange life was: here we were with two different men beside us, brothers who were not Talbotts. "I love you so much, Keeks." I raised my glass and everyone applauded and wiped away tears. I turned to look at Elliot, who kissed my hand. Kiki dabbed her eyes and got up to hug me, and then quieted everyone down.

"I hate to break it to you all," she said to the crowd, "but I will not be tossing the bouquet tonight." Her announcement garnered some disappointed "awwwws," particularly from Eliza. Kiki touched the petals of the pale pink peonies. "Instead, I'll be handing it to my best friend."

She gave me a little curtsy, presenting the bouquet to me, which I accepted. Then I hugged her tightly. "This time next year," she whispered into my ear, as we embraced. "I bet you we'll be sisters-in-law again."

Follow-ups

CASEY SINCLAIR: Broke big-time. Shattering Alanis Morissette's record for a top-selling debut, she rocketed to the peak of the charts and all the journalists were thanking me profusely for helping them predict her fame, and groveling for hot tips on the next big star to break.

CELESTIAL RECORDS: Was bought out in its entirety for a record-setting price and folded into the larger parent music group. The Greene brothers fielded several offers for book deals, and decided to hire me to write their biography.

THE TALBOTT BROTHERS: Were hit badly by the subprime mortgage meltdown in the markets. Their investment in the Ocean Floor Research Institute went belly-up when the treasure they retrieved was filled with not gold ingots from medieval Spain but seaweed. And Black Falcon had a traveler eaten by wild antelopes and despite the fact that the victim had signed his life away, his family sued for wrongful death and won. Shortly after these financial setbacks, Avery set sail for greener (as in money-green) pastures. Tim now resides in Aspen and is dating a ski instructor. Hal lives alone in London.

THE HEDGE FUND WIVES: Some stayed together, some got divorces. Mary's finances, despite the bearish market, were bulletproof, so all was bliss. Posey remained loyal even when they had to bid adieu to flying private, but Emilia, alas, could not live without the sweet white noise of countless ka-chings. She ended up divorcing, then re-marrying a media billionaire, and kept the lifestyle to which she was accustomed. But as she had to shag her spouse, who was eighty-two years old, she was earning every penny.

SHERRY VON: Threw a William Yeoward crystal goblet at Hubert's head, resulting in a wound that required thirty stitches and ended her only real friendship. Hubert sued her in court, declaring Sherry Von "a boss that makes Naomi Campbell look like Mother Teresa," and won a settlement of $10 million from that old crab.

MARK WEBB: Oh, and speaking of crabs, Webb got a scorching case of them from a high-priced hooker and was later implicated in an insider-trading scandal. Thanks to his high-priced lawyer he avoided jail time but lost his license. He then opened a restaurant-slash-lounge downtown and literally "cast" the waitresses to all be smokin' hot. He married one of them, age twenty-two. Chances that will last? The same as a eunuch starring in porn.

LYLE SPENCE: Got a small box for his birthday six months later, which he opened to find a small blue plus sign on a pregnancy test. "I know it's weird to give you something I peed on," said Kiki. "But I'm pregnant." The euphoric couple is having a little girl.

HOLLAND TALBOTT SMITH (ALMOST!): I was proposed to on Thanksgiving Day overlooking the parade and in front of the whole family gathering. The answer was yes, and Kiki's Oracle at Delphi prediction was true: The week of Kiki and Lyle's anniversary the following April, Miles stood as ring bearer as his mommy married her new stepdad. And even though Kiki and I were already true sisters in spirit, as I exchanged rings and kissed Elliot, it became official once again, this time forever.